Claire McNeel is a fifth generation Melbourne Demons supporter/
sufferer, and a former registered nurse and researcher, with a PhD
in Neuroscience. She was a finalist for Best Screenplay at the
Byron Bay International Film Festival, and this screenplay formed
the basis for her debut novel *Darkness Runs Deep*. She currently
lives by the beach on Wadawurrung Country with her dog Homer.

DARKNESS RUNS DEEP

CLAIRE McNEEL

MACMILLAN

Pan Macmillan Australia

Pan Macmillan acknowledges the Traditional Custodians of Country throughout Australia and their connections to lands, waters and communities. We pay our respect to Elders past and present and extend that respect to all Aboriginal and Torres Strait Islander peoples today. We honour more than sixty thousand years of storytelling, art and culture.

First published 2024 in Macmillan by Pan Macmillan Australia Pty Ltd
1 Market Street, Sydney, New South Wales, Australia, 2000

 A catalogue record for this
book is available from the
National Library of Australia

Typeset in 12.5/18 pt Garamond Premier Pro by Post Pre-press Group, Brisbane

Printed by IVE

The author and the publisher have made every effort to contact copyright holders for material used in this book. Any person or organisation that may have been overlooked should contact the publisher.

 The paper in this book is FSC® certified.
FSC® promotes environmentally responsible,
socially beneficial and economically viable
management of the world's forests.

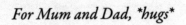

For Mum and Dad, *hugs*

PROLOGUE

31 December 1992

With the night sky the only witness, an inconsolable teenage boy, stumbling towards adulthood, sprinted along a worn, tree-lined track.

As he made his way from the footy oval, the lifeblood of Gerandaroo, to Gundry Crescent, the oldest residential street, the boy struggled to maintain his composure and continue his frenetic pace.

Against the rising moonlight which cast unwanted silhouettes, a lone thought played on repeat: *He's okay. He's okay. He's okay.*

A low-hanging branch ahead would impede an outsider, but like a birthmark this track was an indelible part of him, and he darted to the left. As a young boy he'd played happily in the protective gums that went out of their way to form a crooked line. Now the same trees offered nothing more than whispers of eucalyptus as he passed them by.

Despite increasingly frequent missteps, he was able to steady himself and continue forward with the same determination. His unwillingness to slow down was obvious, his desperation even more so.

Sobbing and out of breath, his dark blond hair matted with sweat, he emerged from the track and headed towards a series of dimmed lights. He staggered down a long familiar driveway, the sandy-coloured stones underfoot slowing him down.

Upon reaching the front door he came to a sudden stop. His breathing was laboured, irregular, and his hands trembled as he attempted to wipe away tears stained with blood.

He's not okay.

The shift in thought caused his body to sway uncontrollably and he collapsed against the door.

'I'm sorry,' he whispered to the night that had already taken so much.

No one heard the two words as they slipped across his lips and left him to drown in the darkness.

ONE

28 August 1993

Despite the frequent signage advising motorists that they were approaching Gerandaroo, the turn-off from the highway appeared suddenly. First-timers would typically underestimate the angle and fail to sufficiently slow down, leading them to hit their brakes with enough force that gravel spat at their car windows.

Bess O'Neill had witnessed this outcome many times. Yet she still found herself speeding up as she approached the exit, rapidly regretting her decision to leave Melbourne for the first time in eight months, and overwhelmed at the thought of returning home.

In a country town like Gerandaroo, taking a breath sometimes seemed like a shared experience, and a common adage prevailed: *In a small town, everyone knows everyone.* As a consequence, what happened in other people's lives rarely just happened to them, it happened to *you*, whether you wanted it to or not.

For Bess, recent events reinforced this experience. She thought about how a single dark moment not only impacted those who were present, but every single person who had previously initiated or participated in some form of abuse. It also impacted the individuals who repeatedly chose to turn away, and those few who always tried to help. The ramifications were far-reaching, with families, friends, colleagues, neighbours – an entire community – linked by a preventable tragedy and struggling to cope.

While this might compel most people to actively pass it by, past residents of Gerandaroo felt an undeniable pull. So, regardless of whether you shed tears the day you left, or had counted the days until you could leave, sometimes coming back was the only way to move forward.

And it was this annoyingly accurate cliché that compelled Bess, against her better judgement, to reluctantly make a sharp left turn, and return home to Gerandaroo.

*

With her blonde hair tucked into a messy ponytail and wearing night-blue Oakley sunnies, Bess drove her mustard-coloured Magna down a deserted road. Her elbow rested on the open window frame, and she rubbed her forehead in an unsuccessful attempt to remove unwanted thoughts.

Catching a glimpse of herself in the rear-view mirror, she stared longer than usual, insecure about her own reflection.

She passed a faded sign that she knew by heart:

Welcome to Gerandaroo – Population 723

Followed by a billboard that she also silently recited, in its entirety:

Home of the Red and Blue Gerandaroo Demons
Premiers 1899, 1905, 1906, 1911, 1913, 1924, 1928,
1933, 1938, 1948, 1954, 1963, 1964, 1968, 1970, 1974,
1975, 1977, 1980, 1982, 1983, 1985, 1987, 1992

Reciting the premiership years was a skill that extended back to her childhood, when she'd taken it upon herself to memorise them to impress her friends. She couldn't explain why she continued to do it; it wasn't as though she rationally believed anything bad would happen if she failed to run through the list of years, and she knew from experience that it couldn't *stop* something bad from happening, but she also couldn't quite bring herself to break the habit.

The premiership sign was always updated within a week of victory, and the recent 1992 entry had been no exception. The population sign, however, last updated some seventeen years earlier, was an ongoing source of irritation for Bess. She wasn't a perfectionist, far from it, but she resented its inaccuracy, as though this somehow translated to a personal deficiency. Her grandfather Percy would tell her that when it came to the town's population, it was best to be cautiously optimistic. Bess would respond that it was better to be pessimistically accurate.

Awkwardly positioned between the increasingly cosmopolitan Denby and the long-deserted town of Melcot, Gerandaroo had struggled in recent times to find its place. The gradual decline in residents had accelerated, and while this caused much angst for the townsfolk who remained, little action had been taken. Despite having first left home for university over five years ago, Bess did not want the town's numbers to dwindle further, and she knew that opting for a 'she'll be right' attitude, out of ignorance or fear, would not help the town survive.

Travelling just above the eighty k speed limit, her peripheral vision was filled with black and white sheep scattered across low-lying farms. Sheep were the dominant livestock in the region, and Bess could easily rattle off the names of prominent farming families, including those who had existed in the area for over a century. She could also reluctantly recount the names of far too many families who had been forced to sell when profit became a distant memory.

She followed a familiar route past the old houses that formed the fringe of Gerandaroo, tired but still standing, with a dozen twice-built owing to a bushfire in the forties that had nearly destroyed much of the south side of town.

Through the town centre, Bess slowed as she approached Green Street, named after early settlers to the region. Here lay the only strip of shops, each a source of comfort but also a sign of resistance to change.

Dominating a large block of land was the general store, which offered the typical groceries along with an eclectic assortment of clothing and knick-knacks. Throughout high school, Bess and her friends had spent an inordinate amount of time trying to convince the owner, Mr Clark, to install a slushie machine, the closest thing to a 7-Eleven Slurpee. But he was a stubborn man who'd lectured them about the cost of electricity and tried to convince them that the variety of ice-creams he offered was more than sufficient to satisfy any sweet cravings. Just after the new year, he'd finally relented, and surprised by the revenue it generated, reluctantly admitted that he should have done it years ago.

A blue and white striped awning flagged Hanks Bakery, with newish plastic chairs and round tables positioned outside for customers to enjoy Meringue Thursday and the long overdue addition of hot drinks. An entire cabinet was devoted to meringues made of different colours and shapes including animals with smarties for eyes and chocolate drops and sprinkles for decoration. Children and adults alike piled in every Thursday to make their selection, and the street would fill with residents milling about, chatting and happily eating their red ladybird or blue lizard meringue.

Next door sat the former bank, recently closed despite overwhelming objection. Adjacent to a pharmacy and opposite the combined post office and newsagency, the Milton auto-shop embraced its aged appearance by keeping an antique Shell petrol pump out the front, accompanied by a *Motor Service Garage* sign that dated back to the thirties.

The two-storey pub rounded out the street, with its recently painted, pale yellow weatherboard exterior complete with a wraparound verandah and outdoor beer garden. It gave a welcoming impression, yet also seemed uncharacteristically quiet.

Various clothing, takeaway, furniture and bric-a-brac shops had come and gone over the years, none able to earn enough to maintain a living. Nestled between the general store and the bakery was the only sign of progress – the hair salon, Just Do's, occupying a space that had sat empty for much of Bess's life.

There was another empty building, one that should always be occupied, but a run of challenging events had led to its seemingly permanent vacant status. The one-person police station was built in the 1920s. The last police officer to serve the town of Gerandaroo had resigned from his position eighteen months ago, leaving behind a haze of distrust and despair. Given the population decline, and Gerandaroo's relatively close proximity to the town of Denby that had a growing police force, the unpopular decision had been made to close the station.

Towards the end of Green Street, a sign for the Gerandaroo Primary School pointed to the left. It was the school that Bess and her younger brother Tom had attended, and that the town repeatedly fought to retain.

Residents were mostly farmers, tied to their land through debt and familial obligation. The typically dominant troughs coupled with the occasional peaks of farming life consumed generations, with most families producing a steady brood of offspring to ensure at least one child remained to continue the family business. The primary school acted as a beacon of sorts, just as the football club always had, and collectively helped create a community everyone was proud to be a part of. Without the school, Gerandaroo would likely be relegated to the history books as another country town that had simply faded away.

Just beyond the town centre, Bess passed a lone feedstock store before making a right-hand turn up a sloping gravel road. As she came to a stop in a makeshift carpark with no white lines, she swallowed hard, jaw clenched. The football oval was empty, highly unusual for a Saturday.

She stepped out of her car, leaned against the warm bonnet and slid her sunnies to the top of her head. In a failed attempt to keep from completely falling apart, she wrapped her arms tightly across her chest. She became acutely aware of the absence of traffic and general busyness that she found comforting from city living. As the country sounds amplified a silence that closed in on her, an uneasiness rose to the surface and hot tears began to fall, reluctantly released after months of suppression.

With limited capacity to focus on anything else, moments from the last game she'd attended came flooding back.

A 1992 Grand Final banner was draped over the steel fence in front of the north-end goal. Bess watched from the boundary, her face partially snuggled under a red and royal blue scarf. Her mum Gayle, with kind eyes and a penchant for waving to her son during a game, and her dad Ian, tall with the body of a retired footy player, stood on either side of her. With pursed lips and hands clasped in front of her face, Gayle shifted anxiously while Ian remained calm, his eyes darting across the oval, ahead of the play. The five-row concrete terrace that wrapped around half the oval was awash with a mix of red and blue for the Gerandaroo Demons, and navy blue and white for the Denby Cats.

They all glanced nervously towards the scoreboard:

Demons	Cats
13.9.87	14.8.92

Bess's cheers joined the chorus of chants from fellow supporters, willing their boys to victory.

'Let's go, Dee-mons! Let's go!'

As the majority of the crowd clapped, the chant increased in intensity.

'LET'S GO, DEE-MONS, LET'S GO!'

Daniel Jacobs, number 23, gathered the loose ball to keep it in play. Hugging the boundary line and with composure and speed, he sprinted away from one defender as another closed in.

'Kick it!' cried Danny's older brother Lachlan.

A shepherd from Rick Russo, number 15 – a midfielder with a determined glare and bearing scrapes and bruises – helped Danny complete a short quick kick to number 10, Tom O'Neill.

'C'mon, Tommo!' Bess cried out in support of her brother.

Tom, a slighter-than-typical full-forward, marked with confidence from inside the right-hand forward pocket in front of goal. But the umpire called, 'Play on!'

Just as several opponents descended, Tom turned to the right and snapped the ball across his body with a left-foot kick. As it sailed high between the goalposts, the siren sounded and the town cheered as one.

Bess reluctantly opened her eyes and clumsily wiped the tears from her face with both palms. Through a blurry lens of overwhelming sadness, she stared at the cracked clay, patches of brown grass and discarded strapping tape. Bess knew that the beloved Gerandaroo football oval waited for players who were not allowed to return.

She continued driving along the backroads before turning into a sandy-coloured stone driveway on Gundry Crescent, where a wooden letterbox engraved with the word *REDLEGS* stood proudly in homage to the Melbourne Demons football club.

Bess was a fifth-generation supporter. Her mum's great-grandfather had founded the Gerandaroo Demons in the late 1890s and football was a deeply held tradition on both sides of her family. Being a Melbourne supporter was practically a prerequisite for a harmonious existence with her father, but in the best possible way. Bess was forever grateful that her dad had taken the time to teach her not just the rules of footy, but how to play the game, and she had subsequently fallen in love with it, only to let it break her heart.

Bess remained in her car. Her hands gripped the steering wheel as she took in the deep verandah of the well-maintained weatherboard house. She instinctively took several long breaths in preparation for a likely challenging reunion in her childhood home.

Bess entered the unlocked house, dropped her bag, and bent down to greet Jinx, her family's fourteen-year-old red merle Australian Shepherd. She'd known he would be waiting for her.

'Hey there, Jinxy old boy,' Bess whispered.

She smiled warmly as Jinx rolled onto his back, a plead for pats.

'Have you been looking after Mum and Dad?'

Jinx wagged his tail in response, the soft thumping a welcome sound. As he wiggled sideways with paws outstretched, begging for the pats to continue, Bess noticed that since her last visit, the deep reddish fur under and above his eyes had continued to fade. As she stroked his belly with a continuous stream of 'such a good boy' and the like, Jinx settled happily.

'Where's Mum, Jinxy? Mum?' she called. When no answer came, she tried again, but louder. '*Mum*!?'

Still no response. Bess stood and walked further into the house, Jinx at her heels. She found her mum hunched in a high-backed chair in the dining room. Her eyes seemed fixated on the seahorse insignia that Bess knew was burned into the edge of the solid oak table. Bess watched her mum gaze out to the left, through the double kitchen windows framed by reddish curtains and into the backyard. Bess remained still. There was something about her mum's sadness that was palpable, and she felt uncomfortable interrupting it. Bess could see that the grass in the backyard was overdue for a mow, and the laundry on the clothesline had long dried.

She looked down at Jinx, now leaning sleepily against her, but still alert. Despite his advanced age, Jinx remained spry when needed and had an unrivalled devotion to his family. Bess thought back to last Christmas when Jinx had placed himself between Gayle and a brown snake she'd inadvertently disturbed from its sun-drenched spot near the letterbox. Without hesitation, Jinx had lurched and snapped at the snake and was fortunate to come away unscathed.

Bess finally approached her mum and gently touched her on the shoulder.

Gayle jumped, startled.

'Oh, Bess,' said Gayle, before she stood and embraced her daughter.

As they held each other, Bess tightened her grip, sensing her mother's need for comfort and wanting to fill her own void. After several long moments, they released each other and sat at the table. Jinx rested his head on Bess's knee. She slowly scratched behind his ears.

'Where's Dad?' she asked, avoiding eye contact.

Gayle hesitated before responding. 'I'm not sure.'

Bess waited for an explanation, her mum not usually one for brevity.

'He just . . . goes out most days,' she continued. 'He doesn't tell me where.'

'Okay,' Bess said slowly. She thought of all the possible places where her dad might be; for a small town, the list was notably long.

'What's happening with the pub? Has he opened it back up yet?' Bess was aware that her voice sounded unnatural and forced.

'No,' replied Gayle, her tone dropping a level.

'Does he plan to?' asked Bess, slightly frustrated, but her concern genuine.

'I don't know,' Gayle said with a slight shrug. 'He just . . . doesn't want to have to talk to anyone. He doesn't know what to say.' She seemed keen to change the topic. 'What about you? It's the middle of the term.'

'Yeah, I know. I just thought that maybe I should be here.'

The strain between them was a stark contrast to their usual easygoing relationship. Bess had followed in her mother's footsteps by becoming a high school teacher, and as adults, the two bonded over challenging students and lesson plans.

'So, have you decided when you'll go back?' Bess asked, with some hesitation.

'Not yet. The Department of Ed appointed an interim principal. He seems to be working out.'

Bess's frown deepened, but she decided against making any comment. By way of distraction, she rose to check the contents of the cupboards and fridge and stared at the near-bare shelves for several moments before turning to face her mum.

'How about you make a list of things you want from the store, and I'll make a run into town?'

'Oh yes, love, I've been meaning to go –'

Bess was quick, too quick, to interrupt her. 'It's okay, Mum, just make a list.'

Gayle nodded, but kept her head low. Although aware of how fragile her mother was, Bess felt impatient and not in the mood to empathise.

She walked down the hall carrying her bag, before coming to a stop outside a closed door. Staring at it, she raised her hand to the doorknob, then paused, hand hovering. She decided against entering, and instead moved to a second door at the end of the hall.

As she stepped into her former bedroom, Bess was regretfully transported back to her younger years. A single photo remained, pinned to a corkboard above her desk. She had long debated whether to take it with her when she first packed to leave for uni, and on every visit home since. She kept it in the same spot, unable to put it out of sight.

She flicked her trusty desk lamp on and off. Its base was covered in stickers of dinosaurs, once bright and new, now long faded and curled at the edges.

Sliding open the top desk drawer, Bess removed an item she knew would be there – a wooden heart with a seahorse insignia burned in the centre.

She held the heart in her hand and, almost reluctantly as her thumb slowly traced over the seahorse, Bess focused on the photo.

A tall, sandy-haired boy hugged her from behind, his arms comfortably across her chest, her hands grasping his forearm, with the wooden heart visible on a leather strap around her wrist. Both looked carefree and had laughing smiles.

Caught in that moment in time, minutes passed before she looked away. Frustrated at the nostalgic influence of this boy and of the heart they shared, she placed it back in the drawer and forcefully slid it shut.

In recent times, Bess had become adept at locking away her feelings, not just under the surface, but burying them under layers of confusion and pain, and sometimes regret. And then she repeatedly covered them with a thick breezy layer of 'everything's fine'. But this tactic could only work for so long.

And she knew it.

After hastily unpacking, Bess headed back to the kitchen, but paused as she watched her mum still sitting at the dining table, her head down. She almost wanted to ignore how undeniably broken this once strong woman had become.

'Mum, how about you come with me?'

Gayle looked up and nodded as a small smile formed.

TWO

A series of farm properties stretched out behind Gundry Crescent, each a reminder that prosperity was measured by the seasons. The paddocks, their lush colour an increasingly common and welcome sight, surrounded near-full dams, one after another after another. Yet the devastating bushfires from the previous decade had created an endless sense of unease, and some farmers predicted that a drought was coming. Everyone hoped they were wrong.

The O'Neills had never been farmers. Bess's paternal grandfather Archie had established the Redlegs pub in Gerandaroo some forty years earlier. His father, a highly educated man, was a chemist with his own pharmacy in the city. His premature death when Archie was only six had forced his family to move from the city to Gerandaroo where his mother Betty had grown up. Bess knew her dad had no intention of leaving – he rarely ventured beyond the surrounding towns, with the exception of watching his beloved Demons play at the MCG a few times a year. He never understood how he'd failed to pass on his deep love for the countryside to his offspring. Although Bess would never admit it, there had been moments over the last year when she'd caught herself longing for an open field with no one in sight.

As they passed a sign to the Trayfords', one of the town's oldest farming families, Bess glanced expectantly at her mum. Passing the Trayfords' farm always prompted a conversation about what they were up to. Gayle, however, did not say a word as she stared out the passenger window with a weariness that made the air difficult to breathe.

'So, how are they?' Bess asked, mainly out of habit but also some interest.

'They're fine,' replied Gayle.

Unsure of how to probe further, Bess remained silent.

*

Near the furthest point from the Trayford family home, Tom's teammate Rick sat cross-legged among dry grass. This had become almost routine for Rick and he knew the Trayfords didn't mind him being on their land. There was something comforting about not having to see people but also knowing that he was still fairly close to home. Rick couldn't make sense of this, how he wanted to be alone, yet still around people. The more he tried to process this idea, the more confused he became, to the point that he frequently experienced a swirling anxiety that made its way around his whole body before settling deep in his heart.

As Rick watched Bess's Magna pass by in the distance, he slowly spun a worn football between his hands. He knew the car well.

He had been staying with the O'Neills when Bess had driven it home, having purchased it without her parents knowing. He and Tom had been so impressed, and they'd begged her to take them for a drive. Bess happily obliged, keen to share her new-found freedom. Despite nearly a five-year age difference, and unlike his own sister, Bess was always genuinely interested in what Tom and his friends were up to. He wondered if her arrival meant something good or something bad.

As Rick's eyes followed the car, his expression remained unchanged. There was no hint that he was actively suppressing an overwhelming desire to chase across the paddock, jump into the Magna and tell Bess to drive him far away from Gerandaroo. He took a deep breath and felt a physical heaviness closing in around him, with a constant stream of 'what ifs' dominating his thoughts.

As the Magna retreated from view, Rick continued to stare ahead, increasingly aware that with each passing day, his friends were slipping further and further away. He knew what he needed to do to feel unburdened. But he also knew that apologising might not be enough.

*

As Bess and Gayle made their way down Green Street, Bess was reminded of all the times as a teenager when she and her friends contemplated drag racing down the strip at night. It seemed too perfectly set up to not at least try. They never did though, and never really came close, but talking about who would win and why must have seemed important because it was certainly a popular topic among them.

Bess parallel-parked in the end spot directly outside the bakery. She wasn't exactly a confident parker. Her dad would tell her that she travelled too close to the car in front and often questioned if she could accurately judge distances. It was for this reason that she'd neglected to share with her parents that two years ago, she'd swung into a friend's driveway a little too sharply and ended up scraping the side of her car against a freshly painted fence.

As Bess turned off the ignition, she watched a group of teenage boys saunter past.

'Is that the Cutler kid?' she asked, gesturing to a tall boy leading the pack.

Gayle nodded.

'Geez, he sure shot up.'

Gayle just nodded again.

'Is he still a brat?'

'He is,' said Gayle, with a slight sigh.

The Cutler family owned the pharmacy in Gerandaroo and the one in Denby, in addition to the Denby general store. They had long been trying to purchase the Gerandaroo general store, but Mr Clark had no intention of selling. *Entitled* was perhaps the most accurate descriptor for Mr and Mrs Cutler's only child, Lucas. Bess remembered how ten-year-old Lucas would falsely and repeatedly claim that his family *owned* Gerandaroo. His parents never bothered to correct him.

Bess and her mum waited the standard five seconds longer than should be necessary to enter the general store, because the sensors on the automatic doors always struggled to do their job. It also meant there was this brief period, and to Bess an uncomfortable one, where you watched the people milling about like they were in a fishbowl.

Once inside, eyes immediately pivoted to them and lingered. Bess bit her lower lip, but Gayle seemed oblivious to the stares.

Despite no longer living in Gerandaroo, Bess was able to locate items easily as Mr Clark never changed the store's layout. This typically irritated Bess as she found the lack of innovation stifling, but today she was grateful for the almost comforting familiarity. They filled their trolley, with Bess making a point of hurrying past several other shoppers as though they didn't exist.

At the checkout, the angelic features of Sam Mills, with her flowing auburn hair and long lashes, were spoiled by her incessant gum-chewing and glazed expression.

Sam did not attempt small talk. 'Ninety-six dollars and fifteen cents,' she told them, her eyes almost closing from complete and utter boredom. Bess suspected that her demeanour could also be a consequence of a recreational habit that likely made small-town life slightly more bearable.

All Bess could remember about Sam was that she and her dad had moved from Denby to Gerandaroo when Bess was halfway through Year 12, as well as a rumour that the family were wealthy, so she was surprised to see Sam working. Bess also recalled something about Sam's mum having stayed in Denby.

The towns were only thirty-four kilometres apart but Denby was far more substantial. With a population nearing twelve thousand and growing every year, it had more shops, a hospital, more houses – just more of everything. Most of the townsfolk in Gerandaroo thought it was a good place to visit but not to live. Bess wondered how Sam felt. She had the outward appearance of someone who longed for a busier scene, but perhaps she secretly enjoyed the solace of Gerandaroo.

*

As Bess and Gayle loaded groceries into the car boot, an old friend of Bess's approached them. Juliet Blackburn was attractive rather than pretty. Her brunette hair was loosely braided in a plait draped over her right shoulder, and as her sheer scarf speckled with small black birds fluttered delicately in the breeze, her green eyes moved intensely between Gayle and Bess.

'Bess! Gayle. I've been thinking of you all.'

This statement said by anyone else would have seemed trite, but from Juliet, it was strong with empathy. Bess was immediately grateful that Juliet did not question why she was in Gerandaroo.

Jules, as she was known to everyone, was unfailingly kind. She immediately hugged them in turn – boundaries had never been her strong suit. But it was a genuine hug that made Gayle smile and caused Bess to experience a pang of regret that she had lost touch with her former best friend.

'Thanks, Jules,' said Bess. 'I got your letters and cards. And messages,' she added, glancing down. 'I'm sorry I never called you back.'

'No worries, B.'

Bess could only manage a nod. Jules' use of her initial rather than her name was almost suffocating. When they were growing up, Bess had struggled to say the letter 'L', so it sounded like she was

21

calling her friend 'Jews'. Instead, she would refer to her best friend as 'J'. To prevent Bess from feeling embarrassed, Jules would refer to Bess as 'B'. It cemented their friendship. Even though they'd seen each other sporadically over the years, they had both stopped using these nicknames. To hear it now, Bess felt a gnawing guilt because she knew that she was the one who had pulled away.

Jules surveyed her friend, her head cocked. 'But maybe we could go out tonight? To the Denby Pub? Just to catch up?'

'No, thanks, I –'

'She'll be there,' interrupted Gayle.

Bess looked at her mum with surprise and slight annoyance. Going out was the last thing she wanted to do.

'Um, yeah, okay. Do you want me to drive?' said Bess, thinking that would at least make it easier for them to leave early.

'That'd be great. Pick me up around seven?'

'Sure,' said Bess, her reluctance not well hidden.

*

Back home, Bess slowly opened the door to Tom's room and stepped inside. Jinx followed and climbed onto the bed, using steps that Tom had made especially for him when his jumping days were over. He sniffed the one pillow that remained and turned in his usual circle before settling into a comfortable spot with his head facing the door.

Entering Tom's room was always a journey of sorts. His walls were covered in framed photographs, many in black and white. They included action and still shots from footy games; domestic dogs keeping watch at front gates and on verandahs; the town at dawn as it slowly stirred awake; chickens, sheep and farm dogs as they went about their day; the farmsteads at dusk when the sky was pink, and many of the town's inhabitants. Intense, beautiful, confronting. Tom captured moments before others even knew they were happening. He saw this as a privilege, to have the capacity to bind a second in time.

Bess perched on the edge of her brother's bed and traced over the diamond pattern on his deep-blue doona cover. She stared at a photo of Tom and his best friend Danny from when they were young boys. They were often mistaken for brothers, both with sandy hair and light eyes – Danny's with a hint of green and Tom's a deeper blue. They shared traits, most notably over-analysing situations and feeling things deeply, perhaps too deeply. There was never a clear leader between them, which set them apart from their friends. Neither wanted to be the dominant one nor in the shadows, so it sometimes seemed that they would take turns to take the lead.

Tom, however, was more naive. He hadn't been through what Danny had and he could not shelter his friend from trauma, nor could he hide his loving family. Tom's good fortune could have created jealousy, and it did, at times, yet the two boys still shared a bond that seemed unbreakable. But as they had recently learned, anything that can be built can be broken.

In the photo they were covered in mud with arms around shoulders, sporting the widest grins, their white teeth shining between their dirt-streaked cheeks. Bess remembered taking the picture just before they ambushed her, and she too had ended up head to toe in mud. They had been using torn pieces of linoleum left over from a kitchen renovation to slide down the grassy banks of a nearby farm following a stormy night. Gayle had refused to allow them in the house until Ian had hosed them off in the front yard.

It was a memorable day, for all the best reasons.

Bess took a deep breath and looked away. The uncomfortable emotions she had managed to suppress for months began to well inside her, and as hard as she tried to push them away, one conversation with her brother from last December spilled out.

'I still can't believe you're a teacher,' said Tom, his amusement visible as he sat on the floor with his back against his bed, Jinx resting beside him.

'I know,' Bess responded, laughing and swivelling in Tom's desk chair. 'I bet I'll keep getting little shits in my class just to make up for all the stuff I used to do.'

Tom looked down at the piece of paper in his hands.

'Top five per cent in the state. Who knew you were so smart?' commented Bess.

'Not I, said the fly,' he replied, and Bess laughed again.

'So, young Thomas, what are your future plans?'

He hesitated before answering. Then, with hands outstretched, he gestured to his photographs. 'This. And uni, and travelling, and writing. And everything in between.'

'And footy?'

'You sound like Dad.'

Bess was on the verge of defending herself, but on seeing her brother's downcast expression, she decided to let him continue.

'It's just a game,' he said quietly. 'And not one that I really wanna

keep playing.' Sensing he wasn't explaining himself very well, he tried again. 'It's just, footy, it makes me feel so . . . trapped.'

He looked around his room and seemed to grow in confidence. 'My photos are an expression, an extension of the world as I see it. They allow me to take in everything that's around us. And they help others to perhaps try and see something they've known their whole life, just that little bit differently.'

Bess tilted her head and looked right at Tom. 'That's rather philo-sophical of you.'

He looked down, embarrassed.

'I get it, Tom. I really do,' she added gently.

'Thanks, Bess,' he responded with a grateful smile.

Bess was jolted back to the present. Even though Tom's photographs provided some comfort, without his voice, his energy, it was hollow. Bess could feel that he hadn't set foot in the room for months.

Hearing the front door open, Bess scrambled to her feet, and with Jinx following, they left Tom's room, Bess careful to close the door quietly behind them.

Her dad stood in the living room, startled by her presence, even though he must have seen her car in the driveway. A brief, awkward moment ensued, before Bess moved forward to embrace him. While Ian returned the hug, his surprise turned to concern.

'What are you doing here? It's the middle of the school year,' he said, a hint of frustration in his tone.

'I was able to take three weeks' leave without pay. And school holidays start straight after,' explained Bess. 'I just felt this is where I should be. For now, at least.'

'You can't put your career at risk,' said Ian, his voice raised, and Bess sensed a lecture about responsibilities brewing.

'Dad, it's fine. The principal approved it. I still have my job, and I am *entitled* to four weeks' leave without pay each year,' she said, her voice rising to match his. Then, aware of the unnecessary harshness of her tone, she allowed it to soften. 'How are things?' she asked.

'Fine,' said Ian. 'We're fine.'

'Okay. Good.'

The conversation stalled.

'So, I'm just about to head out to Denby with Jules.'

'When will you be back? Are you driving? Do you have enough petrol? When was your car last serviced?' Ian barely took a breath.

Bess, anticipating this line of questioning, answered promptly. 'I'm not sure, but I've got my house keys, so you don't need to wait up. Yes, I'm driving. And yes, I have enough petrol. It's due for a service in a month, and it's been running fine.'

Ian looked pained, and Bess could tell he was torn between telling her not to stay out too late and keeping quiet because he knew she was no longer a child.

Bess made the decision for him by leaning over to kiss him on the cheek. ''Night, Dad,' she said, giving him a slight pat on the shoulder. 'Bye, Mum,' she called.

'Have fun, sweetie. Give us a call if you need a ride home,' said Gayle.

Bess resisted the urge to remind her mum she was an adult. 'Will do, Mum.'

THREE

Pockets of smoke-filled haze filled the recently renovated Denby pub, which now resembled more of a club. It used to be a dingy bar that ran a distant second to Gerandaroo's Redlegs in every way possible. The typical weekday patron would drink to excess and there were frequent brawls on the weekend that required police attendance. In contrast, Redlegs had a simple menu of comfort: classic pub food, accompanied by blues and rock, the absence of any pop or disco (except for ABBA), the occasional live band, pool tables, darts and themed trivia nights. The walls were adorned with the town's history, and Ian would often receive photos taken over the years from townsfolk. In addition to those who lived in Gerandaroo and Denby, there was a steady flow of regulars who passed through from across the state, as well as interstate truckers and families making their way up north or down south, who collectively created a loyal base that spanned generations.

After the Denby pub repeatedly failed to match the rustic charm of Redlegs, a new owner decided to modernise, with a focus on cocktails, dancing, and playing music at an unhealthy decibel level. With the prolonged closure of Redlegs, the Denby pub attracted more visitors from Gerandaroo, particularly the younger crowd, much to the chagrin of their parents. The Victorian government had started airing ads focused on preventing drink-driving a few years earlier, and the line 'If you drink, then drive, you're a bloody idiot' had become a common part of parental lectures delivered as their children piled into cars and drove off into the night.

Tonight, as patrons continued to drink, the noise level steadily rose, a mixture of conversation, laughter and the occasional broken glass. For a brief moment, Bess felt she was back in the city on a typical night out with friends. She glanced at the Geelong Cats clock on the wall that read ten past eight and wondered where she truly belonged. Was she far from home? Or close to it?

She returned her attention to the lone pool table tucked away in the back and watched as Jules lined up for her shot.

'So, why haven't you applied?' asked Bess, desperate to switch off the debate she was having with herself. 'Your portfolio's ready, isn't it?' Bess used to be envious of Jules' ability to draw pretty much any and everything. But now, she was more frustrated that her friend had never followed through with her long-held plans to study Architecture after her undergrad degree.

'Yeah, I guess. I mean it *is* finished. It's just, I keep meaning to, but...'

'Are you just gonna stay in Gerandaroo?' Bess was aware that her tone was bordering on exasperated, but made no attempt to rein it in.

Without taking her shot, Jules straightened to face Bess. 'You make it sound like I'm doing nothing.'

'That's not it. I know you work hard on the farm. It's just . . . you always swore you'd never stay,' said Bess.

'I know. But things change,' Jules responded with a heavy sigh.

She returned her attention to the table but missed her shot, and they both watched as the number 7 solid maroon ball ricocheted back towards her.

'So, just apply,' Bess said with a shrug. 'See what happens. You've talked about doing it for years.'

'I know, but we can't all just leave,' Jules muttered.

'What's that supposed to mean?' said Bess, her tone rising.

'Nothing,' Jules replied hastily, avoiding her glare.

'It must mean something or else you wouldn't have said it,' Bess fired back.

Jules locked eyes with her before taking a deep breath. 'You just left.'

'So did you!'

'No, I came back. Even when I was at uni, I came home a hell of a lot more than you ever did.'

'It's not my fault that your brother took off,' Bess shot back. 'Or that you refuse to even consider selling the farm.'

'First of all,' said Jules, 'you know that's not the situation and I'm not going to defend my brother to you. And second, *you're* the one pushing me to do something else. You're the one who acts like working on the farm isn't good enough.'

Just when Bess thought Jules was done lecturing her, she continued, her voice quiet. 'And even after what happened, you only stayed for a week. And then you left again.' Jules paused before adding the final blow. 'It was as though you couldn't wait to get away from us.'

Bess placed her pool cue on the table, frustrated by the turn the conversation had taken. 'I'm getting another drink,' she said, having given up on the prospect of being able to drive but with no thought as to how she and Jules would get home.

Jules dropped her head slightly and a sadness seeped in, crowding their already complicated space. Despite recognising that Jules clearly had things she needed to say, things she had been holding on to, Bess knew she didn't have the capacity to support her friend. Nor did she have the insight to justify how she had acted in the past.

As Bess walked past Jules towards the bar, she stopped, then turned back. 'Do you want another beer?' she asked pointedly, but with a slight smile.

Jules turned to face her oldest friend and smiled knowingly. 'Sure.'

*

Gayle busied herself in the kitchen for longer than necessary. Tea was ready, but the prospect of another silent meal weighed heavily on her. She placed a bowl of spaghetti bolognaise in front of her husband and watched him once again avoid eye contact.

'Thanks,' said Ian quietly.

Gayle sat opposite and reached for the shaker of parmesan at the centre of the table. Ian reached for it at the same time, but pulled his hand away.

'Sorry,' he said, his voice still low.

Gayle used the parmesan and passed it to Ian. She spoke suddenly, but her words suggested she had been holding her thoughts in for some time. 'Before Ruth died, we promised her that we'd look after the boys.'

Ian continued to avoid looking at his wife, and instead shifted awkwardly in his seat.

'We didn't, did we?' continued Gayle.

Ian moved his spaghetti around without taking a bite.

'Ruth was my best friend. She was *our* best friend.'

Without looking up, Ian offered the only response he could to his wife of twenty-five years and best friend since primary school. 'We did the best we could, given the circumstances,' he said, his voice trailing off before he spoke again. 'You reported your concerns, *multiple* times, for Daniel *and* Lachlan. And nothing ever came of it. What more could we have done?'

Gayle wasn't convinced, and as she watched her husband, she knew he wasn't either. She felt increasingly isolated from him, with no idea how to bridge the ever-growing void between them. Although she had no appetite, she took a mouthful of spaghetti, and they finished their meal without another word spoken.

*

Several streets over, Rick lay on top of his doona as he tossed a tennis ball into the air. He stopped as he heard footsteps approach.

'You right, love?' called his mum. 'Are you sure I can't make you something to eat?'

'Nah, Mum. I'm fine. I'm not hungry,' he replied, aware that his mum was on the verge of entering his room. ''Night, Mum.'

There was a brief pause. ''Night, love. I'll see you in the morning.'

Rick could hear that his mum was desperate for reassurance.

'Yep,' he replied, because he didn't have the energy to say anything more. He listened as his mum waited another few moments before walking back down the hall.

Rick continued to toss the tennis ball to himself, resigned to the knowledge that it would be hours before his thoughts slowed enough to permit sleep.

*

The Cats clock had just passed ten thirty, and with Jules and Bess perched on stools at the bar, the discussion turned to football as it inevitably always did.

'You know Denby have a women's team?' said Jules as she stirred her freshly made gin and tonic with a straw. 'Deb started it.'

'For real? Who do they play against?'

'No one. Yet.'

'I guess it makes sense – Deb's the only one who could organise something like that. She was always so bloody competitive. And bossy,' Bess added with a hint of jealousy.

'Remind you of anyone?' Jules smirked.

'Who?' demanded Bess.

'Seriously? Bess, come on. She's practically your personality doppelgänger,' said Jules, failing to suppress her laughter, a consequence of straddling the line between tipsy and drunk.

Bess smirked back, unable to think of a snappy retort. 'Remember when we tried to get a team going and the boys absolutely cracked it? They kept saying "we don't play netball, so you can't play footy", like that was a logical argument,' said Bess.

'They were such dicks. Except for Lachie,' replied Jules.

'And Ryan,' they said in unison.

The familiarity of the two names brought a shared smile, but it was fleeting. These were the boys they'd grown up with, shared first kisses with, had their first drunken night on the footy oval with, first no-adults-allowed camping trips, and who they'd sat next to on their first day of kinder and final day of high school. But as adults, they had all experienced the common drift that made them question if these friendships had been genuine or only formed out of proximity.

Bess bit her lower lip, eyes downcast. 'Yeah, they were always good about that stuff. They were just good guys. There aren't really too many of them around these days. Remember how we'd play Marks Up in the street for hours?'

'It seems like forever ago,' said Jules. 'You know, Ryan doesn't even talk much about footy anymore.'

'Is he still working construction?'

'Yeah. He's doing a job out at Wylie Creek for a few months and is staying with his cousin. He comes back to town every now and then. I see him here sometimes,' she added, briefly scanning the pub.

'And the two of you . . .?' For as long as she had known Jules, there had been a Jules and Ryan. Even when they were in primary school there was an intensity around the two of them, but they also never seemed to quite fit.

Jules shrugged. 'I dunno. We keep trying to make it work, but he doesn't think I'm here to stay.'

'Is he right?'

'That's just it. I really *don't* know.'

Bess believed her, but couldn't think of any advice to offer.

'He still makes me laugh,' Jules continued, somewhat wistfully. 'No matter how annoying he can be. So, whenever we see each other, it's just . . . he's like a habit. And sometimes I think he's the best kind of habit and other times, he's possibly the worst.'

The two women sat lost, or perhaps trapped, in shared memories from years gone by.

*

As a child of Gerandaroo, Rick had only ever lived in the one house, so he knew that the distinctive creaks in the dead of the night were not from an intruder. His sight had adjusted to the darkness, and with moonlight seeping beneath the blinds, he could make out every shape, every corner, every surface. With the likelihood of sleep drifting further away, Rick did the only thing that seemed to help. He slid off his bed, changed into trackpants and a hoodie, and slipped out his bedroom window. He moved slowly down the side of his house so as to not wake his parents; if they knew he went for late-night runs, they would only worry more. Once on the street, he broke into a jog, his body almost thanking him for the chance to move and his mind grateful for the distraction.

*

Back at the Denby pub, the clock ticked towards midnight.

'You started it!' Jules shouted in a joking manner.

'I did not!' said Bess, equally loudly.

Jules looked at Bess and Bess looked away, trying in vain not to laugh.

'Okay, okay. Yes, I started it,' Bess surrendered, hands raised in the air.

'Grade 5 with Mr Ling. You dared Lachie to lie on the floor of the class and refuse to sit on his chair until he got a pink cushion to sit on,' said Jules, pointing at Bess.

Bess doubled over with silent laughter. 'I got him in so much trouble back then. Remember the pledge we came up with? It took us *sooo* long. We didn't do an assignment –'

'A book report,' Jules interjected.

'Yeah, that's right. And we handed it in as a group,' continued Bess.

'Yep. You, me, Ali, Rach, Lachie, Fi, Eva and Ryan,' said Jules, the names flowing out with ease.

'And Mr Ling gave us all bin duty for two weeks,' said Bess.

In unison, they recited the pledge: 'I pledge to honour each dare. To let no force, be it parent or teacher, interfere with my quest. For if I fail to complete a dare, bad luck will come in multiples of three, ending only at a time when I complete the dare that you, my friend, have set for me.'

They both collapsed against the pool table and continued their moderately drunken laughter despite the stares from those nearby.

'Remember when everyone started to get involved?' said Bess. 'The parents were pissed. And we'd write them down, so it was all formal?'

'I've still got the exercise books.'

'Okay, top ten dares. Go,' said Bess as she lined up for a shot.

'There are just too many to choose from,' said Jules, pretending to be serious. 'I'd have to say, one, when you dared Ryan to make and wear a condom packet necklace to the Year 10 formal.'

'If I recall, he insisted I said it had to include one *used* condom,' said Bess.

'Yep, and I nearly helped him out with that.'

'Jules, you *did* help him out.'

. 'Yes. Correct. I did,' said Jules as the laughter continued. 'But, as you well know, the necklace he wore did not include *that* condom.'

When Bess couldn't stop laughing, Jules tried to move on. 'Two, when Fi dared Lachie to repeat everything Coach Macca said during the prelim final in Year 11.' Jules paused to take her shot. They both watched the number 9 yellow and white striped ball head towards the right-back corner pocket, and fondly remembered the interaction between Coach and Lachie.

Macca, the Gerandaroo Demons coach – who also used to own the feedstock store before moving interstate – was an imposing man with an impressively deep voice and absolutely no hair on his head. It was as though he'd never had hair; he was simply born bald and remained bald.

The players were huddled around him, breathing heavily and throwing back water as he delivered the three-quarter-time talk. They all focused intently on him, the adrenaline palpable. Supporters, including Jules and Bess, had gathered around the group, eager to hear what Macca had to say.

'Use the middle,' instructed Macca, who did not need to yell to be heard.

'Use the middle!' Lachie repeated.

'Tackle with purpose, stick to your man.'

'Tackle with purpose, fellas, gotta stick to your man!' shouted Lachie.

'You've put in the hard yards.'

'Hard yards!' Lachie echoed.

'For Chrissakes, Lachie! What the hell are you doing?' Macca barked, his voice now raised.

'Just getting pumped up, coach, just getting pumped up!' said Lachie, bouncing up and down in the process.

The team, unable to control themselves, doubled over with loud laughter.

Macca looked at them, exasperated, but not angry. 'Let me guess, Gerandaroo dare?'

Through more laughter, Jules kept recounting the top dares.

'Three, when Ali dared Eva to unroll and then glue together the top sheets of all the toilet paper in her house.'

'Eva's mum nearly banned us from ever visiting again after that,' said Bess, shaking her head.

Jules took a sip of beer. 'Four, when Rach dared you to steal your dad's remote during the '87 Grand Final.'

Bess nodded. 'He absolutely *hates* listening to the ads. And most of the commentary. So he always bloody mutes and un-mutes the telly – it drives Mum crazy,' said Bess. 'But I think Dad just resigned himself to putting up with those dares. He never punished us,' she added philosophically as they made their way back to the bar stools.

'Yeah, your dad was always so good like that. Except,' said Jules, as she reached for the counter to steady herself, laughing hard, 'for that time when . . .' She tried to go on but couldn't get the words out.

'No, don't,' said Bess, 'don't mention the green paint.' The words rushed out as every muscle seemed to spasm with laughter.

'Okay, okay.' Jules raised her hand. 'I promise not to talk about it.'

Bess exhaled slowly. 'You've given me a bloody cramp,' she said, clutching her stomach.

'I'm sorry.' Jules smiled widely. 'So, six,' she said, forcing a serious voice, 'when you dared Eva and Fiona to wear face paint for the Year 12 English exam.'

'Eva the lion and Fiona the bear,' added Bess. 'They were the only two who could get away with it.'

'So true,' Jules agreed. 'Seven,' she continued, 'when Ryan dared us to steal the hubcaps from Lachie's dad's car.'

'Now that one was pretty dangerous,' Bess conceded.

'Really, you think?' said Jules sarcastically. 'I mean, Mitch *was* a police officer. But other than that, no danger at all.'

'Well, he was a corrupt and abusive cop, so he bloody well deserved it,' said Bess, the happy tone of the evening souring.

'Bess,' Jules said with a hint of warning.

'What? You know it's true. Why do you think he quit? He was about to be fired. And –'

'I don't want to talk about him, okay?' Jules interjected with force.

Bess stared at her, frustrated because Jules was the one who'd brought up the dare involving Mitch. But for once she decided not to push it. Despite their recent absence from each other's lives, Bess still knew where Jules' limit lay.

*

As the night drew to a close, Bess lined up for her final shot, but Jules interrupted her focus with a surprising proposition.

'I dare you to put together a women's team to play Denby, in Denby, the week after the Grand Final.'

'Well, that came out of nowhere,' Bess commented, amused.

Jules fixated on her. 'Well?'

'Well, what?'

'Are you refusing the dare? Do you really need bad luck in your life right now? Times three?'

'Jules, seriously, come on,' said Bess, still laughing it off.

'I'm deadly serious. What about this – if you miss the next shot, you have to complete the dare.'

'And if I make it?'

'If you make it, I promise to talk to my parents about selling the farm.'

Bess felt a smile form on her face. 'Got a pencil?' she asked, although she already knew the answer. Jules habitually carried a pencil and notepad for sketching.

She nodded, and Bess reached for Jules' handbag.

'Why do you have this?' She held up an eyebrow pencil.

'It's an eyebrow pencil,' said Jules.

'Yes, I realise that,' said Bess. 'But why do *you* have one? You have eyebrows.'

'It's just, I just do.'

Bess started laughing. 'Oh, my, goodness. Jules, is this because of that time in Year 11 when you over-plucked your left eyebrow and your mum had to show you how to fill in the gap with an eyebrow pencil? Do you just wanna be prepared in case it happens again?'

Jules grabbed the pencil. 'Maybe,' she said, pretending to be offended.

But she too couldn't help but laugh.

Bess found a sharpened pencil and notepad and wrote down the dare, which they both signed. Then she picked up her cue and steadied herself with a few deep breaths as she focused intently on her target. She knocked the white ball and watched it collide with the solid blue number 2 ball. As the blue and white colours spun towards the left-back corner pocket, Bess had no inkling of what was to come.

FOUR

35 days to Game Day

Bess lay asleep, reclined in the passenger seat of a once-white but now permanently dirt-coloured Toyota ute. She woke with a start, and, as she raised a hand to shield her eyes from the unwanted intrusion of the early-afternoon sunlight, recognition set in.

'You've got to be kidding,' she muttered, and reluctantly breathed in the cigarette smoke that clung to her clothes and hair. She swallowed a few times and ran her tongue over her teeth to try to erase the feeling of cotton balls in her mouth, asking herself why she always seemed to sleep with an open mouth after drinking.

She tried in vain to find the lever to bring up her seat. Frustrated, she opened the door and awkwardly slid out. Standing tall, she stretched and vowed never to drink again. Or perhaps just not as much.

The ute was parked at a familiar spot close to the Gerandaroo Lake. She had been camping in the area since she was an infant. As a

41

teenager, finally being allowed to stay overnight without an adult was a Gerandaroo rite of passage, one that she and her friends had revelled in. Her uni and city friends could never understand the appeal of camping. They had all grown up holidaying in hotels or at the very least a caravan. She had come to realise camping was an acquired taste, one she sorely missed, and that she had zero chance of convincing them that sleeping in a tent could actually be enjoyable.

She paused and looked towards the lake, hesitant to approach the man standing at the water's edge. Lachie Jacobs, tall with sandy hair and wearing a tired red and blue checked shirt, was as affable and genuine as a country boy could be.

He was skimming stones with his back to Bess. 'Mornin', sunshine. Still strugglin' to hold ya liquor?' he called without turning around.

Bess smirked, irritated in equal measure that it had to be him and that he spoke with poor diction only to annoy her.

Glancing down at her jeans, she closed her eyes and tried to remember the night before.

'We didn't . . . did we?' she asked.

'Have sex?' he replied, mildly amused. 'Well, you did force yourself on me. Several times, in fact. But I wasn't in the mood.'

Lachie expertly skimmed another stone and they both watched as it bounced four times across the glassy surface.

He turned to face Bess. 'Nah, you tried to drive home, so I took your keys and made you sleep it off. I didn't really fancy taking you home drunk. Again. And getting yet another lecture from your dad.'

Past events came flooding back as Bess stared at Lachie, embarrassed, but slightly relieved.

'I called your mum and told her you went home with Jules.'

'Where is she?'

'I'll give you one guess,' he said.

'She went home with Ryan?' An obvious rhetorical question.

'Just like old times,' said Lachie, looking nostalgic.

'Yeah. Old times,' added Bess, not as keen to take a stroll through their shared adolescence.

'I don't remember seeing you at the pub,' she commented in an almost accusatory tone, as though Lachie was in the wrong simply for being in the same place as her.

'I was only there for the final drinks call and to catch up with Ryan. Just in time to see you and Jules down some shots. Many, many shots.'

'Right. Well. Just like old times then, I guess.' There was a hint of resentment in her voice, mostly directed at herself, but also at Lachie.

'There's water in the back if you're thirsty,' he offered with a nod towards the ute.

'Thanks.' Although she was in dire need of a drink, Bess was also too stubborn to accept anything else from Lachie.

Still, as she struggled to swallow with such a dry mouth, she reluctantly fetched Lachie's decades-old blue water cooler. She had last used it at this very spot, camping with their younger brothers. They were meant to come alone, but Danny and Tom had begged to be allowed to tag along, and they relented.

It had been over eight years since they first camped here, just the two of them. It wasn't exactly with their parents' permission, as in, Bess told her parents she was staying at Jules' house and Lachie 'borrowed' his dad's ute while Mitch was on night duty, with Danny spending the night at Rick's. Yet surprisingly, nothing had happened. At the time, they both felt ready but also not. The best part of knowing someone your whole life was those moments when you were truly in sync. Six months later and their dynamic shifted. It was subtle, a slight tension had invaded their previously uncomplicated relationship bubble; seeing your best friend naked will do that. But they never discussed it, how being together seemed just that bit harder, not as solid, and less reassuring.

To an outsider, and even those who knew them both well, they remained 'perfect' for each other. Bess hated this comment. She maintained that nothing in life was perfect, not a person and certainly not a relationship. This perhaps contributed to her pulling away from Lachie, not intentionally, but almost out of self-preservation. The expectation that they would always be together was more of a hindrance than a blessing. She felt that it created a barrier between who they were and who they could be. Lachie had tried, consistently, to talk with Bess about their relationship. She'd resisted, not because she wanted to stay together and not because she wanted to break up, but because she knew she didn't have the confidence to do either.

The tension had escalated in the weeks after they finished high school. Before Bess left, they never officially broke up, nor did they say goodbye in such a way that implied they were still dating. And then their lives diverged, for the first time since they'd napped side by side on the quilt Bess's granny had knitted in the months before they were born. They went from being a constant in each other's lives in every conceivable way, to that person you *want* to call when you have good news or bad but can't because you're not meant to rely on them anymore.

So now, Bess kept her distance from Lachie – not from fear of danger, but rather fear of comfort. She examined the two wooden outdoor chairs tied down in the back of the ute, Lachie's distinctive seahorse insignia visible on the back right corner of each.

'These are beautiful,' she murmured.

'Always with a tone of surprise,' he replied with a wry smile.

Bess caught Lachie's eye but was quick to look away.

'They're for Sophie and Luke,' he added softly.

'Really? I thought they'd moved back to Adelaide?'

'They leave on Friday.'

Bess wanted to believe that in that moment, she knew what Lachie was thinking and feeling. But she was acutely aware that that was a privilege she perhaps no longer had.

'So, how have you been?' she asked, each word coming out forced and uneasy.

'I'm okay.'

'And, your dad . . .?'

'I don't know where he is,' Lachie said rapidly, his jovial tone completely gone.

'I know you don't,' Bess replied equally fast, 'but did you think of looking for him –'

'No,' he said, cutting her off and shaking his head. 'If I found him, I'd –'

This time Bess cut him off, fully aware of what Lachie would do to his dad if he saw him again. 'It's okay, we don't have to talk about him,' she said, chastising herself for having even mentioned Mitch.

They both skimmed several stones before Lachie spoke.

'How's city life?' he asked, his voice lifting a beat.

'Good. Busy.'

'But you're back?'

'Ahh, sort of. Not really. I mean, I am, but just for a bit. I'm not like *back* back. It just . . . it seemed like I should be here. For now.'

An awkward silence followed her rambling. There was, however, a brief moment when their eyes met and Bess thought about mentioning Danny, and she was sure that Lachie thought the same about Tom, but neither of them did.

'Um, do you think you could drive me to my car?' she asked instead.

Lachie stared at her, but Bess clumsily avoided his gaze. She could sense that he was overthinking her return home and was perhaps desperate to ask her something. She knew her answers would be insufficient. Her eyes darted back to him, checking to see if he was still staring.

He was.

'Sure,' he replied as he headed to the driver's side of his ute. Bess tracked him, his long stride so familiar, and despite being subtle, the whispers of woodchips that followed Lachie created an unwelcome feeling of intimacy. Her first thought was that he hadn't changed, not at all. But her second thought was that he had. And that her sudden reappearance and presence in his life, however peripheral, might do more harm than good.

As they drove, the radio, tuned to Triple M, acted as a filler of sorts. When a new song started, the sound was instantly signifi-cant – so much so that Bess squirmed noticeably. Dave Faulkner's voice was uncomfortably clear and direct.

'Good Times' had been released in the middle of their final year of high school. Bess did not know anyone except Lachie who would claim this as their favourite Hoodoo Gurus song. And she knew exactly why, but always pretended not to.

Secretly, there was a part of Bess that wanted to believe Lachie when he said they would always be in each other's lives. He was definitely the more romantic one; unlike Bess, he'd remember anniversaries the week before rather than the day of. Lachie seemed to want to make sure that the people he cared about knew it. She'd once asked her mum why he acted this way, and Gayle explained that the death of his mum when Lachie was only twelve might have created a space that he needed to fill by showing as much love as he could. Bess had never experienced the death of someone in the way Lachie had; even though Bess had loved Lachie's mum, she knew it wasn't the same.

As the lyrics triggered unwanted sentimental feelings, she couldn't help but steal a sideways glance at Lachie. To her surprise, his expression was static, not even a flicker of nostalgia for the song he used to insist they play over and over.

Even though she'd never told him, it was her favourite Hoodoo Gurus song too. But if listening to it again in her presence had impacted Lachie in any way, he hid it well. Moments later, Bess nearly reached out to smash the radio as U2's 'With or Without You' invaded the car.

Why did it feel as though the station was sending her not-so-subtle messages about their relationship history? Was Lachie thinking the same thing? Was he even thinking about her at all?

The next song was more comically kismet. Even though Lachie smiled so slightly that you could barely notice, Bess still sensed that he relaxed his body, however briefly, and she was certain he was replaying the same memory.

'Don't Change' by INXS was the last song they'd listened to together, in this very car, driving home from the lake over five years ago.

*

On arrival at the Denby pub, Lachie turned off the engine. He seemed on the verge of saying something, but Bess beat him to it.

'Okay, so, thanks for the ride, and, you know, for last night, or not last night. You know what I mean,' she said, stumbling over the last few words. Rather than wait for a response, she quickly exited the ute.

'Yeah, no worries,' Lachie said as Bess shut the door, leaving him to stare after her.

Bess waited in her car for a few minutes to make sure she wouldn't have to travel behind Lachie the whole way home. Despite the brisk country air, she opened her window and also blasted the radio as she drove, both to help her stay awake and to try to create some distance from the feelings that threatened to resurface.

*

Once home, Bess entered the house as quietly as possible. She closed her bedroom door and flopped face first onto her bed, groaning loudly into her pillow. A crumpling sound from her jeans prompted her to roll onto her side and sit up on the edge of the bed. She reached into her pocket and removed two pieces of folded paper.

As she read the dare, the realisation of what she had signed up for generated a nausea that did not mix well with her hangover. The second piece of paper was a recruitment flyer Jules had designed. Bess had absolutely no recollection of her doing this. Even drunk, Jules had enormous talent. Despite only being in pencil, her hand-drawn picture of a female footy player taking a specky looked like it could jump off the white page at any minute. Underneath were the words: *Join Gerandaroo's First Ever FEMALE Footy Team! First Training Tuesday Night 6 pm. Contact Bess O'Neill for more details*, complete with Bess's home number.

Not only did she not remember the flyer, but she definitely did not recall organising a training session for two days' time. In that moment, her dominant thought was that this was a pipe dream, a dare that would go unfulfilled. However, there was also this small thought, seemingly determined to have an impact, that insisted she could do this, that she could make this work.

Starving, Bess decided not to engage any further in her vacillating thoughts, and instead headed to the kitchen to fix something to eat. She spent the rest of the afternoon with the house largely to herself. Her mum was gardening out the front with Jinx, her dad off somewhere in his car.

As Bess climbed into bed that night, she was desperate for sleep to come and hopeful that her recurrent nightmare – the one that had plagued her since her last visit home over Christmas – would take the night off.

Bess stood on the verandah, the sharp chill in the air cold enough to drive her inside under normal circumstances, but all she could taste and feel was fear. As it coursed through her body, it pervaded her thoughts and crushed her heart. Tom emerged from Bess's car, his t-shirt and hands covered in blood, and he seemed unable to stand without swaying.

Bess rushed down the steps and embraced her little brother tightly.

As he let out a cry that cut through the air like a wounded animal, Bess repeated herself through tears. 'It's okay, Tommo. Everything will be okay. Everything will be okay.'

Suddenly, Tom was gone and Danny stood in his place. Eyes wide with fear, he held up his hands and they both watched as blood spilled, staining the sandy-coloured stones a deep red.

Bess woke with a start, her breath catching sharply, almost painfully, in her throat. She reached up to wipe the sweat from her forehead and tried to slow her breathing. She glanced at her bedside clock. The neon outline of 2.27 am made her sigh heavily. With still so much night to endure before morning, she wondered if she would make it.

*

With her eyes fixed on the ceiling, Gayle lay awake. Her mind was plagued by an interaction with Danny from nearly two years ago.

Gayle sat at her office desk, Danny opposite her. A bluish-black bruise surrounded his left eye.

'Daniel, how did it happen?' asked Gayle.

'Just copped a stray elbow at footy practice,' he replied. 'It was probably Tom,' he added, trying to make a joke out of it.

Gayle furrowed her brow in a concerned, motherly way as she leaned forward. 'Danny, you know you can talk to me. Are you sure there isn't something you'd like to tell me?'

'Nah, I'm fine. No big deal, just a black eye.' He kept laughing it off. 'Can I go now?' he asked, already rising from his chair. 'It's just I've got phys ed.'

Gayle leaned back, frustrated and certain that Danny was lying but unsure of how to proceed without losing his trust. 'Yes, Daniel, you can go. But you're coming for dinner tonight, after training?'

'You bet. Thanks, Mrs O'Neill.'

Gayle rolled over in bed. Ian knew that his wife hadn't fallen asleep, because she'd been tossing and turning for half the night. He too lay awake, his thoughts on Danny and an incident midway through the last footy season.

Mitch Jacobs was a tall burly man in need of a shave and unsteady on his feet from a night of heavy drinking. He pushed past his youngest son.

'Where's that bloody umpire? Wouldn't know how to call a game if his tits were on fire,' he slurred.

'Dad, let's just go,' pleaded Daniel. He attempted to push his dad back towards their car, but Mitch aggressively shoved his son to one side.

'If you can't take care of these things now, you're never gonna stand up for yaself. Or do you want people to keep talkin' about you and . . .' His voice trailed off as he threw his hands in the air. 'Holding the ball and bloody high tackles. And he was fucking wrong. Every fucking time!' he yelled, his voice rising with each outburst.

'Dad, come on, it's not worth it.'

'Not worth it?' cried Mitch as he swung around and nearly face-planted in the process. 'What sort of man are you?' he sneered, getting closer and closer to his son. 'Ya can't even stand up for yaself.'

Ian, having witnessed the exchange, walked with purpose towards Mitch and Daniel.

'Hey there, Mitch, how about Dan comes and stays with us tonight and I'll get someone to drive you home?' said Ian, trying to defuse the situation.

'Why don't you fuck off there, Ian, and worry about your own kids for a change?' Mitch shot back. He turned to Daniel. 'Get in the car. We're goin' home,' he ordered.

Ian spoke directly to Daniel. 'Dan, grab your stuff and head over to my car.'

'Don't you tell my son what to do!' Mitch shouted as he moved towards Ian, gearing up for a fight.

Other families were now staring. Daniel, embarrassed by the attention, rebuffed Ian's help. 'Nah, we're fine. Come on, Dad, let's go. I'll drive,' he said.

Daniel attempted to lead his dad towards their car, but Mitch tripped over his own feet and landed heavily on his knees. Daniel grabbed his dad around the waist and tried to lift him so he could stand.

Ian moved forward to help. Daniel looked at Ian, a pained expression filling his face. 'Mr O'Neill, please just leave. You're only making it worse.'

Ian hesitated, concerned about leaving Daniel alone with Mitch but not wanting to embarrass him further.

'Ahh, there you have it!' Mitch raised his arms. 'The boy's got some fight in him after all.' He stood and patted Daniel on the back, and finally allowed his son to guide him away.

Daniel helped his dad into the passenger seat and jogged around to the driver's side. He got in without looking back at Ian, who stood and watched as Daniel, despite only having a learner's permit, reversed at speed and drove away.

As Ian climbed into his car, his own son glared at him. 'How could you let him leave with his dad?'

'What would you have me do, Tom?' said Ian, exasperated. 'Drag him to our car?'

'You could have tried harder.'

'He's not my son,' Ian said reluctantly.

'But he's my brother,' replied Tom. He turned on the radio and pushed the volume way up.

Ian knew what Tom meant because he felt the same way. He saw Danny as a surrogate son just as Tom saw him as a surrogate brother, and he'd failed to protect him. He'd failed to protect them both.

FIVE

The O'Neill family danced around each other and engaged in brief conversations with little substance. They all seemed to be actively avoiding any prolonged interactions, making meal times particularly challenging. Bess decided to wait until she heard her parents finish in the kitchen before getting up for breakfast. It wasn't that she didn't want to see them, at least not entirely, it was more that she just had no idea what to say.

Besides their strained relationship, Bess had noticed a change in the town's dynamics. Residents had always stopped in the street for a chat, even crossed the road for a quick hello. And dropping by a neighbour's house unannounced was commonplace and typically welcomed. But in the time Bess had been away, this behaviour had noticeably diminished. Without the everyday conversations, the town began to drift, with connections forged over decades now seemingly severed by silence.

This made small town country living unbearable. Bess knew

it was driven out of fear of saying the wrong thing or refusing to accept what had happened, and more importantly *why* it happened. But knowing that didn't make it any easier. And it certainly didn't mean she was actively attempting to change things by interacting with anyone.

This had happened before – an unwanted stillness had blanketed the town about ten years earlier, but it hadn't had the same lasting domino effect and it wasn't born out of violence. That time around, it was because the men were struggling to consistently field a full team. Despite their best efforts and with Ian leading the charge, they'd had to concede defeat and withdraw from competition. The players had experienced a run of injuries, and the impact of record-breaking bushfires also meant many of the men just couldn't make training or matches. How could playing a game be a priority when their livelihood was at stake? It was only meant to be temporary, one season at the most, but they'd never returned. And Ian stopped trying to make it happen, so the town's entire hopes had come to rest on the Under 18s. Bess found it irritating that the premiership billboard did not differentiate the premierships won by the senior side compared to the boys. She and her dad used to argue about it.

'It's not wrong, Bess, so what's the problem? Gerandaroo won all the premierships listed,' Ian had insisted.

'I never said it was wrong,' she'd countered, 'it's just not as accurate as it could be.'

It remained an unresolved issue between them.

*

Aside from reluctantly placing the flyer in the window of the general store early that morning, with little belief that anything would come of it, Bess had no desire to go anywhere else. She realised how easy it was to fall into a routine that didn't require her to talk to people. And despite knowing that wasn't a good thing, she felt unwilling to do anything about it.

Back in the city, Bess would have been up at 6.30 am and at school most mornings by 7.30 am to help run athletics training in Term 1 and cross-country training in Term 3. She enjoyed her involvement with the school sports teams and found it helped her develop a stronger rapport with the students. As a new teacher, she spent her evenings over-planning her lessons and had a habit of becoming anxious when trying to pre-empt what questions her students might ask. She was slowly realising that she needed to let them sit with the content for a while, and that more often than not, it was better if they *had* questions, because at least that meant they were engaging with the material.

However, Bess sometimes struggled to keep her frustration hidden when students derailed a lesson. Earlier that term, on a particularly shitty Friday afternoon during the last period of the day, a Year 10 student had repeatedly turned around to chat to his friends, ignoring her instructions to face the front and pay attention.

After asking him for a fourth time to stop talking, Bess slammed her fist on the table. 'Damn it, Peter! Out, now!'

The room fell silent. She had lost it. Not completely, but close enough that the students knew better than to laugh.

Peter was quick to gather his things and leave the room. Her voice

56

shaking, Bess continued with the class, but all she wanted to do was walk out and not come back.

That incident was the catalyst for Bess to realise she needed a break, because she wasn't in the mindset to be teaching anyone, least of all impressionable youth. Her principal was supportive and encouraged her to return home to Gerandaroo.

*

After another awkward breakfast, Ian left the house under the pretence of needing supplies from the hardware store to fix a broken pale in the back fence. But there was no broken pale, and he had a toolshed with everything he could possibly need. Instead, he drove to the feedstock store and parked his car. Despite the crisp air stinging his face and hands, he took his time as he made his way along the side and backstreets towards the town centre.

He had walked these roads since he was a child, and had taken to running at an early age. There was never any thought of danger, so his parents were content for him to go any and everywhere, just as long as he was home by six o'clock for tea. It meant that he knew every street name, every turn, every slope. He learned which farmers were happy for him to explore their land, and which weren't. He knew the quickest route home from school, and the longest. And he knew how to get lost and find his way back home again.

As he walked past the general store, he slowed his pace, eyes straight ahead, trying to process what he thought he saw. He backtracked and stared at a handwritten flyer in the window. He stood motionless for a few moments, anger rising in him, before he marched inside and ripped it down. Half a dozen people watched him do it, but no one dared tell him to put it back.

*

On his return home, Ian stormed into the kitchen where Bess was reading the paper and slammed the flyer down on the table.

'What the bloody hell is this?' he yelled, in a tone Bess had seldom heard.

'Right. Okay. I thought you might see that,' she said, trying not to be put off by her dad's anger.

Ian stared at her impatiently.

'Um, well, I'm putting together a women's footy team,' she explained. As she said the words out loud, she suddenly thought how foolish she sounded, but continued talking nonetheless. 'We're going to play a match against Denby on the third of October.' She drew out her words, eager to calm her father down.

'Like hell you are!'

Bess was shocked by her dad's increasingly aggressive behaviour and wondered if she should even bother responding. The chances of her forming a team in time to play a game were slim to none anyway.

Gayle entered the kitchen and surprised them both by saying, 'Do you have any players yet?'

'Um, two. Me and Jules,' replied Bess, glancing apprehensively towards her dad.

'Well, that's a start.'

'A start?' Ian looked incredulously at his wife before turning his attention back to his daughter. 'Why are you doing this?' he asked, his tone more subdued.

Bess knew better than to tell her dad it was only because of a dare. But as soon as she'd engaged with the prospect of actually playing a game, that small insistent voice had gleefully danced its way to the forefront of her mind.

When she spoke, her voice was gentle. 'Because . . . because I think that maybe we need it,' she said, surprising herself.

'Who? Who needs it?' Ian said impatiently. 'Is this another one of those bloody dares you did as kids?'

'I . . . Dad, maybe it'll help? For the town to be around footy again? And maybe . . . maybe we can talk about what happen—'

'No, Bess. No,' he said with a firm shake of the head, emotion boiling over. 'It's too soon for anyone to play on that oval. It's not right,' he added, his voice no longer angry or loud, but broken.

An uncomfortable silence descended that no one knew how to break. After a minute or two, Ian let out a deep sigh and walked out, with Jinx following closely; he let the wire door slam, causing Bess and Gayle to jump.

When they couldn't hear the car engine, Bess knew her dad was just sitting in his car. He'd taught her and Tom to never drive angry, a lesson passed down from his grandfather, whose best mate had died in a single car-crash following a heated argument with his parents.

Bess felt a pang of guilt, but it was not strong enough to pull her outside to try to reconcile with her dad. She also felt frustrated, and his refusal to talk to her ignited a desire to justify the need for a women's team.

'Would it really be such a bad thing?' she asked her mum. 'I mean, surely Dad knows that we're not trying to deliberately upset anyone?'

'You don't have to convince me,' said Gayle. 'But your dad, he feels things so deeply.'

'Just like Tom.'

'Yes. Just like Tom.'

It was the first time since Bess had returned home that either of them had mentioned Tom, and saying his name made his absence even harder to bear.

*

Ian eventually reversed down the driveway and travelled through the town, with Jinx sitting faithfully on the passenger seat, his head poking out the open window. On the outskirts of Gerandaroo, they turned up Bannon Lane – a hilly and longish no-through road that appeared suddenly and was typically only accessed by locals. Ian stopped outside aged iron gates that were permanently half closed, with yew trees either side. He slowly opened his door and stepped out, Jinx close behind.

The cemetery was nearly a century and a half old and surprisingly well maintained. Pine trees bordered the area, and sunlight edged through to create a calming effect.

Ian slowly lowered himself, his knees cracking from repeated football injuries, and sat slightly uncomfortably on the dewy ground in front of Ruth's headstone. Jinx settled beside him, and as he gently stroked Jinx's soft ears, he thought about the day after her funeral.

The O'Neills had woken up to an early-morning phone call from Lachie who told them his dad wasn't home and the car was gone. Aware that Mitch was still inevitably drunk from a day of heavy drinking at the wake, and not wanting to expose the boys to his homecoming, Gayle was quick to pack the family esky and they took the kids to the lake.

Ian and Bess sat on folding camping chairs, Danny and Tom were playing fetch with Jinx, while Gayle was laying out the food on a large tartan rug.

Lachie had rolled up his pants and was standing in the darkish water up to his knees.

Ian took in his daughter's features as her gaze remained fixed on Lachie.

'He's so sad,' Bess murmured.

'I know,' Ian replied. 'It'll take time.'

'For what?'

'For him to feel a bit better.'

Bess picked up a stick and traced it through the dirt. 'I don't think so.'

'You don't think he'll feel better?'

'No. I think he'll just pretend. If Mum died, I'd never feel better. But everyone expects you to. Like when Teddy died, and you pretended.'

Ian was taken aback by his daughter's insight, especially considering she was only eight when the family's first dog had died.

'Why do you think I was pretending?' he asked curiously.

'I could tell. When you came home from work and he wasn't there to say hello, you were always so sad. But you never said you were.'

'You're right. I was very sad, but I didn't want to upset you.'

'But I was sad too. So was Tom, even though he was really little.

And then we got Jinx and you were happy again. Lachie can't get a new mum,' she added after a beat.

'Maybe that's something you can talk to Lachie about. Share with him that it's okay to be sad and that he can talk to you about how he's feeling. Do you think that might help?'

'Maybe,' Bess conceded.

Ian thought how grown-up his daughter seemed. He knew she'd always been perceptive, but now she was acutely aware of how cruel the world could be, and that sometimes there was very little you could do to change that. Still, he didn't want her to grow up believing that she couldn't make things better.

'It may not make much of a difference right now, but over time, letting Lachie know that he has a friend, no matter how sad he might feel and how awful life might be, it'll help, Bess. I promise.'

'You said never to promise unless it's a promise you can keep.'

'I know.'

Bess stood, rolled up her pants, and walked towards Lachie.

Gayle came and sat beside Ian. 'They'll be okay,' she said.

'Maybe,' Ian replied.

With Jinx asleep by his side, Ian's thoughts drifted to his father. Ian had been close to his dad, although he sometimes wished he had pushed him more, perhaps expected more.

Ian's parents did not have an easy marriage. Archie experienced extreme anxiety, likely the result of being an aerial gunner in the RAAF. While he was not the type to share war stories, the effects were visible and his hands would often shake. During the 1987 Melbourne v Hawthorn preliminary final at VFL Park, he suffered a near-fatal heart attack, after which he could not bring himself to return and watch a game live. He maintained his MCC membership, though, and was a lifelong Melbourne Demons supporter, a tradition passed down from his mother, who'd loved footy and encouraged her children to be passionate supporters.

Ian was a bit of an anomaly among his friends growing up, torn between being a rough-and-tumble country kid and a quiet academic. He excelled in English and History, but was also an outstanding full-forward, one of the best Gerandaroo had ever produced. Gayle encouraged him to strive for something more than just staying in Gerandaroo after school finished. But he struggled to set academic goals when his male friends openly mocked him for wanting to study rather than play or train with them every night. The majority of his footy team were stereotypical country jocks, who played with a brutish intensity that crossed over into their daily lives. With the exception of two mates who voluntarily enlisted in the army in 1966, the rest had little desire to experience anything beyond what Gerandaroo had to offer.

While he enrolled at a teachers' college along with Gayle, he quit after a year. He developed anxiety from living in the city and was eager to return to Gerandaroo and take over Redlegs. He had no regrets about this phase of his life, because it was only after they both left Gerandaroo that he and Gayle fell in love. She finished her training, and after two years at a large public school in the city, she returned to Gerandaroo and took a position at Denby High, where she became principal about twenty years later.

Despite surgery, Archie's heart never recovered, and he died aged seventy-three. Ian's mum succumbed to pneumonia a month later, her death particularly hard to accept given how stoic she had always been. Gayle's parents, who shared a close bond with both Gayle and Ian, had died unexpectedly years earlier. First her dad following a tractor accident on a friend's farm, and then her mum only six months after being diagnosed with breast cancer.

As Ian blinked away hot tears, he thought of his parents and Gayle's parents with affection. He wished they were here. He wished for someone to take care of him. To tell him everything would be all right. Even if it was a lie.

SIX

Rick checked his yellow and navy Casio watch, a recent gift from his granddad, and noted he'd been running for forty-one minutes. He never used to wear a watch; he relied on the two bell system to make it to class on time, used the wall clock to count down until home time, and always seemed to just make it through the front door for tea at exactly six o'clock. All his friends ate tea at six, and after years of playing outdoors, they all knew that when the sun sat just above the town's peak, it was time to head to their respective driveways.

Rick was surprised by how much he enjoyed timing his runs. Being the fastest or the strongest had never been a goal of his, but now he needed something to look forward to, something to aim for, and besting his times and running further had helped to fill an unwanted void.

As a country boy, Rick had grown up with the surrounding bush as the ultimate playground, and the only dangers he cared about were environmental – fire, flood, drought. He thought back to days spent running all over town, without any real worries, and how he and his friends, including Tom and Danny, would create obstacle courses on the track using whatever was at hand. On one occasion they dug a deep hole and tied a rope to what turned out to be an unstable branch above it. They took it in turns sprinting towards the rope, jumping on it, and seeing who could swing the furthest. By the time it was Rick's turn, the branch had had enough and snapped cleanly just as he hovered over the hole. The result was a fractured wrist that required a cast, which was what all his classmates wanted. His parents were less pleased, but Rick thoroughly enjoyed the attention and getting everyone to sign it. As a bonus, it meant two weeks without having to hand in any homework. But what he remembered most from that incident was that all the boys tried to take the blame so Rick wouldn't get into any trouble. They each spoke with his parents to explain that Rick had not wanted to jump (even though he had), that he'd advised them not to do it (which he hadn't), and that they'd forced him to jump (which they hadn't). It created a bond between the boys that stayed with them.

Rick enjoyed country life; he never planned to leave or at least, if he did, not to go very far. But lately, he felt his upbringing had perhaps created a false sense of safety, and there were other threats, far closer and more personal than he dared imagine. Until recently, he had never acknowledged that harmful words could lead to harmful actions. And as that feeling of comfort and safety and belonging started to erode, he worried he would never get it back.

As Rick approached Gundry Crescent, he slowed to a stop, his legs and breathing heavy. He watched in the distance, hands on hips, sucking in air, as Bess reversed down her driveway. He hadn't meant to come this way, but his mind often wandered when he ran. A few months earlier, he'd ended up halfway to Denby where he'd pulled his calf muscle and had to hobble back. His mum, furious with worry when he arrived home nearly three hours later, made him promise not to be gone longer than an hour without telling her exactly where he planned to run. He agreed, and knew he was on the verge of breaking that promise, so he turned and ran in the opposite direction, determined not to let his thoughts overwhelm him.

Or at least not too much.

*

In the hours leading up to the first training session, Bess engaged in a circular self-debate about whether she would, could, or indeed should form a team. There were numerous cons and they flowed with ease: her dad was against it, which meant most of the town probably felt the same way; it was going to take a huge amount of energy and effort to both recruit players and to get them match ready; and she knew she would need to have some conversations with people she had avoided for years.

The pros she always came back to seemed far simpler: she loved footy and was fed up with only being able to enjoy it from the boundary. But perhaps more importantly, she also knew that country footy created its own pulse and gave life to her small town. Until it returned, Gerandaroo would continue to beat out of sync and possibly fade away. Acknowledging this spurred her on, however reluctantly, to not only put the flyer back up in the general store, but also to head out to the oval for the first training session.

Leaving the house had been a trial of sorts. Bess had never owned footy boots but was certain Tom had kept an older pair that were about her size. She had uncharacteristically neglected this task until the last minute. Entering Tom's room for a second time, Bess felt like an intruder, particularly when she had to open his wardrobe and move things around. With no luck, she bent down to look under the bed and immediately thought about all the times she'd done this in the weeks after Tom had started kinder.

Four-year-old Tom, who at the time slept in a much smaller bed, was convinced that some unknown person planned to replace him with another 'Tom', and the only place that person could hide would be under his bed. It took some prodding, but Bess finally established that Glenn, a boy from kinder, had told Tom this was going to happen. Apparently, Glenn's thirteen-year-old brother Kyle had told Glenn the plot of *The Omen* – a film entirely inappropriate for both Kyle and Glenn. Being four years old, Glenn misunderstood most of what Kyle told him, but relayed enough to scare the crap out of Tom. To help settle her brother, Bess slept on a mattress beside Tom's bed for a week. She told Tom that if he got swapped out for 'another Tom', she'd make sure she went with him.

Bess saw the boots close to the wall, and had to half-crawl under the bed to reach them. Ian watched her emerge from Tom's room, but said nothing. Jinx became very excited upon smelling the boots, clearly equating them with the imminent arrival of Tom.

Bess could only apologise as she patted Jinx. 'I'm just borrowing them, Jinxy,' she explained.

*

When she pulled into the gravel carpark, Jules was already waiting for her, her socks high and her hair pulled back in a long plait. She smiled wide and waved to Bess, which both irritated and amused her. They really were polar opposites. Bess had a tendency to expect the worst, not because the worst always happened, but because it made for a nice surprise when things worked out. As a consequence, others sometimes perceived her to be sullen or even a tad bitter. With Jules, it wasn't that she was all sunshine and light, it was more that she gave people the benefit of the doubt. She could forgive without anger and show compassion when it was undeserved. And this shone through in her gentle eyes.

As Bess stepped out of her Magna, she and Jules both glanced at the group of boys huddled on the north-east side of the boundary. Lucas Cutler, with sharp, some would say handsome, features, leaned into the fence.

'Great-looking team, girls! Are you gonna bring us home the premiership?' he yelled, his black t-shirt and the latest Nike Airs still perfectly white, out of place among the raggedy teenage boys that surrounded him, their shoes scuffed, their t-shirts grubby.

The boys laughed, that arrogant, snide laughter that all women find grating. The type of laughter that made you want to punch the guy in the face or knee him in the balls. Preferably both. In quick succession.

'I didn't really think we'd have an audience, did you?' Bess threw a sideways glance at Jules, her focus still on the boys.

Jules responded hesitantly, 'Um, no. I did not. But I doubt they'll stay much longer. I'm sure they have things to do,' she added with unfounded optimism.

'Yeah, I'm sure their calendar's full of things to do. In Gerandaroo. After school. With no football training. In a town where nothing happens. And where there's absolutely nothing to do.'

'Okay, point taken,' replied Jules. 'No need to be such a dick about it.'

Bess tried to stall by taking her time removing a gym bag filled with footballs from her boot. One toppled out, with *Geran Primary* visible in black marker on the side.

'I see you've done some late-night pilfering.' Jules grinned.

'Not quite.' Bess chuckled. 'Although there are a few footies in here from the primary school that somehow made their way to my house.'

After gathering the gear, they headed towards the fence. Bess stopped abruptly, her gaze fixed on the centre square.

'You right?' asked Jules as she followed Bess's gaze.

'Yeah. I just . . . I haven't been on the field . . . since . . .'

'I know. Neither have I.'

They continued to stare at the oval.

'Hey,' Jules said suddenly, 'do you remember that game against Wylie Creek? When all our balls were missing?'

'You mean stolen?' said Bess with a short laugh. 'It was like the first time that it *wasn't* us,' she continued, 'or someone we knew.'

'Yeeaahh,' said Jules, looking down sheepishly. 'So it actually was someone you know.'

'What?' Bess turned to face Jules. 'It was that dropkick Lionel. Remember? They found several in his bag and the rest under his seat on the bus.'

'Only because I put them there.'

'You did what?' said Bess, her shock spreading into a wide smile. 'How did I not know this? And how did you get away with it? And why did you do it?' The questions tumbled out amid her laughter.

'Well, so, you remember the previous season when Lionel knocked Ryan out behind the play? And then he laughed about it?'

'Yeah, he was a real arsehole.'

'He absolutely was. And I guess I just wanted some payback. So, I framed him,' Jules explained matter-of-factly. 'It was pretty easy in the end. Two of his teammates helped. Most of them couldn't stand playing with him. Or even being around him.'

'I can't believe you kept that a secret all this time,' said Bess.

'Are you mad I didn't tell you?' asked Jules.

'Mad? More like impressed. I always knew you had a Machiavellian side.'

'More like a revenge side.'

'Good enough,' Bess replied with a smile.

'So, together?' Jules nodded towards the oval.

Bess bit her lower lip, but nodded, albeit reluctantly, and they approached the fence.

'Wow. Why is this so hard to do?' asked Jules, as her right leg hung awkwardly over the fence before she found the ground.

'I know, I suddenly feel very *very* old.' Bess placed the ball bag on the oval side and attempted to follow it by straddling the fence. She immediately regretted not using the gate a few metres away.

As they landed on the oval and looked at each other, both were smiling in a comforting sort of way, but the moment was broken by a loud voice from the boundary.

'Come on, girls! Show us your kick!' Lucas called.

Jules glared at him. 'He sounds like Simon,' she said, her voice quiet.

'Yeah,' Bess agreed after a beat, equally quiet. 'With so many good players finishing last season, he probably expected this to be his year. I'm guessing he's pretty pissed that the league decided they couldn't have a team this season.'

'That doesn't give him the right to be an arsehole,' said Jules.

For reasons even she couldn't fully understand (but was sure were linked to the fact she was now a teacher and some warped sense of protection for students, *any* students, had overcome her), Bess continued to defend Lucas, a position that was more typical of Jules.

'Footy's probably the only thing he's good at.'

'I wouldn't say that. He's pretty good at being a well-dressed dick.'

They headed towards the faintly painted centre circle, within an equally faint centre square.

'So maybe we wait a little bit and see if anyone shows up?' suggested Bess.

'How many are coming?'

Bess tried to look busy, fumbling with the opening to the bag. 'Um . . . a few. I think. I don't have a final number.'

'Did anyone actually tell you they're coming?' asked Jules.

Bess hesitated. 'Well, no, not really.'

'Not really or no?'

'No,' said Bess.

'Have you talked to Lachie yet?'

'About what?'

'About the team.'

'Why would I talk to Lachie?' Bess asked, bordering on defensive.

'Um, I just thought that maybe he could help out?'

'I don't think that would be a good idea.'

'Okay, it was just a thought,' Jules replied.

'Okay.'

'You know, it doesn't matter if things are a bit slow to start with,' said Jules. 'There's still plenty of time for you to form a team.'

Bess looked at Jules, slightly irritated. 'How exactly am I supposed to do that?'

'Did you think only putting up a single flyer was gonna cut it?' asked Jules.

'Well, I didn't see you do anything,' Bess countered.

'You mean other than come up with the idea and create the flyer? Besides, it's not my team, B.'

Jules picked up a ball, jogged about twenty metres to the left of the square and prepared to kick.

Bess did not seem surprised that Jules' kick landed directly in front of her for an easy mark. She returned the kick and the two continued, falling into a familiar rhythm of moving closer and further apart. A fumble by Jules a few kicks later drew derisive laughter from the boys on the boundary.

'You do realise you need more than two to make a team?' Lucas yelled.

'You do realise you're an arrogant fuckwit?' Jules yelled back.

The other boys laughed.

Lucas's expression darkened. He was not used to someone challenging him, least of all a woman, and he was definitely not accustomed to others laughing at his expense.

'Tell you what, sweetheart,' he drawled, his snide nature shining through as he jumped the fence and headed towards Jules, 'if you wanna play on our field –'

'Your field? Since when is this your field?' said Jules. 'We've been playing on it for longer than you.'

'When you play for the Gerandaroo Demons, the field is yours,' he shot back. 'And I don't recall you ever having played an actual game? You know this little kick-to-kick thing you're doing doesn't count, right?'

'Well, you don't play for the Gerandaroo Demons anymore, right?' said Jules, mimicking his tone.

Bess cringed; Jules had gone too far. But nothing could have prepared her for Lucas's response.

'Yeah, cos that fucking gay kid –'

Jules didn't allow Lucas to finish. She lunged and shoved him in the chest, causing him to stumble and fall awkwardly to the ground.

The boys on the boundary howled with laughter.

Lucas jumped to his feet, now fired up, and furiously brushing dirt from his t-shirt. 'Crazy bitch! What the fuck's your problem?'

Bess watched, paralysed.

Jules and Lucas glared at each other as though they were in a forced stare-off. 'Get off our field,' she told him, her voice low but even.

Lucas continued to scowl at her, his nostrils flaring as he struggled to formulate a response. He shook his head, clenched his jaw, then left the field, his stride long and pissed off.

The other boys followed him like sheep.

Bess watched them go, then turned and began walking away.

'Where are you going?' called Jules.

'I'm not doing this.'

'What do you mean? We haven't even started!'

'Well, look around.' Bess threw her arms out wide and spun around to face Jules. 'No one came. And we're getting laughed at.' The tears she had fought to suppress for so long seemed incapable of remaining hidden now she was back home. With her eyes welling up, she continued. 'Being here, knowing what happened, it's just too hard. It's too much.'

Jules softened. She walked over to Bess and placed a hand on each shoulder. Bess slowly lifted her gaze.

'Bess, that's exactly why we have to do this. Why *you* have to do this.'

Bess lowered her head, not convinced, but acutely aware that something had to happen for things to change.

She just didn't think she was the one to do it.

In fact, she was certain that she wasn't.

SEVEN

Around lunchtime the next day, Bess stood in front of the auto-shop receptionist, Jen Milton. With her hair tied back in a tight ponytail and wearing no make-up, Jen's plain white shirt, black slacks and black shoes meant you'd likely forget her as soon as you turned your back.

'I just noticed a clinking sound yesterday and it's due for a service,' explained Bess.

'Dad can take a look in ... probably an hour?' said Jen as she ran her finger down a large diary. 'Can you leave it here for the afternoon?'

'Yeah, that'll be fine. Thanks.'

As Bess turned to leave, Jen surprised her. 'I saw your flyer in the general store. Are you still looking for players?'

Bess turned back and paused. Her immediate thought was that she could easily justify not pursuing the team any further – thought she'd decided not to, in fact – but that stubborn ripple of defiance cut through again: *Don't give up so easily. Gerandaroo needs something to cheer for.*

'Ah, yeah, I am,' she said finally.

'I used to help my brother practise. Before he moved to Sydney for uni.'

'Oh right. Was that Tim?'

'Yeah, he's studying medicine.'

'Wow, smart guy.'

Jen smiled in a proud sort of way.

Although Bess hadn't set up another training session time with Jules, she tried to make herself sound as organised as possible. 'We train tomorrow night at six. Do you maybe wanna come check it out?' she asked, actively wondering how wrong it was to imply that the collective 'we' represented an actual team and not just her and Jules.

'Okay,' said Jen, before she reached for the phone that had just started to ring.

'Okay. Great,' replied Bess, still surprised as she turned away.

Bess stood on the pavement outside the mechanics, feeling conflicted. She had intended to head straight home, curl up on the couch and watch a movie. If she failed to take further steps to recruit players, she would only disappoint Jules and Jen. But Jules' words from the night before kept niggling at her, gentle but insistent. Bess considered how Jules consistently went out of her way to make everyone around her not only feel better, but become better people. Even though they hadn't spoken much over the last few years, just the thought of letting down Jules created a rush of discomfort that Bess knew would fester into regret. And Jen asking to join the team proved that there *were* women who wanted to play. So, Bess took a deep breath and turned to the left, away from home, and towards an old friend.

*

On the other side of the street, Rick sprinted past. His faded yellow t-shirt clung to his chest and sweat was visible across his forehead. He pounded the pavement at an unsustainable pace, but only began to labour as he reached the backstreets beyond the town centre. As he approached the oval, he stopped and spat on the ground, hard, desperate for a drink of water. He felt that his body was collapsing with each breath, so he gripped the fence with both hands to steady himself. Despite being surrounded by nothing but space, he had the familiar sensation that the country air was almost crushing. Rick briefly closed his eyes, but the moment had already started to overwhelm him.

He glared at the oval, and as adrenaline collided with anger and regret, he lashed out and kicked the fence.

And then he kicked it again.

And again.

And again.

He wanted answers but was met with silence. He turned awkwardly and fell to the ground, his back sliding painfully down the fence. He sat uncomfortably still, his knees bent, palms resting on the gravel, breathing deeply. Remaining stationary for too long made his thoughts jump around at a rapid pace and he couldn't handle much more of it.

He allowed only a few moments of what he felt was undeserved self-pity, before he jumped up and sprinted away, careful not to turn back.

*

On Green Street, Bess stood near the doorway of the hair salon Just Do's and waited to talk with the owner. Andrea Wilson was doing the finishing touches on Mrs Jenkins, who held regular appointments for a wash and set.

Andy was honest, which people often mistook for rudeness. Her school reports were filled with terms like 'rebellious' and 'impertinent', but she was far more capable than her teachers ever gave her credit for.

As Andy walked Mrs Jenkins to the cash register, Bess found herself standing a little straighter. As the former primary school principal, Mrs Jenkins ruled with authority in an 'I care about you, but you will do as I say' type of way. No one had ever felt comfortable calling her anything but Mrs Jenkins, including adults.

'I'll see you in two weeks,' said Andy.

'Yes, thank you, Andrea.'

With a slight nod of the head, Mrs Jenkins gave Bess a wry smile. 'I do hope you're staying out of trouble.'

'Doing my best, Mrs Jenkins, doing my best,' she replied as she held the door open.

Bess turned to face Andy, whose black hair streaked with violet rested perfectly on her shoulders.

'So, Bess, one guess why you're here.' Andy stood with her head slightly cocked.

'You've heard?' said Bess.

'I have.'

'And?'

'Sure. Why not?' she replied with a shrug of the shoulders.

'That was easy.'

'Bess, I've literally wanted to play footy for years. I even tried to get a team going.'

'Seriously?' asked Bess.

'Yep. It was around the same time I was your peer support leader.'

Andy gathered some wet towels and made her way to the back of the salon.

Bess followed her. 'So, what happened?'

'There was definitely interest. Denby, Wylie Creek, Yalop and even Brendalee started to put together teams so we knew we'd be able to play at least a few games.'

'But you never got to?'

Andy opened the washing machine door and placed the towels inside. 'Nope. Parents were concerned we'd get hurt. Girls decided they didn't wanna play, especially after the boys wouldn't stop making fun of us. And so it just . . . fizzled out. Same thing happened in all the other towns.' She set the dial for a quick wash and dry.

'Well, that's depressing. I can't guarantee this time will be any different,' said Bess.

'I know. And I also know you'll need to do more than just put a group of women together for it to work,' she stated candidly.

Bess sensed an opportunity to pass the buck. 'Would you prefer to be in charge?'

Andy laughed. 'Not a chance, Bess.'

'You can be decidedly unhelpful.'

Andy just smiled in a knowing sort of way.

'So then I'll see you tomorrow at six?' said Bess.

'You will,' said Andy.

*

As Bess made her way through the streets, she struggled to pass a single one without her mind being clouded by childhood and teenage memories that she hadn't thought about in years. She resented the intrusion, but wasn't sure why, given they were mostly happy memories.

She couldn't help but smile walking past the ever-growing gnome family outside the Leveys' house. As thirteen-year-olds, Bess and her friends, on a group dare, replaced them with oranges decorated with hand-drawn smiley and frowny faces, and then moved the gnomes to the front yards of neighbouring houses. They all had to work on Jules' farm for a weekend as punishment.

She quickened her pace when crossing the Bowmens' driveway. In Year 9, Ryan had 'borrowed' the starter pistol from Denby High, used for the school athletics carnival. Ryan and Jules took turns firing it while a bunch of them raced their bikes down the street. Unfortunately, it scared the crap out of the family's whippets, to the extent that one of them dug under the fence and went missing for two days; the Bowmens had, understandably, never forgiven them.

The houses lining Windem Street were versions of the same model. Mostly built in the thirties, only a few had been renovated in the last decade. Signs of family living were prominent, with basketball rings above garage doors and yards littered with bikes and balls.

Bess rang the doorbell at number 19 where the lawn had been freshly cut. Eva Riles threw open the door. She was a tall woman with a thin, slightly fragile frame but a strong face. Her little boy, Toby, was perched contentedly on her right hip.

'Bess! Hi!' exclaimed Eva. She seemed genuinely happy to see Bess and she extended an arm to embrace her before ushering her inside.

'Wow, he's got so big,' said Bess as she tickled Toby's toes.

'Kids do tend to grow,' a laughing Eva responded.

'Right. I still can't believe you have kids. Plural.'

Eva smiled. 'Well, you know that Jesse wasn't exactly planned, and Toby here was also a bit of a surprise.'

Bess just nodded, suddenly feeling self-conscious. She had last been in Eva's house when she attended a baby shower during her first year at uni. Since then, she'd only had brief encounters with Eva, usually at footy games or in passing along Green Street when she was home for the holidays. And although her mum kept her up to date with how Eva and the kids were doing, this was the first time Bess had thought of Eva as an actual mum. It made Bess feel that perhaps, unlike Eva, she had only *pretended* to be an adult these last few years.

A knock at the front door broke the awkward moment.

'That'll be Fi,' said Eva.

'Oh, sorry. I should have called first.'

'Bess, it's just Fi.'

Fiona Roberts, with a gym-honed body and the sort of face you would not want to cross, entered the hall with her immaculately dressed twin girls, Daisy and Lily, in tow.

'Oh, hi, Bess,' she said, her words forced. She threw an annoyed glance in Eva's direction.

'Hey there,' said Bess, bending down to greet Lily and Daisy. 'Look at how tall you both are!'

'I'm, I'm a bit taller,' exclaimed Daisy.

'No, not true. Mummy said we are the same!' Lily looked pleadingly at her mum.

'You're the same height,' said Fi. 'Daisy just likes to stand on her tippy-toes. Now go find Jesse,' she instructed as they scurried away. 'Share, please! And that doesn't mean share toys with yourself!'

'I just thought I'd drop by,' Bess said, hoping to come across as casually as possible. She turned to Fiona. 'I was actually going to come and see you as well?' she said as though she was asking Fiona's permission.

'Let's all go into the kitchen,' suggested Eva, seemingly unfazed by the underlying tension.

Fi sat opposite Bess at the kitchen table, while Eva busied herself by making a pot of tea and placing Tim Tams on a plate.

Fiona and Bess avoided eye contact by watching the kids play.

Bess gestured towards the girls. 'They look just like you did in prep.'

Fiona smiled, a genuine smile. 'Let's just hope they don't start eating grass like I did at their age,' she remarked.

'To be fair, we all ate grass,' said Bess.

'So, Bess, how's work going?' asked Eva as she joined them.

'Pretty good. I lucked out and got some great kids this year.' Bess glanced at Fiona, reluctant to expand.

'Shouldn't you be in school now?' Fiona said bluntly.

'Um, yeah, I should. But I took some leave.'

The women said nothing for an excruciating minute before Bess spoke again. 'Look, I know I didn't really stay in touch,' she said briskly.

'That's an understatement,' Fi shot back.

'Okay, you're right, it probably is. But when I moved to the city, I didn't expect to feel so different. It's just . . . I can't explain it,' said Bess.

'We get it,' offered Eva. 'Our lives changed as well.'

Fiona looked sideways at Eva. 'Falling pregnant right out of high school wasn't really what we had in mind either,' she said. 'We were *both* meant to study teaching, remember? But everything was harder because you never made any effort. Not even when you were on break. When you left, it felt like we lost a friend. It was like you thought you were too good for us.'

'I didn't think that,' Bess said. 'I *don't* think that,' she added forcefully.

Fiona scoffed.

'Okay, maybe I did, back then. But not intentionally. You both had newborns. And then, Eva, you had another kid and I was going in a completely different direction. And it was exciting, not being in such a small town where everyone knows every little thing about you. And every time I came home, it felt like I was going backwards.'

'But even when you *were* here,' said Fiona, 'after everything that happened, you stayed for what, a week? And then you left. *Again.* Like our town didn't matter. Like *we* didn't matter.'

Bess looked down at the table. 'I couldn't stay. If I did, I'd never have left again.'

'You mean you didn't want to stay and end up like us?' said Fiona.

Eva remained silent as Bess looked up to face her friends, hoping they still were her friends.

'That's not it. I just wanted . . . I don't know what I wanted. But I know I was wrong, to leave the way I did. And to treat you both the way I did.' Bess looked back down at her cup. 'I have friends in the city,' she mused, slowly stirring her tea, 'but they don't really *know* me. Or they only know the me that I *want* them to know. I miss having friends who have seen me at my worst. And who helped me to be my best.'

'I'd miss me too,' Fiona said with a wry smile.

They all laughed, which broke the tension slightly.

'We've talked about it,' said Eva, glancing at Fiona.

'About what?' asked Bess.

'Bess, we know you're here to recruit players,' said Fi.

'Am I making a mistake?'

'No,' Fi said with unexpected force.

Even Eva seemed shocked by Fiona's response.

'How many times,' Fi continued, 'did we talk about starting a team? But we were only ever shut down by the rest of this town. And now the boys aren't even playing. And everyone's just . . .'

'Trying to hang on,' offered Eva quietly.

'Exactly,' Fi agreed with a firm nod. 'So, we're in.'

Although pleased, Bess couldn't help but express one thought. 'Why didn't you let me know, or come to the first training?'

'We wanted you to take the time to actually *ask* us, Bess. Rather than just assume we'd come running back to you,' said Fi.

Bess could not contain the smile that spread across her face.

EIGHT

Bess had stayed and chatted with Fi and Eva, and was easily swayed by the kids to play hide-and-seek multiple times. By the time she made her way towards the O'Sheas' place a few houses down, school had been out for over an hour. Bess opened the gate of a picture-perfect white picket fence and made sure the latch caught behind her. The manicured front garden, complete with a water feature and vine-covered arch, might have seemed pretentious to an outsider, but to those who knew the occupants, it was tended to out of care and patience.

Bess knocked several times on the oak wood door with large panels of deep-red stained glass. The last time she'd visited was for a retirement party that lasted until the early hours of the morning. After a short wait, Mr O'Shea opened the door. He was in his late sixties, with honest eyes framed by square-rimmed glasses and wearing a collared long-sleeved shirt and tailored pants.

'Ms Bess O'Neill,' he said, his voice pensive even with such a simple greeting.

'Mr O'Shea,' Bess responded with a slight nod. 'How are things? Enjoying retirement?'

'Well, I no longer have to discipline young students with a flair for finding drama.'

Bess looked down sheepishly.

'No doubt you're becoming accustomed to the other side. As educator rather than agitator?'

'Something like that,' she replied with a reluctant smile.

Mr O'Shea led Bess to the outdoor patio, his right-sided limp slightly more pronounced than she remembered. She never thought of Mr O'Shea as being old, just older than her parents. On the very rare occasion that he used a cane, it only served to make him seem somewhat mystical, as though he was a character from a well-loved children's story. He wasn't one to dwell on the past, and Bess only knew snippets about the cause of his injury from her mum. Mr O'Shea had served in the army during World War II and sustained multiple injuries from heavy shell fire. The resulting nerve damage had led to the limp – not that it slowed him down. He could still kick a left-foot torpedo punt and bowl a bouncer better than almost anyone in town.

They settled with a cup of tea on newish wooden chairs. A small seahorse insignia was visible on the back of each of them.

'So, Bess, how's your mum these days?'

'She's okay, I guess,' Bess replied without making eye contact.

Mr O'Shea tilted his head and looked directly at her.

'Well, not really okay, but . . . to be honest, I don't know,' she said, finally looking up. 'She doesn't talk to me.'

'Do you talk to her?' he gently prodded. The genuine concern in his voice matched the expression on his face.

'No,' she responded quietly. 'I mean, I do, but just not about . . . that.'

Mr O'Shea took a long drink of tea and seemed content to let Bess's comment settle between them.

Bess was well acquainted with Mr O'Shea's extremely patient nature. He had an uncanny ability to encourage students to be honest without ever becoming frustrated with them. He had been her principal throughout high school, and she and her friends had a habit of finding themselves in situations that required some explaining. And a visit to Mr O'Shea's office. Thankfully he wasn't a fan of detention but he definitely enjoyed a good discussion, which was an annoyingly effective approach. Bess had tried this with some of her students when they acted out, but she lacked the patience required and usually ended up giving a longwinded lecture that had little impact. Followed by detention.

'Your mum,' he said slowly, 'was the best teacher I ever had the privilege to work with. Mentoring her was the finest way to end my career.' He took another sip of tea before continuing. 'What happened was an absolute tragedy. And it's not something we will simply move on from. Nor should we try to.' He turned to Bess. 'Your mum needs someone to talk to.'

She looked away. She could feel the sudden brimming of emotion and was determined not to cry.

'The same goes for you,' he added.

The comment nearly pushed her to tears, but she swallowed hard a few times and kept her composure.

'I don't know what I'm supposed to say,' she replied, her voice shaking slightly. 'What if I make things worse?'

'What if you make things better?'

At that moment, Mr O'Shea's seventeen-year-old granddaughter Lou came outside, still dressed in her school uniform.

'Hey, Lou,' Bess said.

'Hi, Bess,' responded Lou as she settled on a nearby deck chair.

When Bess was in high school she'd babysat Lou many times, and had never met someone who was so shy. Lou's father had left when she was only three, and even though she had the right to be pissed off, she never seemed to be. Her mum was a nursing officer in the army, so her grandfather was heavily involved in raising her. It was no surprise that Lou was so much like him. Despite their quiet manner, they were exactly the sort of people you'd want in your corner.

'So, how's Year 12 going?' Bess asked, trying to sound upbeat.

'Pretty good.'

'Any plans for next year?'

'Um, I think, maybe studying Archaeology at uni.'

'Impressive,' said Bess. 'So, where's your mum posted these days?'

'Somalia. She should be home by the end of the year.' There was a noticeable sense of pride when Lou talked about her mum.

'That's great. I bet she really misses you. You know,' Bess continued, 'I'm actually here to see you.'

'Me?'

'Yep. How would you like to play footy for a women's team? You might have heard that there's a match against Denby planned for the week after the Grand Final.'

Lou nodded. 'Yeah, some of the girls at school were talking about a flyer they saw. But I don't know if I'd be any good. I haven't ever played . . . like, a proper match, I mean. I only kick the ball around with Granddad, and sometimes at school. Maybe I shouldn't. I don't want to let anyone down.'

Bess had anticipated this level of hesitation. 'Tell you what, just come to training and see what you think. No pressure.'

'Um, yeah. I guess that would be all right –'

'Excellent,' Bess interjected. 'I'll see you at the oval tomorrow night at six.'

'Okay,' agreed Lou.

'You know, it was never considered a good idea for girls to try footy,' commented Mr O'Shea. 'The general consensus was that you would get hurt and should just stick to netball.' He paused, and Bess was about to launch into a tirade about why women could, and should, play footy.

'Good to see you'll finally get to play,' he said with a smile. 'But just be prepared, Bess.'

'For what?'

'For this town to push back. You'll have to show people why it matters. Not just to you, but to them too.'

She nodded, hoping he was exaggerating because she wasn't entirely sure she knew what he meant.

As she walked through the gate, Mr O'Shea called after her. 'Bess, encourage your mum to come and see me.'

She turned to face him and nodded, but there seemed a mutual understanding that this would not happen.

*

A few streets over, Bess trekked up concrete steps that cut through an overgrown front lawn and knocked on the door of a tired house.

Sounds of roughhousing could be heard from within.

The door swung open, and eighteen-year-old Billy Blake, muscular and strong-jawed with a mop of light brown hair, stood with a Vegemite sandwich in one hand and a disinterested look on his face.

Behind him, three younger boys, all Billy's brothers, were wrestling on the floor.

'What?' said Billy.

'Pleasure as always, Billy,' said Bess as she groaned inwardly. 'Is Rach home?'

'No,' he replied bluntly.

'Do you know where she is or when she'll be back?'

'No.'

The play-fighting increased in intensity, but was momentarily interrupted as one of the boys crashed into the hallway wall and a vase on a side table wobbled precariously. The boys stared at it for several seconds, and when confident that it would remain upright, they returned to pushing and shoving as though they were fighting for a very real prize.

Billy moved to close the door and Bess reached out to stop him.

'Could you tell her I came by?'

He took a bite of his sandwich. 'Probably not,' he replied, his mouth full as he pulled the door shut.

Bess made her way back down the steps. As she turned onto the footpath, movement down the side of the house caught her eye. Bess approached Rachel who was folding laundry; she was a stocky woman, aged beyond her years with tired eyes and dark, unwashed hair.

'Hey, Rach.'

Rachel jumped, startled. 'Bess! Hi!' Her response was one of surprise but also scepticism.

'Um, so Billy said you weren't home.'

'Typical,' muttered Rach. 'He's meant to be at work,' she explained. 'Dad got him an apprenticeship in Denby, but he called in sick. And he's definitely not sick. If he does it again, he'll lose his job.'

She bent down and placed a folded towel into a wicker basket. Bess reached out and unpegged one end of a pale blue sheet hanging on a rotary clothes line.

'So, you're back?' asked Rachel as she removed the aged plastic pegs from the other end of the sheet.

'Um, yeah, but just for a bit. I've taken three weeks' leave. And then it's school holidays.'

'That must be nice. To be able to take such a long break.'

Bess knew that Rachel had never been on a holiday.

After neatly folding the sheet, Rach spoke again. 'I can't.'

'Can't what?'

'Play.'

'Why not?'

'Because nothing will get done around here if I do.'

'Rach, surely your brothers can do some things for themselves by now.'

'Don't do that. Don't pretend that you don't know what it's been like for me.'

'I know it must be hard –'

'Hard? Seriously, Bess?'

'Okay, I know.' Bess glanced down. 'I'm sorry. I just . . .'

'You just what?'

She looked up at Rach. 'I just remember how good you were. Before your mum . . . I mean, before she left . . . you just, you were so good. At *every* sport.'

'Yeah, well, we don't always get to do what we're good at.'

They finished removing the rest of the linen in silence.

'I guess I'll get going,' said Bess. She turned and walked back down the side of the house.

'What's it like?' Rachel called after her.

Bess turned back.

'Being on your own, in the city?'

Bess was taken aback by the question. 'It's different.'

'Better?'

She paused. 'Sometimes.'

Rachel nodded slowly, her eyes briefly downcast. 'I'm sorry.'

Bess nodded in return and bit her lower lip, aware that Rachel's apology had nothing to do with playing footy.

With a slight wave, Bess turned and walked away.

*

On the east side of town, Bess reached the end of a street and was met with a familiar scene. Against the backdrop of a pink sky, the sun slowly setting, a group of kids were playing an unnamed game involving a lot of running and yelling.

Ali Jungarai was sitting cross-legged on the grass nearby reading a worn book. Despite the cool weather, she was wearing thongs. She looked up and, on seeing Bess approach, placed her book down and stood to greet her friend.

'Hi, Bess.'

'Hey, Ali. It's been a while. Still got you babysitting?' Bess asked, gesturing to the horde of kids.

'Pretty much. But only on my days off.'

'Lucky you. How are things at the hospital?'

'Busy. But in a good way. I'm in Emergency now,' said Ali.

'Oh, that sounds terrifying. And your mum's still working in the ICU?'

'Yep. And still nurse manager.'

'I'm surprised she hasn't tried to recruit you.'

'Oh, believe me, she tries daily. But I can't stand it up there, Emergency is way better.'

They stood side by side and watched the kids run around each other, the rules of their game still unclear.

'Please don't ask me to play, Bess,' Ali said suddenly.

Bess turned to face the woman who had been her friend since kinder. 'Ali, seriously? You have to! You trained with your brothers. Your dad was the best full-back this town's ever seen. And you *love* footy.'

'Bess,' she started, 'I'm also part of the only Aboriginal family in town. Suffice it to say I love footy *from the boundary*. You know what it's like when my brothers and cousins play. And how hard it was for my dad.'

'Yeah. Yeah, I remember,' Bess responded uncomfortably.

'Do you?' said Ali. 'Because it doesn't seem like it.'

'Well, maybe it'll be different for you?'

'Bess, come on. The locals will have a fucking field day.'

Bess secretly loved it when Ali swore. She wondered how she curtailed it at work. The two women watched as a border collie pup rolled in freshly mown grass and several of the younger kids decided to do the same.

'Do you *want* to play?' asked Bess.

Ali watched her youngest cousin giggle with his whole body as the pup jumped around him. 'Of course I do,' she replied.

'Then you have to play. Just come to training. Please, Ali. I can't do this without you.'

'Bess –'

'Okay, before you say no, do you remember in Year 11, when you really, really, *really* wanted to ask Dean out? And you were so nervous, and you just kept talking yourself out of it?'

Ali grinned. 'Vaguely.'

'And I told you that the worst that could happen was that he might say no, which would be no big deal. But, if he said *yes*, it'd be a huge deal. Massive! Colossal! The best thing ever, right?'

'Right.'

'And so, you asked him out.'

'And he said no.'

'Correct. And Jules and I took you camping to console you, and we had one of *the* best nights ever.'

'I remember. It was rather epic,' Ali agreed.

'If you'd never asked him out, we never would have had that night.'

'Bess, what does playing footy have to do with being rejected by Dean?'

'It's about regret. I told you to ask him out so you wouldn't regret *not* doing it. And it all worked out because he really was a bit of a knob.'

'I think he became a car salesmen in Yalop. Or he sells funeral insurance. It's definitely something in sales,' said Ali.

'Well then, you clearly dodged a bullet.'

Ali shook her head but she was smiling.

'Did your brothers or cousins ever think about *not* playing?' Bess asked.

Ali nodded. 'But they've never given in. I think they just expect that there will always be some people who don't want them to play. And they've learned how to tune it out, at least a bit.'

'Do you think that maybe they could give you some advice on how to handle any abuse?'

'Probably. But I'm not sure I want to put myself in that position in the first place,' Ali explained.

'Yeah, I get that. And I know that I don't have any idea what it must be like. So, I promise I won't try and convince you to play.'

'But?'

'Okay, yes, there is a but.'

'I knew there would be.'

'*But*, I will say that I've never known a Gerandaroo Demons team that didn't have a Jungarai team member.'

'Me neither,' said Ali, half-smiling.

'So, maybe something to think about?' Bess asked.

Ali took a deep breath. 'How is it that you always get me to say yes to things so easily?'

'Because I'm delightful.'

Ali laughed. 'You're fucking full of it. But I'll do it. Dad's been on my case about it since he saw your flyer. I think he's more excited about the prospect of watching me play than he is about watching my brothers.'

'Because you're better than them?'

'Pretty much, yeah. Just promise me we won't look like idiots.'

'If only I could,' said Bess as she placed her hand on Ali's shoulder, and the two laughed.

*

Rick walked aimlessly around town as he did most days, having long finished his run. He watched Bess enter the auto-shop and was tempted to say hello; she had been a constant presence in his life throughout primary school and was far cooler than his own big sister.

He remembered an unfortunate yet gratifying incident from when he was nine years old, playing a game of backyard cricket with Bess, Tom, Danny, Lachie and Billy. Danny bowled a slow looping ball and Rick, unable to control himself, smashed it through the O'Neills' kitchen window. He was shocked, and recalled becoming instantly cold as the colour drained from his face and the bat felt like a weapon in his hands. This was around the time he seemed to be in a lot of trouble at school, always getting told off by Ms Denise. And even though breaking the window had been an accident that he was unlikely to get in any real trouble for, he was technically meant to be home at that very moment doing homework that had been due the previous week. And homework that had been due the week before that. And, naturally, homework that was due the next day.

Bess was playing wicketkeeper and, having witnessed Rick nearly collapse out of fear, grabbed the bat when her dad came storming outside and pretended she was the one who'd hit the ball.

'Sorry, Dad!' Bess had called, bat raised. 'I promise I'll help you fix it!'

'Do you think perhaps you can all try to aim towards the giant field that's on the other side of the fence?' Ian said, his tone firm but non-threatening.

Rick asked her why she'd taken the blame, and Bess explained that she would have done the same for Tom; it's just what sisters do. Rick knew his own sister never would have done that, because she never took the blame even when she was the one who had done something wrong. In that moment, he developed a crush on Bess that had never really gone away.

Rick watched Bess glance both ways before she exited the auto-shop driveway. He knew she'd seen him, and that she'd looked away. He knew in that moment that any interaction would be awkward, and despite honestly believing that Bess could be one of the only people to make him feel better, he also knew that it was not up to Bess to do that.

*

Bess felt surprisingly optimistic as she left the auto-shop. She'd been tempted to share with Jen that they actually had more players, but had decided it was best to wait and see if they all showed up before getting too excited. And she was quick to remind herself that they were still well short of a full team.

As Bess parked outside the general store, she was conscious not to look back at Rick. She was disappointed, but more unsettled that she'd automatically turned away from him. She always used to have time for Rick. Out of all of Tom's friends, he was the one who would make her laugh and pester her with questions about things he was too young to understand but desperate to know.

Despite her optimism, there was a nagging sense that all of today's efforts could be for nothing. Although others would sometimes comment that she was a pessimist, she saw this as simply being practical. And she wasn't *always* like this, or at least her thought processes weren't always so black and white. She rationalised that thinking this way was a reasonable act of self-preservation – if you didn't expect too much, you didn't fall as far when things didn't work out.

As she descended into her usual spiral of overthinking every interaction and questioning if she was making a mistake, Bess barely noticed the stares directed her way when she entered the general store.

It was her turn to prepare dinner and although she knew her mum was always happy to try something new, her dad resisted unfamiliar dishes. She decided to stick with a tried and true lasagne that she had been making since she was fourteen. As she wandered past the baking section, the sight of bags of flour triggered a memory.

Several days before she left for uni, Danny had dared her to bake exactly one hundred and ninety-nine Anzac biscuits. She happily obliged and took about a hundred with her on her first day at resi. They were a huge hit after the opening get-to-know-you event, in large part because everyone was suitably drunk, and biscuits and milk soon became the standard post-drinking snack among the students on her floor. She always thought Danny had helped ensure that she made friends right away.

She turned towards the frozen section at the back of the store, where the brief interlude of happiness was interrupted by Mrs Finch, an overbearing woman with a permanently furrowed brow. Her son Andrew was a year below Tom and was a pretty decent kid. He kept to himself and was more interested in computers than being outdoors. Yet Mrs Finch insisted that he play footy and cricket, despite his repeated objections. He was the sort of kid who was counting down the days until he could leave, but he wasn't bullied, at least not by the Gerandaroo kids. The boys from Denby were a different story. Andrew had a slight frame and was quiet, so being excluded and called a nerd was a common occurrence.

Mrs Finch resented the fact that the Gerandaroo and Denby teams couldn't play this season. Her loyalties seemed more aligned with supporting Denby, who'd rallied against the ban, than with her own town, who had agreed that the boys shouldn't compete. She was almost eager to take her frustrations out on Bess.

'You've got a lot of nerve,' said Mrs Finch, her large frame towering over Bess, her index finger thrust in her face.

'Excuse me?' Bess took a step back.

'Coming back here and starting a girls' team when our boys can't even play. Girls don't play football, only boys do. And men,' she lectured.

'Well, actually, that's not true, is it? Because even though I've never been part of a team, I've still always played footy. I played as a girl and now I play as a woman.'

'You're not a woman. You're one of them lesbians, aren't you? The city's full of 'em.'

'Okay, so let me get this straight,' started Bess, 'because you think I'm a lesbian, that means I'm not a woman? Even though lesbians are women attracted to other women?'

'I always knew you'd grow up to be trouble,' said Mrs Finch, shaking her head.

'Oh, really? Psychic, are we? Is that a skill you developed over time or something you were born with?' Bess knew she was baiting a bull, but she just couldn't help herself.

Mrs Finch fumed, nostrils flaring. 'Don't you dare talk to me like that!'

'Why the hell not? I'm an adult. You're an adult. I don't owe you respect. You've never shown me any.'

'You're just like your mother. Acting all high and mighty. Thinking that you own the place.'

'Don't ever talk about my mother that way. She's saved your kid from getting the crap kicked out of him more times than you could possibly imagine. And if you wave that finger in my face one more time, I'll bite it off.' Bess pushed past, making sure her elbow grazed Mrs Finch's arm.

'Did you see that? She pushed me!' Mrs Finch cried out to no one in particular.

Bess continued on her way, her breathing now rapid as adrenaline overwhelmed her senses. She opened a glass freezer door and leaned forward slightly, the cool air acting as a circuit breaker, and she felt her breathing slow.

Still distracted when she approached the checkout, she paid little attention to Sam, the same teenager who'd served her last time.

'Hey,' said Sam.

Bess glanced up. 'Hi,' she replied. She was hopeful for as minimal an interaction as possible.

Sam scanned the items and placed them in a plastic bag. Only the barcode beep and her gum-chewing could be heard, but she kept glancing at Bess.

'That's nineteen dollars and ten cents,' said Sam.

Bess handed over the exact amount and collected her solitary bag, increasingly aware that Sam was staring at her.

'I'd like to play,' Sam stated.

Her comment caught Bess off guard and she didn't respond right away.

'That's what you're doing, right?' continued Sam. 'Putting a team together?'

Bess nodded.

'Well, I'd like to play,' she repeated.

'Have you ever even played footy?'

'Loads of times.'

'Okay.' Bess wasn't sure if Sam was being serious.

'My boyfriend said I'm not allowed to join your team.'

'So, does that mean you only want to *pretend* to join? To piss him off?'

'No!' Sam replied. 'I've always wanted to play, but there's never been a team.'

Bess was starting to feel more convinced.

'I've got a few friends who think that maybe they'd like to join, too. Can they play?'

'Of course,' said Bess as a voice echoed within her: *I knew it! I knew there were women in this town who want to play football!* 'We train at the oval tomorrow at six,' she added, trying to keep her voice even and not as excited as she felt. 'Bring along anyone you think might wanna play.'

'Cool.' Sam turned away and began scanning items for the next customer.

Bess left the store looking and feeling perplexed. She wasn't often surprised, but she really did believe, at least to some extent, that this could actually work.

NINE

31 days to Game Day

As Bess closed the boot of her car, she noticed that the air was unusually mild; the typically cool breeze had apparently decided to take the night off. This was the sort of evening she missed the most from city living. A calmness had descended over the town, and everything and everyone seemed to slow down just that little bit.

She closed her eyes and breathed deeply as whispers of lemon flooded her senses. It was the scent of the soap she used, and her mum would always pick some daphne for her room when she knew Bess was coming to visit. It was also the flower that Lachie had placed on her front doorstep every birthday from age five, tied with string and accompanied by a handwritten note. She knew he did it the first time because his mum had told him if he ever liked a girl, he should try to do something nice for her on her birthday. It was a tradition Lachie would never break, at least not until Bess left home.

She opened her eyes and glanced at the nearby clusters of mauve-pink daphne in her front yard, toxic if ingested.

She decided against picking some.

*

Arriving to an empty oval, Bess stood on the north-east side of the centre square with the bag of footballs at her feet. Just as she checked her watch, she heard chatter in the distance.

She looked up as Jules, Andy, Lou, Jen, Ali and her younger cousin Tully – tall and toned and the only one holding a football – walked towards her in a row.

They were closely followed by Sam, who, as promised, had brought along some friends Bess recognised, all in their final year of high school. To Sam's right was Charlie Lewis, who had a swagger of confidence to her step and a voice that could be clearly heard. Next to Charlie was Abby Mitchem, slight and the shortest of the group by far, with a pixie haircut. Her grey t-shirt sleeves were rolled up and she wore long red and white striped socks. The first thought that came to mind was *Where's Wally?* Finally, there was Kat Evans, with deep red hair and covered head to toe in freckles; she was bouncing around like she was going to a dance rather than footy training.

Bess noticed Lou glancing back nervously at the girls – the tell-tale sign of a student who wanted to be part of the popular group but wasn't.

The women reached Bess and instinctively formed a semicircle around her.

'Hey, guys,' she greeted them with a smile, 'glad you could all make it. We're just waiting on two more,' she added, gesturing to Fiona and Eva who were jogging towards them.

'Sorry,' said Fi, slightly breathless, 'the girls didn't want me to leave. They're basically piranhas when they each take hold of a leg.'

'And my husband was acting as though he'd never worked an oven before.' Eva rolled her eyes.

'All good, you're right on time,' said Bess.

As she looked around, she was unsure of what to do next. 'Um, so maybe . . . ahh, we could start by going around just to make sure everyone knows everyone?'

She anticipated some solid nods of validation, but the women fidgeted awkwardly and avoided her gaze. It was an unwelcome flashback to her first teaching placement, where the majority of the class were mouth-breathers who also seemed to have the capacity to sleep with their eyes open.

Out of the corner of her eye, she watched as Lucas and his lemmings sauntered up to the fence and leaned on it. She groaned inwardly and hoped the rest of the team didn't notice them.

'Maybe we could just say our names?' Bess prompted loudly. She looked to Jules with a pleading expression, hoping she'd get things going.

'Hi, I'm Juliet, but everyone except my mum calls me Jules.'

The others followed.

'I'm Fiona, but I go by Fi.'

'Andy. Call me Andrea and I won't ever kick to you.'

'Eva.' She gave a small wave.

'I'm Jen.' Jen smiled nervously.

'I'm Tallara but get called Tully.'

'Really?' exclaimed Charlie. 'I always thought your name was actually Tully.'

'Nah, my older brother couldn't say "Tallara" when I was born, so he always just called me Tully. And it kinda stuck,' she said with a shrug.

Charlie and Tully smiled, a shared acknowledgement that despite having lived in the same town their entire lives, and with Tully only a year level below, they had never really talked to one another.

'I'm Ali.'

'See, now, I thought *that* was short for something?' said Charlie.

'It is. My full name's Alinga, which means the sun or the sun goddess. But only some of my family call me that.'

'I like it. It's different. Charlotte means a pudding made of stewed fruit.'

All the women laughed.

'Are you sure it's not just that the dessert is called Charlotte? I don't think that's what your name actually means,' said Fiona.

'Oh. Right. Yeah, that does make more sense.' Charlie grinned with sudden realisation. 'So, I'm Charlotte, as you now know, but I get called Charlie by everyone. Except my teachers when I'm in trouble. Which is often.'

'Um. I'm Lou, short for Louisa. You can use either.'

Bess gave her an encouraging smile.

'Samantha. But I only, and I mean *only*, go by Sam.'

'I'm Katrina, but pretty much only get called Kat.'

'I'm Abby. Or A. Or Abs. Or Able. Or Bee, or –'

'Yeah, we get it, Abigail, you've got a lot of nicknames,' said Charlie.

'So that makes thirteen of us, which is a great start.' Bess looked around at their feet. 'And I see you've all got footy boots, which is excellent. I wasn't expecting that.'

'Yeah, I'm wearing an old pair of my brother's,' said Ali.

There was a chorus of 'I'm wearing a mate's' or 'These are my brother's' and 'Same here' or 'Me too'.

'So how many more players do we need?' asked Abby.

Bess hesitated. 'Um, well, a team has eighteen on-field. And typically, we'd have four interchange, but I don't think that's going to happen.' The last three words dripped with trepidation.

'So, we'll have to play the whole game?' questioned Fi.

'Basically, yeah,' said Bess. 'But I'm working on it. And it would be a *huge* help if you could all talk to anyone you think might wanna play.'

'And full quarters?' asked Tully.

'Not quite. So, Deb Phelan – do you guys know her? She lives in Denby and works for the council?'

Fiona grinned. 'Don't you mean *Drop Punt*?'

'Oh man, I bet no one's called her that in *ages*,' Bess responded.

'Is that because of her initials?' asked Kat.

'Partly. I think Lachie gave her the nickname in, what was it, Year 7?' said Bess, turning to Fi.

'Yep. It was after she did that kick at recess and the footy smashed through the staffroom window and the teachers wouldn't give it back.'

'The boys were pissed,' said Eva.

'Probably because they'd never kicked that far before,' said Andy.

'Well,' Bess said, 'she's organising the Denby side, which means they'll *definitely* have their shit together. We thought it would be best to do fifteen-minute quarters with no time on. So, it's –'

'Sorry, what does "time on" mean?' Kat interrupted.

'Seriously, Kat? You said you watched footy all the time,' said Sam, possibly regretting having brought her along.

'I do,' Kat responded pointedly. 'But that doesn't mean that I pay attention to the rules. I just like watching the guys run around.'

'Oh, for god's sake, Kat,' said Sam, but the rest of the group were laughing.

Kat just grinned and gave an exaggerated shrug.

Bess and Jules shared a side smile. Bess was pretty sure they were thinking the same thing: Kat and Sam were behaving exactly like Fiona and Eva did in high school.

Kat riled Sam up some more. 'Is there some edict that says I have to know every rule to enjoy the game?'

Sam just let out an exasperated sigh and shook her head. 'You didn't even know the word *edict* existed until English class last week,' she said.

'Neither did you,' Kat shot back, and they all laughed.

'You guys good? Or do you wanna go another round?' Bess joked.

'Nah, we're good,' said Sam.

'So, Kat, and for anyone else who doesn't know, when the guys play, the clock stops for injuries and when there's a score. And all of that time is then added on so that the time spent actually playing is meant to equal twenty-five minutes. Does that make sense?'

'Um, yes. And I now realise why the game goes on forever,' replied Kat.

'Yeah, it can be pretty long. But for us it'll be four fifteen-minute quarters, with a five-minute break after the first and third quarters, and fifteen minutes for half-time,' explained Bess.

'I can't remember the last time I exercised for that long,' said Eva, which drew murmurs of agreement from the older players.

'I can't remember the last time I wore shorts for that long,' added Jen.

The younger ones seemed undeterred.

'I think this is going to be fantastic!' Sam exclaimed. 'I'm so sick of the guys telling us we can't play.'

As if on cue, jeering from the boundary invaded their happy bubble.

'What are you ladies doing? Planning a tea party?' Lucas shouted through cupped hands as though merely yelling wasn't enough.

The women largely ignored him, but Sam fixed Lucas with a prolonged glare, a mixture of annoyance and frustration, but also, Bess noticed, some disappointment.

'What about umpires? They have to get paid, right?' asked Jen.

'Yeah, that's a good question,' said Bess. 'Deb spoke with the league and is just waiting for them to confirm some of the details. But she doesn't think it'll be a problem. So, what do you guys say? Ready to get started?'

*

As Jules led them through a warm-up of stretches and some jogging, the mood was upbeat. It reminded Bess of all the times Jules would take over at netball training because their 'coach', Mrs Ware, who struggled to remember all the positions, would tune out five minutes in and sit on the sideline reading a romance novel that was really just soft porn.

Despite the smiles and laughter that surrounded her, Bess waged an internal battle with an increasing list of worries and things to do: *Do they all know the rules? What about fitness? Could they all last a full game? Could I last a full game? And tackling! How will I teach them how to tackle safely in such a short space of time? And marking, and kicking. And handballing can bloody hurt if you don't use correct form. And we still need at least five more players. How on earth am I going to pull this off? What have I got myself into?*

She felt jittery as a surge of unwanted energy rushed through her body, sparking a sudden urge to just flee the oval and not look back.

Why do I need to do this? Does it even matter?

She stopped herself from completely spiralling by listening to her dad's voice telling her to take a few deep breaths. It was always her dad that she heard in these fight or flight or freeze moments. This surprised her as much as it would likely surprise him, if she ever told him.

Just breathe, Bess. Just breathe.

She looked around at the other women and realised that their presence and their enthusiasm was more than enough to keep her going. At least for the time being.

Bess decided to start simply, so she set them up to handball in pairs.

As Kat held the ball in her palm, she connected with a tight fist and managed to half-handball, half-throw so far over Sam's head that Sam couldn't even reach it with a high leap.

'Christ, that hurts!' Kat cried, shaking her right hand.

'Well, that's actually impressive,' said Sam. 'You managed to miss me entirely. You do realise that I'm not ten feet tall?'

'Your attitude certainly is,' Kat quipped as Sam fetched the ball and handballed cleanly to her.

'So, Kat, cradle the ball in your hand, and when you make a fist, always have your thumb on the outside,' Bess explained.

Kat nodded as she followed Bess's instructions.

'Now, just lower your left hand a bit, and try and strike the ball here,' Bess went on, pointing to the juncture where the thumb formed a V-shape. 'You also wanna step forward and direct your foot to where you want the ball to land.'

Kat swung through with force as she punched the ball, stepping towards Sam. The ball was just off to the left, but the action was spot on.

'Exactly!' Bess exclaimed, surprised that Kat had responded so well to corrections.

'It still bloody hurts,' said Kat. 'But it's also oddly satisfying.'

'Glad to hear it.' Bess thought how refreshing it was to be around someone so honest.

She wasn't surprised that each player displayed strong hand-eye coordination. While the boys played cricket or footy competitively and the girls were unofficially restricted to netball and basketball, and soccer when they could field a full team, it didn't stop them from playing footy, and indeed cricket, with friends and family. Bess had met a woman at uni who'd played in boys' teams until Under 12s. Looking back, she realised that even though she would have loved to play footy, she'd never even considered asking to play on the boys' team. She highly doubted that it would have been a viable option in Gerandaroo anyway, but still, the more girls and women who tried to play, the easier it would be for the next generation. And it was this thought that pushed its way through her doubt to settle in the forefront of her mind.

Aside from Kat, and Abby (who it seemed had never actually held a football), the rest had at least tried to handball before, and the group were able to move on to handballing in groups of three, and then four. For over ten minutes, no one spoke, and the only sounds they all focused on were fists punching footballs and the claps of successful catches. The jeering continued, but the less attention they gave the boys, the more distant their insults became.

After that, they did some running drills with loose footballs on the ground so Bess could get a better sense of their skill level. One player stood about twenty metres away, and as another did a short kick or handball to the space between them, two others would sprint forward, try to collect it, and then handball to the stationary player. Most of them either ran too fast so they went over the ball and missed it entirely, or they became entangled with the other player, or they were too hesitant to try to pick it up. This last outcome was slightly amusing when *both* players were too hesitant.

'I'm sorry' became a far too common phrase. Bess decided to let it go, but she knew she would have to toughen some of the players up a bit. Her dad had taught her that you should always respect your opponent, but that did not extend to being a pushover.

After numerous fumbled attempts, Bess asked Jules and Ali, two players who seemed to really understand the drill, to demonstrate. This time, however, Bess instructed them to be a bit more aggressive when trying to block each other out, but to still pick up the ball and pass it off cleanly. With both releasing some pent-up frustration, they were able to do just that.

The others gradually began to see how to position themselves, and after about twenty minutes, Bess decided to assess their kicking ability. In pairs, the players attempted to kick the ball back and forth – 'attempt' being the operative word for some of them. If you'd never kicked a football before, you'd likely be in for a bit of a shock, especially if you tried doing it on the run.

Aside from Bess, the most consistent were Ali, Jen, Fi, Tully and Andy, while Jules and Eva had correct form but lacked a bit of power. The others, particularly Sam, struggled to drop ball on boot at the right angle and follow through with enough force to get any sort of distance.

Sam was becoming increasingly frustrated with herself. 'Why doesn't it just drop the way it's meant to?' she complained to Bess.

'It took me ages to learn how to do it,' Bess reassured her.

'That's not helpful,' Sam responded. 'You know, considering we have only a few weeks until the game.'

Sam tried again to kick accurately. The ball sprayed awkwardly off her boot and nearly hit a nearby Jules in the head.

'Oh Sammy, just give up!' Lucas called. 'You're not built for this! And you look ridiculous!'

Sam tried to ignore him, but the more he yelled, the worse she kicked.

Charlie ran past her. 'Tell him off, Sam! Seriously, why do you let him be such a dick?'

'Mind your own business, Charlie!' Sam shot back.

Recognising that the longer this went on, the worse it would get, Bess decided to finish with a game of Marks Up rather than draw more attention to Lucas and the other boys.

With Ali starting them off, the game shut the boys up for a least a few minutes – her form was near perfect. As the others jostled to mark the ball, the women found themselves laughing more than anticipated, and Bess realised it was the first time she'd had fun all year.

After about ten more minutes, fatigue started to kick in. 'I think we'll call it a night,' said Bess. 'But really great start, guys. I hope you'll all come back?'

She was immediately apprehensive that some players, if not all of them, would decide it was going to be too much work.

'Are you kidding?' said Kat. 'That is without a doubt the most fun I've had in ages.'

'Definitely,' Ali chimed in.

'Absolutely,' said Eva.

'Okay, um, great,' said Bess, her surprise genuine. 'So, same time on Monday?'

The players nodded in agreement.

As they walked off the field, Bess watched Sam approach Lucas. She shrugged off his attempt to drape his arm possessively around her shoulders.

But she still left with him.

TEN

Each player attempted to recruit more women from Gerandaroo to join the team. Their approaches varied wildly. While Lou politely asked girls at school and swiftly retreated when she was told no, Charlie harassed them. She maintained that repeatedly asking the same question did not amount to harassment and could not understand: one – why the response was a consistent and emphatic no; two – why she had not been able to wear down the other girls to the point where they responded with a yes; and three – why they didn't want to play in the first place. When Charlie's approach failed, Sam mildly threatened every girl she knew. Sam was someone who always seemed to know little facts about the other students, and she wasn't afraid to use this knowledge to her advantage. In the end, Abby and Kat had to intervene and remind both Charlie and Sam that getting people offside probably wasn't the most effective way to go about things.

Andy planned to discuss it with some of her customers,

but business had slowed recently and she couldn't risk alienating anyone. There were a few times when she felt sure a customer would at least be willing to talk about the team, but was immediately put off by throwaway comments along the lines of: 'It will only end in tears' or 'What are you trying to prove?' For the first time, Andy felt out of place in the town she had grown up in.

Jen also considered talking to customers about the team, but found herself stumbling over the words and unable to come out and ask directly if they wanted to join. Instead, she placed a flyer on the reception desk. After more than a few looks of derision were thrown her way, she reluctantly removed it, not yet brave enough to persist.

Ali worked mainly with women from Denby and surrounding towns, as Denby's hospital was the largest in the region and the only one with a trauma centre and ICU, so there wasn't really anyone for her to ask.

Tully seemed the most insightful of the school-aged players on the team, and explained that the other girls were perhaps too concerned with how they would look and what people might say to even give footy a go. The older women agreed, and were aware that these concerns did not just disappear the moment you left the confines of high school. Jen was also unexpectedly perceptive, and proffered that they all wanted to present an image to their community of the type of person they thought they should be, and that didn't necessarily match up with their true selves. So, if they wanted acceptance, playing footy for a town that staunchly believed that only boys and men should play wouldn't really help with that, even if deep down, playing and being part of a team matched more with who they truly were.

Bess was confident there were more women in Gerandaroo who would relish the chance to play a full game of footy and be part of the team. But the risk was great, the likelihood of abuse high, and the reward too uncertain.

So despite their best efforts, no one was successful. Bess hoped that word of mouth might have enticed a few women to at least come and check it out. When this didn't occur, she decided to employ the tactic of ignoring the problem in the hope that it would simply resolve itself.

*

Midway through their next training session, the players were spread out across the oval participating in separate drills. Given their time constraints, Bess decided to try and develop their skills across some areas of weakness. Or, as Abby put it, focus on their 'soon-to-be-awesome skills'.

Bess knew that if they were to have any chance of making it through a game, they needed to be able to kick and handball with a modicum of accuracy, and at least attempt to bounce the ball. But as the evening progressed, she wasn't overly confident that any of this would occur.

At the south-end goal, Tully was giving Lou, Charlie and Jen tips on kick-to-kick accuracy. Lou had developed good form but lacked power with her follow-through, leading to kicks that always fell just short of the mark. It was as though she pulled back right at the last second. With each less-than-adequate attempt, she became increasingly discouraged.

'I don't think I can get this,' she whispered to Tully.

'Lou, you will. I promise. You just have to keep your head up. And keep trying,' said Tully, her voice upbeat.

Lou nodded, sceptical, but appeared to be willing to keep going.

Charlie's attempts matched her intensity. She was determined to kick strong, but repeatedly dropped the ball at bizarre angles, resulting in a couple of shin strikes. Where Lou became quietly frustrated, Charlie was far more vocal.

'Oh, come on!' she cried out as her kick splayed to the right, a good twenty metres away from Jen who was her target.

'It just comes down to how you hold your body and the football, and how you drop it on your foot,' Tully called as she jogged over to Charlie. 'That time you let it go too soon and it hit the outside.' She pointed to the side of her right shoe. 'But the aim is to hit here in the middle.' She patted the football across her shoelaces. 'Remember to guide the ball down. So, place each hand either side of the laces and make a V-shape like this,' she said, grasping the football confidently between her hands. 'Then bring your body forward a bit, rather than pulling back, and use your right hand to guide the ball as you release it.'

Charlie watched with both admiration and slight annoyance as Tully expertly guided the ball so that it landed effortlessly in Jen's arms for an easy chest mark.

'Yep. I can totally see what I need to do. And I am totally confident that I will never *ever* be able to do it,' said Charlie.

'Well, at least you're realistic,' Tully replied with a smile.

'How are you so good at this?' asked Charlie.

'I kick a footy around with my cousins most nights,' said Tully.

'That must be nice,' commented Charlie. 'To have family who like to play sport.'

'Your family doesn't like sport?'

'Not even remotely. My mum will be furious when she finds out that I'm playing footy.'

'What does she think you're doing at night?'

'She works the evening shift at the aged care home in Denby, so she doesn't get home till ten.'

'What about your dad?'

'He's oblivious to most things. I just tell him I'm going to Kat's to study. He doesn't even notice that I'm in workout clothes when I leave.'

'Oh,' said Tully.

'It's okay, Tully, really. I'm used to it.'

'Okay,' said Tully, clearly not entirely convinced. 'You should come over and play footy with my family one night. You can stay for tea. Dad always cooks way too much food. It's like he thinks we're never gonna eat again.'

'That actually sounds really nice,' said Charlie.

They turned their attention to Jen. It was clear that she had a solid kick, but compliments and any sort of attention seemed to make her uncomfortable. It therefore seemed unlikely that she would be able to perform well in front of a crowd.

Bess asked Sam to help Kat with bouncing the football – something Sam was surprisingly good at. Bess watched from about a metre away as Sam threw her hands in the air in frustration, before she took a deep breath and again instructed Kat on how to bounce.

'You've got to hold the footy like this,' explained Sam, her right hand towards the top of the ball, 'and strike it on the ground at about a forty-five-degree angle.' She demonstrated with a few clean bounces while stationary.

'Why does it look so easy when you do it?' Kat complained. 'And how on earth am I meant to be able to actually run and bounce *at the same time*?'

'It just takes practice,' said Sam. 'And Lucas actually showed me how to do it back in Year 10 when we first started dating.'

'You're kidding? So that's, like, the one good thing he's ever done.'

'Why do you do that?'

'Do what?'

'You only ever talk crap about him.'

'That's because ninety-nine per cent of the time he's a complete dick,' insisted Kat.

'Maybe he wouldn't be if people didn't say mean things about him.'

'Okay. I'll stop saying mean things as soon as he stops being a dick.'

Bess stepped forward to intervene, mindful that boys could ruin friendships between girls, but thankfully, Sam redirected the conversation back to footy.

'You need to pay a bit more attention to what your right hand is doing,' she stated pointedly.

Kat tried again and couldn't help but laugh as the ball dribbled an inch or two from the ground before coming to a pathetic stop.

'Really, Kat?' said Sam. 'Is this going to be like that time in Year 7 when I tried to teach you how to braid your hair and you only ever managed a wonky plait?'

'That says more about your teaching skills than it does about my ability to pay attention,' replied Kat. 'And if you recall, I *did* manage a braid. That one time.'

'Yeah, on *my* horse!'

They both burst out laughing.

'Okay, let's try again,' said Sam with a bit more patience. 'But stand beside me so you can see what I mean by getting an angle. And use a bit of force. No more of this "drop and watch it dribble" bullshit.'

In an attempt to hone some defensive skills, Fiona was waving her arms and jumping around in front of Eva while she took a shot at goal. She motioned for Abby to take her place and do the same. Abby seemed both embarrassed and also highly amused that this was required.

'What on earth does this even do?' she asked. Laughing, she dropped her arms. 'It just seems like a waste of energy.'

'It's all about distraction,' Fi explained. 'So, we need to make sure someone is always on the mark, looking like a bit of a fool. I think you'll be good at it.'

'Wow. Thanks,' said Abby. 'Do I have to do this every time a Cats player gets the ball?'

'Um, do you watch footy at all, Abby?' asked Eva.

'Nope,' replied Abby. 'I've seen bits and pieces, though. But the game's too long.'

Fi and Eva exchanged an incredulous look.

'So, um, yes, Abby, if the player you're on marks, you have to go back and raise your arms in defence,' said Fi.

'How long can they hold the ball for?'

'That's actually a very good question.'

'I have my moments,' said Abby.

'As soon as a player marks, the umpire will blow the whistle, you then need to stand on the mark.' Fi paused, then pre-empted Abby's next question. 'The mark is the point where the player actually caught the ball. So, you stand on that point, and the player has about ten seconds to dispose of the ball. They can kick it or handball, and as soon as the umpire blows the whistle for a second time, you can move off the mark and try and tackle them if they are still holding the ball. If you put your arms up, you can try to block a kick or intercept a handball. A player can also run off the mark. If they do, you're also allowed to try and tackle them. But if a player marks and is taking a shot at goal, they get longer.'

Abby stood silent; Bess could sense her mind working overtime to process the information.

'So that is yet another reason why games are literally like a never-ending story?' asked Abby.

'Oh! That was such a good film,' Eva chimed in, unable to help herself.

'It was. It really was,' Abby agreed.

Fiona threw Eva a *don't encourage her* look, but Eva chose to ignore it.

'The death scene involving Artax still haunts me,' said Eva.

'Me too! That was just so brutal,' exclaimed Abby. 'I couldn't leave my horse alone for weeks after that.'

'What sort of horse –' started Eva, before Fi interjected.

'Do you think we could save the chitchat for the cool down?'

Eva and Abby suppressed a laugh before plastering on serious faces and continuing with the drill.

Towards the south-end fifty-metre line, Andy, Jules and Ali were practising some fast-paced handballing while running. The ratio of clean catches to fumbles was lower than Bess would have liked, but progress nonetheless.

*

As training came to a close, Sam approached Bess as she collected the footballs.

'So, the game's in like, four weeks,' said Sam.

'Yep,' replied Bess.

Sam stared expectantly at her.

'And?' Bess prompted.

'*Aaaand* it's gonna be pretty shitty to play with only thirteen people. Literally no one I spoke to wants to play. They think it's some big joke. And without enough for a team, what's the point of training?'

Bess glared at Sam, jaw clenched. She wasn't annoyed about what she'd said; she was annoyed that she was right.

'Just sayin',' said Sam, putting her hands up in surrender.

With that, Sam jogged off to meet Lucas who, as usual, was standing on the boundary.

*

Alone in his work shed, which was just a converted garage, Lachie stood back to survey his latest project. Rocking chairs had become something of an obsession and he was trialling a few different approaches to get the balance just right. He frowned, concerned as he rocked it and it swung forward too quickly.

Lachie was a mostly self-taught cabinet-maker, having learned the basics from Mr West, an elderly neighbour who'd noticed Lachie's talent in woodshop before he retired. When he died, Lachie inherited all of his tools. He started an apprenticeship in Denby after Year 12, but his father's frequent, sudden and prolonged absences meant Danny was often required to get himself to school and plan dinner when he got home. This wasn't a new situation in itself. Lachie and Danny had banded together to get everything done that needed to be done, but with Lachie working long hours and commuting to and from Denby, more was demanded of Danny, and he was only thirteen. Lachie didn't want his brother to have the same experience that he did in high school, where permission slips went unsigned, he often went hungry because there was not enough food for breakfast or lunches, sometimes both, and he missed sporting matches because his dad would promise that he would take him, only to go on a bender and be too paralytic to drive.

So, Lachie quit. After that he became a more formal surrogate father to Danny. He made sure Danny completed his homework and set him a reasonable curfew, particularly around exams, to ensure his brother was well rested. He even volunteered at the school canteen with the mums to make sure Danny had a horde of women looking out for him. He taught Danny how to use the washing machine and the importance of fabric softener, how to open a bank account and balance a chequebook, how to change a tyre, and how to cook a not-too-awful-tasting meal with pasta or rice and tinned anything (except sardines; they both learned that the hard way). Lachie did all the things for Danny that he had not been afforded, all the things that his peers took for granted.

Mitch had tried multiple times over the years to force Lachie to sell the tools Mr West left him. Some were antiques and quite valuable. Lachie returned home one evening after footy practice to find his dad with a random bloke from Yalop, a few towns over, negotiating a sale price for all the items. Lachie went ballistic at his dad, and both ended up with black eyes. Although Lachie managed to prevent anything from being sold, he had to temporarily move all the tools to Bess's house to keep them safe.

Despite his father's lack of standing in the community, Lachie had managed to build a solid reputation as reliable and skilled. He had a reasonably steady flow of work, mainly for outdoor furniture, but also for dining tables and chairs. It was enough to keep paying the mortgage on the house, which his father had graciously left Lachie to manage for over five years. Even in high school Lachie was skilled enough to work as a handyman and made enough money to pay for groceries, and to almost cover the electricity and water bills when his dad either gambled or drank his pay packet away, or did both.

Lachie's favourite part of finishing a job was searing his seahorse insignia into the wood. He was often asked why he used a seahorse, and he never gave a detailed answer, except to say that he thought it looked good. He kept the origin of the insignia story close to his heart because he felt that's where it belonged and it was just for him to know. But he often reminisced about the reason why.

One day in kinder, his teacher had asked all the kids to draw a picture of the water creature they would like to be. Most of the children drew a shark or a whale, some drew a fish or an octopus. But only two students independently chose to draw a seahorse. The bond between Lachie and Bess had always been there as their mums were best friends and they had already journeyed through the first few years of life together. But on that day in June 1974, as they held up their seahorse drawings for the class and each other to see, it seemed they were kindred spirits, which would be lovely if either of them believed in that sort of thing.

The first item Lachie made that he placed the insignia on was a bracelet for Bess. He carved a perfect heart from a piece of red cedar and drilled a hole right through the centre to hold a thin strip of leather. He remembered tying it on Bess's right wrist on a warmish autumn night in Year 10, and telling her that he loved her. He remembered her leaning up to kiss him and seeing her smile the way she always did right before they kissed. The smile was how she told him she loved him, not the kiss, and she never said the words. Although sometimes he wished she had.

He stood back again and rocked the chair. He knew it still wasn't right, but he couldn't figure out what he was doing wrong.

*

Bess climbed her verandah steps, taking them two at a time, and wiped the wet soles of her runners. She entered the living room where her dad sat in his recliner chair, the TV on low, Jinx settled contentedly beside him.

'Hey, Dad.'

Ian glanced over and watched as Bess sat on the couch and began untying her laces. Without a word, Ian stood up, disturbing Jinx in the process, and walked out the front door.

Bess stared after him with a mixture of confusion and hurt. She gestured for Jinx to come to her. The dog seemed equally miffed at the abrupt departure of their dad.

Ian returned after about an hour, without saying where he'd been. He simply sat at the kitchen table. Bess placed a plate of grilled chicken and salad in front of him, and then her mum. She brought her own plate to the table and watched as her parents essentially ignored each other.

After several minutes, Gayle broke the silence with an unexpected question. 'How many players do you have now?'

With the mention of the footy team, Ian stood and left the table, plate in hand. He sat in his recliner chair and turned on the TV without saying a word.

Gayle seemed oblivious, or had perhaps just chosen not to indulge her husband's indignation. She looked at Bess and waited for a response.

'Um, thirteen,' Bess said quietly.

'So, you need at least five more?'

Bess nodded, distracted by her inner voice: *It's my fault that Dad's upset*. She thought back to family dinners where her dad would entertain them with footy trivia. Her favourite tidbits included how in 1858, the first year of competition, there was no time limit for a game, rather, the team that first scored two goals won. And in 1860, if there were no umpires available, the team captains made the on-field decisions regarding any infringements. She used to imagine what it would be like if current games had no umpires. She was pretty sure there would be an all-out bloodbath. And one of her absolute favourites – that before 1955, white handkerchiefs rather than whistles were used by boundary umpires.

As the O'Neill family continued to eat their dinner in a silence they were all reluctantly becoming accustomed to, Bess's eyes shifted from her dad's empty chair to Tom's empty chair, and she felt her body become heavy, her mind building layers of unwanted possibilities. All because she had decided to come home and stir things up. She exhaled slowly.

Just breathe, Bess. Just breathe.

She tried to focus on one line of thought: *I came home because I miss home. I miss endless cups of tea with my mum, and watching movies and talking about any and every sport with my dad.* Bess reminded herself that for most of the year, she'd felt like she was drifting into someone else's life, and to break that pattern something had to change.

But now, her presence had made things worse for her dad, so perhaps not going ahead with the game was the only change she needed to make.

ELEVEN

25 days to Game Day

Two days later, twelve players stood on the oval, shivering slightly as the afternoon rain left its mark. Bess was nowhere to be seen.

'All right, guys, um, Bess told me she couldn't make it today, so I'll run training,' Jules improvised.

The players made no attempt to start warming up.

'Why couldn't she make it?' asked Sam, eyes narrowing.

'Um, she just felt a bit out of sorts,' Jules replied.

'Out of sorts? What the hell does that mean? Has she gone back to the city?' questioned Charlie.

'What? No! Of course she hasn't!' said Jules. 'Why would you even think that?'

'Well, we've just, we've heard some things . . .' Kat said reluctantly.

'What things?' asked Eva.

Kat and her friends looked uneasy. None of them seemed willing to elaborate.

'Seriously, guys, come on. What are you talking about?' prodded Jules.

'She just . . . has a tendency to leave. When things get a bit difficult,' explained Sam. 'I mean, that's right, isn't it? Or at least that's what we've heard.'

'And who told you this?' Fiona demanded.

Sam inadvertently glanced towards the boundary, but immediately looked away. 'Um, no one. It's just something that's going around.'

'Right, so that dickhead Lucas told you?' Fi had followed Sam's eye line. 'You can tell him that he doesn't know the first thing about Bess. And if I hear another rumour, I'm gonna make a larger head hole in every polo shirt he owns to fit that giant nob of his.'

Eva and Jules exchanged a knowing glance. Despite how she challenged Bess, Fiona was extraordinarily loyal.

'Okay,' acknowledged Sam.

'Let's start warming up,' Andy suggested, and the players fell into line.

As they started to jog around the oval, Jules watched Lachie drive up and emerge from his ute. He wore an army-green beanie, and leaned into the fence to scrutinise the passing group.

'Jules,' he called, 'where's Bess?'

She broke off from the team and approached Lachie. 'Um, she said she just wasn't feeling that well.'

Lachie scoffed. 'Jules, seriously?'

'Yeah, I know,' she replied.

'I don't know why you always cover for her.'

Jules met his eyes and simply shrugged.

'Yeah, I get it,' said Lachie with a sigh. 'Just keep training, okay?'

'We will. But Lachie, don't be too hard on her.'

He nodded, but his sharp reverse down the gravel path moments later was a clear indication that he was not happy.

*

Bess lay on her living room couch, headphones on, her walkman resting on her chest, eyes closed with Jinx stretched out beside her. Despite the high decibel level of 'Rhinoceros' by The Smashing Pumpkins, her eyes shot open at the sound of insistent knocking.

She swung open the front door. 'What the hell, Lachie?' said Bess as Jinx slipped out to greet him. Rather than invite Lachie in, she stepped outside and closed the door behind her, avoiding eye contact.

'Is there a reason you're not at training?' Lachie asked, his tone heated but his hands gentle as they ruffled Jinx's head.

Bess looked up to face him. 'Since when do I have to answer to you?' she shot back, her tone rising to match his.

'This isn't just about you, Bess. This team is for Gerandaroo. You know, the town that you *left*.'

Bess blinked back tears and took a deep breath.

'Why aren't you at training?' repeated Lachie.

'Look . . . my dad . . . he just . . .'

When she failed to finish her sentence, Lachie prompted her. 'Your dad what?'

'He just . . . I can't do it, okay, Lachie? I can't play. Dad's so upset by this whole team thing. And I . . . I can't keep hurting him. Not after everything he's been through.'

She knew that last comment was unnecessary. Her dad didn't have a monopoly on suffering. Lachie had suffered; they all had.

'So, you're quitting? Just like that?'

Bess was becoming increasingly upset that he was questioning her with such aggression. 'Lachie, who really cares if we play a game of football or not?'

Bess immediately regretted what she'd said, seeing the hurt in Lachie's face, his eyes. Eyes that she still knew so well.

But an apology was not forthcoming.

Lachie scoffed, gave Jinx a final pat, and walked down the steps. He was almost at his car door before he turned back. 'You know, Bess, you and I, we always wanted the same things. And the only reason it didn't work out was because you could leave but I couldn't. And you knew that. And you *still* left.'

He sounded as though he was saying all the things he wished he had said years before.

'But you can't always run away, Bess,' he added.

She walked down the steps towards him. 'Did you expect me to just stay here forever? Because you wouldn't leave?'

'*Wouldn't* leave? Wow. Really, Bess? Is that how you see it? Do you seriously think I would do that to my brother? Just leave him to fend for himself?'

Bess was ashamed of her outburst, but was too stubborn to backtrack.

'And no, Bess. I stopped expecting things from you long ago.

So, I'll tell you what, you just do what's best for you, all right? You seem to have got pretty good at it.'

For several agonising moments, their eyes locked; Bess was the first to look away.

'Bess, please stop acting like you can't make a difference.' Lachie's voice was gentle and sincere, the way she had always known him to be.

Rather than wait for a response, he left, this time without glancing back. Even if he had stayed, Bess had no idea what to say to him. Or even what he wanted her to say.

Still, as she watched him go, she was torn between a strong desire to run after him or to never see him again.

*

Shortly after, Gayle answered the home phone. 'Jules, love,' she said, 'how are you?' This was followed by a pause. 'I'm glad to hear it. Have you heard from Jake lately?' Gayle offered murmurs of understanding. 'Well, you give him our best if you hear from him.'

Bess watched the conversation unfold and thought back to high school when Jules would call her despite the fact that they had spent the entire day together. Her dad used to ask what they could possibly have to talk about. Bess would tell him that a lot of thoughts can happen in a short amount of time, and would he prefer to be the one she shared all of those thoughts with? He declined, good-naturedly. Ian would always talk to her friends when they came over, which was often. He was more involved than the other dads, some of whom never even bothered to learn anything about their own kid, let alone their kid's friends. Ian helped them build cubby houses when they were younger, he would do the morning drop-off after sleepovers so they didn't have to walk home lugging sleeping bags and pillows, and he always brought orange slices to their netball games in case the designated parent forgot.

'Sure, she's right here,' said Gayle. 'Say hi to your mum for me.'

Bess took a step backwards as her mum tried to hand her the phone. Gayle paused, and Bess pleaded through her eyes with a shake of the head.

Gayle drew the phone back to her ear. 'Jules, hon, sorry, she's just hopped in the shower. Can I get her to call you back? Okay, thanks, love.'

Her mum returned the phone to the cradle and surveyed her daughter.

'Thanks, Mum,' said Bess. She had no intention of calling Jules back.

*

An hour or so later, there was a knock at the door.

'Hey,' said Jules as Bess opened the door.

'I didn't call you back,' Bess said.

'I know.'

'But you still came over?'

'I did,' said Jules. 'I knew from the tone of your mum's voice that you were standing beside her when I called.'

'I'm sorry.' Bess dropped her head slightly.

'I know,' Jules reassured her. 'Come on, let's take Jinxy for a walk. It's been ages since I've seen him.'

Jinx was overjoyed to see Jules. If ever a dog had a crush on someone, it was Jinx for Jules.

They walked side by side down Gundry Crescent, Jinx between them, slightly ahead, setting a gentle pace. He veered towards a garden bed, enticed by a strong scent, likely blood and bone that the neighbours used in copious amounts.

'Do you remember when your dad brought him in to school for your show-and-tell?' asked Jules as Jinx continued to amble along.

'He was such a good puppy,' said Bess. 'Always so calm. Like he knew what the world was about.'

'Yet he still did that giant wee in the hallway.'

'Oh, you're right.' Bess laughed. 'I'd totally forgotten about that.'

'He's still the best dog,' said Jules, scratching behind Jinx's ears. 'Or at least tied for first with Molly,' she added. Molly was Jules' red kelpie.

'Why did you call?' asked Bess, not entirely sure she wanted to know the answer.

'I know you have doubts,' said Jules. 'About the team and about coming home. And I guess I just don't want you to make a decision without talking to someone.'

Bess nodded slightly but definitively. 'I appreciate that.' She thought for a moment before continuing. 'Back in the city, everything was on track. Like my *life* was on track. I had my degree, I love the school I work at, I've got pretty great students and the staff are supportive. And then, I just . . . couldn't really process what happened here. I knew I didn't want to *be* here, watching everyone struggle, and I thought work would distract me. That's why I left so quickly. But then . . . I was . . . drifting, I guess, is the best way to describe it. Nothing felt stable or certain or clear. And you know how much I like to plan things.'

Jules chuckled. 'I do.'

Bess turned to face her. 'Starting this team has upset my dad so much,' she admitted. 'And I just don't want him to feel that way.'

'I understand,' Jules replied slowly. 'But maybe, that's something *he* needs to work through. And if you stop now, before we've even been able to play a match, well, you'd be hurting a helluva lot more people.'

The two friends continued to walk, aware that the certainties they had grown up with, the belief that people were good and kind and decent, had slipped away from them. And although they were equally unsure if that trust would ever return, they at least took comfort in knowing that they did not have to suffer alone.

*

After a hectic day shift that involved a near record number of admissions, Ali was looking forward to training that night. It was a chance to expend some of the built-up nervous energy that came with her job. She was a good nurse, but with a mother who was one of the most respected nurses in the region, she felt burdened with the weight of expectations.

Some of her nursing colleagues were playing for the Denby team, and they peppered her with questions about how the Gerandaroo players were getting on. Mindful that Bess and the others wouldn't be too happy if she mentioned that they were yet to form a full team, she kept her responses vague, but she was happy to engage in light banter.

As she pressed the green exit button to leave the Emergency Department, she was unprepared for what came next.

'Hey, Ali,' called Sean, a senior nurse who had been her preceptor when she transitioned from the surgical ward to emergency nursing. 'Hold up a tick,' he said, jogging towards her.

'Did I forget to do something?' asked Ali, immediately worried.

'No, no, nothing like that.' Sean shook his head. 'Um, it's actually about the footy game.'

'Okay,' Ali replied slowly, intrigued but a tiny bit concerned.

'So, I don't know if you've heard, but there are some people who apparently don't want the game to go ahead.'

'What do you mean? What people?'

'Some folks on the council, and from the high school, and parents.'

'Why don't they want us to play?'

'I'm not entirely sure. But apparently there's a petition going around.'

'A petition?!' exclaimed Ali. 'What? To ban us?' She was almost laughing at how silly that sounded.

'Well, yeah,' said Sean, his voice low and disappointed. His comments wiped the smile from Ali's face.

'I just thought you should be prepared, maybe tell your team?'

'Yeah, yeah, I will. Thanks for letting me know.'

'Of course. I'll see you in . . . is it two days? For the pm shift?' he asked as he turned to head back inside.

Ali nodded, her thoughts already cycling through possible outcomes. She decided not to tell the team. At least not until she had more information.

*

Sam had arrived at training about fifteen minutes early and was helping Jules set out some cones. Jules got the impression Sam was attempting to make amends for her comments about Bess.

'So, how's Year 12 going?' Jules asked her.

Sam shrugged. 'It's going.'

'Yeah, I remember that feeling.'

Sam looked up, surprised.

'It can be tricky,' Jules continued, 'not really knowing if you want the year to end or not.'

'Yeah, that's pretty much exactly it,' said Sam. 'I mean, of course I want high school to be *over*. Who doesn't? But when it is, I have to make a decision.'

'About what to do?'

Sam nodded and placed several cones on the oval, about ten metres apart.

Jules waited, not wanting to pry or press for any more information than Sam felt comfortable sharing.

'It's not really my choice,' Sam said as she returned to stand near Jules. 'I mean, it is, but my mum and dad, they have very different ideas about what I should study and where.'

'Like it isn't hard enough already,' said Jules.

Sam grimaced. 'Exactly.'

'If you could forget about what your parents want, what do *you* want to do?' Jules asked gently.

'That's just it – I dunno. But I'd like to be able to have some time to figure it out. And it's not that I don't want to go to uni, because I do. But I'd like to maybe take some electives in a more general degree.'

'Have you told them this?'

'Sort of. But it never comes out right.' Sam picked up a nearby football and started to bounce it on the spot. 'They need a clear reason *why* I would do that, rather than doing a degree that leads straight to a job. And I don't have a reason.'

'Seems to me you have a pretty good one,' said Jules, but Sam looked unconvinced. 'Sam, knowing what you *don't* want to do is just another step towards helping you figure out what you *do* want.'

'You work on your family's farm, right?' asked Sam as she and Jules started to handball back and forth.

'Yep.'

'Is that what you always wanted to do?'

'Um. Not really. Especially not after uni.'

'You went to uni?'

'Yeah, I have an Arts degree and did the whole live-on-campus thing.'

'So, what happened?'

'You mean why would I give up the city life for a farm?'

'I'm sorry . . .' started Sam as she caught the football and paused.

'It's okay, I know what you mean.' Jules waited a moment before continuing. 'My brother, Jake, he became pretty unwell.'

'Oh right. Yeah, sorry, I knew that,' said Sam with a long blink.

'It's okay. Everyone knows.'

'How old is he?' she asked, handballing again.

'Twenty-nine.'

'And you don't know where he is?' Sam queried. 'I mean, that's what I've heard,' she added hastily.

'He called about four months ago. But he didn't say where he was living. He used to always let us know, or at least let *me* know. But in the last two years, he's become pretty distant.'

'Does he have a job at all?'

'He actually tries really hard to find work. Usually it's pretty short-term stuff in hospitality. And as soon as we find out where he is, we try to send money. Last October I found him up the coast and got him back on his medication. But that . . . well, that only lasted about six weeks. He has such a hard time . . . um, just with following a schedule and things like that. And there doesn't seem to be a whole lot that we can do.'

'Oh.' Sam thought for a moment. 'Why does he stop?' she asked. 'Taking his meds?'

'Yeah.'

'He starts to feel better,' Jules explained, 'but he doesn't make the link between the medication helping with that. And he thinks everything will be all right, so he stops. And then nothing is all right.'

Sam just nodded, seemingly trying to process the information.

'In the beginning, when my parents were looking for places that could provide treatment and they were trying to convince Jake to come home, they were spending so much time away from the farm that things were falling through the cracks.'

'So, you came back?'

Jules nodded. 'I thought it would only be for a little while. You see, Jake, he was the one who always wanted to take over the farm. And we sort of hoped that that might still be possible. But it doesn't . . . um, it doesn't look like it'll happen. At least not at the moment. So, I'll stay for as long as I need to.'

'But that could be forever!' Sam exclaimed, nearly dropping the ball.

'Yep. It could be.' Jules nodded again. 'And if that's what needs to happen, then that's what I'll do.'

'But how can your parents make you do that?'

She laughed. 'They're not *making* me do anything. In fact, they'd prefer to sell the farm and move to the city. *I'm* the one who wants to keep it, so that it's here for Jake.'

'Oh,' said Sam, frowning.

'Jake loves the farm. And I guess I just hope that one day, he'll be able to come home and enjoy it again.'

'What did you wanna do? I mean, before all of this happened,' asked Sam.

'I wanted to be an architect. I planned to do a master's after my undergrad.'

'Really?'

'Yeah, while I was at uni I worked in admin at an architecture firm and I have a portfolio. But the timing never seems right. And sometimes things end up being a bit different from what you expected.'

'I guess,' said Sam, avoiding eye contact with Jules but continuing to handball.

'I don't resent my brother, if that's what you're thinking.'

Sam looked at Jules. 'Yeah, that's exactly what I was thinking,' she admitted.

'Jake's a great brother, I mean a *really* great brother,' said Jules. 'Mum and Dad were always so busy with the farm, which is part of the reason why they wanna sell it, but it meant that Jake always looked after me. And it's not his fault that he's sick. If it had been me, he would be doing everything possible to get me well again.'

Sam nodded. 'I get it.'

'Hello, stranger,' said Jules, as she handballed high over Sam.

Sam turned to see Bess standing behind them, looking a bit sheepish as she caught the ball.

'Don't think for one second that I'm going to set up for you every training,' said Sam, who couldn't help but smile.

'Wouldn't dream of it,' replied Bess.

As the rest of the team gathered around them, the chatter came to a close.

'So, what's on for tonight, Bess?' asked Andy.

'Well, I think we need to go over the rules a bit more.'

'What about positions?' asked Ali.

'It's a bit hard when we're still short on players,' said Charlie.

'Are you sure about that?' said Jules, who was facing the town. She gestured with her head to something behind Bess.

'What are you talking about?' asked Bess as she and the others turned around. A fast smile formed. 'Yeah. Yeah, maybe we *should* talk about positions.'

*

Gayle was striding towards them with a wide grin; it was the happiest and most relaxed Bess had seen her since she arrived home. Her mother was flanked by three women who, despite their varied physical appearances, all radiated a tenacity that warned onlookers not to question their decision to play or they'd sorely regret it. To her right was Diane Carson, tall with perfect posture and manicured nails painted a bright red. Beside her was Meredith Harron who, despite skilfully bouncing a football, had lanky limbs that gave the impression she could trip at any moment. To Gayle's left was Nora Phillips, already slightly breathless and wearing an ill-fitting t-shirt, but beaming as she approached the team.

Horror filled the faces of Kat, Sam, Abby, Lou, Tully and Charlie.

'Oh, man,' said Kat.

'You've got to be kidding,' added Charlie.

'What? What's the problem?' asked Andy.

'They're all teachers!!!' they exclaimed in unison.

'We can't play with teachers!' cried Sam.

Taking in their pained looks of indignation, the older players laughed.

'Guys,' said Bess, 'you realise that *I'm* a teacher.'

'Yeah, but, you're not like a *teacher* teacher,' explained Charlie.

'I don't know if I should be offended or flattered.'

'Come on, guys,' said Andy, 'at least we have a team now.'

'Almost,' added Eva. 'We're still one down.'

'Yeah. I have an idea about that,' Bess said in a tone that left the others to exchange inquisitive looks.

She informed the team that practice was not going to take place on the oval and to change out of their footy boots. As she jogged towards the boundary, the players followed.

*

The expanded team of seventeen slowly made their way along the back roads. All were jogging comfortably, or in Nora's case, half-walking, half-jogging. Jen hung back so Nora wasn't running alone.

They stopped outside the Blake house and started to play Marks Up. It was quite the sight, with sixteen women huddled on one side facing Bess, who kicked the ball high so they could contest the mark. Meredith nearly caught it, her long arms reaching above the pack, but Tully got a hand to it and the ball ricocheted towards a nearby Commodore. Fi collected the ball and kicked it to Bess, who fired it long, forcing the team to take a series of steps back.

After the third kick, the ball was marked cleanly by Andy, who swapped with Bess to become the kicker.

The Blake brothers emerged from their house, the sounds of the women joshing about and the smack of the ball acted as a pulley of sorts. As they gathered on the nature strip, the mockery was close behind.

'What the hell is this?' Billy scoffed, hands on hips as he observed the women.

Rachel was the last to emerge, tea towel in hand. She stood back and watched as her brothers derided the women, her lack of expression gradually morphing into a furrowed brow.

Lou fumbled a mark and the ball bounced off her chest.

'Ohhh, this is just too good,' Billy chided loudly. 'You girls are gonna lose *soooo* badly.'

As though suddenly filled with courage, or perhaps rage, Rachel threw down the tea towel, stormed into the street, and marked the incoming ball. The rest of the players, rather than cheer, simply smiled, sharing small glances, and watched as Rach swapped with Andy.

Rachel shanked her first kick and the ball landed on her front lawn.

The Blake boys, now perched in a row on the gutter, laughed and slapped each other on the back. None of them made any attempt to retrieve the ball.

Rach hurried to pick it up, her face beet red.

'This is boring,' proclaimed her youngest brother as he stood up and stretched. 'Rach, what's for tea?'

Rather than answer, Rachel lined up for another kick.

'Rach, tea?'

'That depends,' she called.

'On what?' asked Billy.

'On what you decide to make.'

Billy stood up. 'Rach, come on. This is getting silly.' His raised voice was impatient.

'Car!' Jen called. The group moved to the side of the road as a beat-up white seventies ute pulled into the Blake driveway.

Rachel's dad John, aged in his early fifties with a permanently weary expression, slowly got out of his car.

He walked around to the back and removed his tools from the tray. He was a man of few words, and the sort of bloke who helped his mates whenever they needed it. He let customers pay late or gave them discounts, despite the strain it caused his family. He was the first to make sure his elderly neighbours were prepared for bushfire season, and despite working long hours, he always offered to keep score at his sons' footy and cricket matches.

Rachel watched him and held on to the ball without moving to kick it.

'Dad,' whined the second youngest brother, 'Rach said we have to cook tea.'

'Well, if you wanna eat, you'd better think of something to make,' said John with a hint of amusement.

The brothers shared a look of incredulity.

As John walked towards the front door, he offered his daughter some advice without turning around. 'Remember, you need to guide the football as you kick it, don't just drop it.'

Rachel turned to face her teammates and followed through with a textbook kick.

*

Later that evening, Ian sat at Tom's desk with his head in his hands.

The room was dark except for a small bright light coming from the desk lamp.

His thoughts were unable to shift from a night over a year ago.

'What do you mean you're not going?' Ian bellowed. 'No son of mine is gonna just walk away from an opportunity like this!'

'Dad, for the last time, I don't want to be a footballer.' Each word

Tom spoke was deliberately emphasised. 'I'm moving to the city next year to study and become a photographer.'

'Thomas, photography is not a plan for life. It's a hobby. It's time to grow up.'

Exasperated by the conversation, Tom turned to leave.

'Don't even think about walking away!'

He turned back to face his father.

'This is your chance to follow a childhood dream. One that every boy in this country has,' Ian pleaded.

'Whose dream, Dad? Because it certainly isn't mine.'

Ian was taken aback, and Tom's expression showed that he knew the hurt his words had caused.

'Dad, I love that you taught me to play footy. And I know how much it means to you, to watch me play. But I've told you before that I was never going to do it past high school.'

Ian, his hands outstretched, tried to reason with his son. 'When you're older and you've experienced life, you'll regret not taking every opportunity that came your way. You're just too young to understand that. They invited you, Tom, they want you to try out for them. You need to trust me on this and not waste this chance.'

Tom stared right into his father's eyes. 'Dad, why did you buy me a camera last Christmas?'

'Because it's what you asked for,' said Ian.

'But I've asked for lots of things that you never bought. Like a Game Boy, or a BB gun. So why did you buy the camera?'

Ian furrowed his brow and sighed deeply. 'Look, I don't know where you're going with this, but it doesn't have anything to do with playing footy.'

'It has everything to do with it,' said Tom. 'You gave me the camera because you knew how much it would mean to me. You did it because you knew that I'd found something I love to do. And now you're scared. You're scared because I'm not doing what you planned for me. And you don't want me to be disappointed if things don't work out. But just because you can't see where my life might be headed, it doesn't mean that it's wrong.'

'I just don't want you to regret not doing something you're good at,' Ian explained. 'You've played football your entire life, Tom, and all that hard work has paid off. Now's the time to focus on the opportunity that's right in front of you, rather than chasing after something that you'll lose interest in.'

'What do you think of my photos?' asked Tom.

'It doesn't matter what I think of them. Because that bloody creative world you think you wanna be a part of, it'll only disappoint you,' he said, frustration rising.

'Then I'll be disappointed.' Tom shrugged before turning and walking out the front door.

Jinx attempted to follow him, but the door closed in his face.

Ian stared after Tom before turning to Gayle who was leaning against the hallway wall.

'He's going to those tryouts. He's just confused. It's too overwhelming for him. But he'll go,' said Ian, nodding, 'he'll go.'

'No, love,' Gayle replied gently as she walked towards her husband. 'He won't.'

Ian turned the desk lamp off and left Tom's room. As he climbed into bed, he watched Gayle, still awake, turn and face the wall.

He lay on his back for a few moments before he turned onto his side and stared at the other wall.

Ian visited Tom's room every night. And every night, the silence that followed was deafening.

TWELVE

17 days to Game Day

Bess was surprised that she began to look forward to training, and the other players seemed to as well. It was partly because they were doing something new, which made it a bit exciting, but also because they were a part of something that they couldn't achieve on their own. They were dependent on each other to show up and participate. It created a welcome sense of responsibility and camaraderie.

Unfortunately, the players were subject to some absurd 'feedback' from the community, with Mrs Finch at the top of the list. She arrived at Denby High one Thursday afternoon, hell-bent on speaking with Nora Phillips about the team. After nearly twenty minutes of non-stop lecturing, Nora had had enough.

'So, like I said, I promise to take your feedback on board, and I'll also pass it on to the other teachers,' said Nora as she rose from behind her desk and headed towards the classroom door.

Mrs Finch remained sitting at a student's desk for a few seconds before she reluctantly followed. 'I really must insist that you consider the poor example you're setting for your students,' she lectured bluntly. 'Running around trying to play football, especially at your age. As if this town hasn't been through enough. Football is a game for men.'

'According to whom?' Nora raised her voice to match the intensity of Mrs Finch's outrage.

Mrs Finch narrowed her eyes, unable to formulate a response.

'If women want to play, and it's clear they do,' Nora continued, her tone respectful but defiant, 'how is that hurting you? And no one is saying *all* women have to play footy or that you have to support the team, but some of us quite enjoy it. There really is absolutely no harm in that.'

Nora stood holding the door open, and Mrs Finch finally left the classroom, clearly miffed that her impact had been insignificant. As Nora closed the door behind her, she let out a deep breath, exasperated, but slightly proud that she hadn't flipped her lid the way she'd wanted to.

*

'I have something very important to share with you all,' Charlie announced loudly as the team warmed up that evening.

Intrigued, the women momentarily stopped stretching, anticipating some grand proclamation.

'The name Charlotte means "free man", and is actually the feminine form of the male name Charles.' She looked around, anticipating a surprised response, but was met with suppressed laughter as the women looked anywhere but at her. 'I have decided I will continue to believe that Charlotte means a pudding of stewed fruit,' she added.

'That's great, Charlie,' said Andy. 'I'm so pleased you shared this vital piece of information. Now I can sleep at night.'

No longer suppressed, the group fell into infectious laughter.

'Well, I just thought you should know,' said Charlie, indignant but still smiling.

'I think a more pressing issue is, what are we going to wear for the game?' Abby mused.

'Yeah, I was thinking about that last night,' said Ali. 'Maybe we can try and borrow guernseys from family or friends, and just wear white shorts?'

'Or maybe basketball shorts, like we do for phys ed?' Tully chimed in.

'The guys' tops never fit right,' Sam complained.

'How do you know that?' asked Charlie.

'I tried on Lucas's once,' she said with a shrug.

'Bet he loved that,' Kat muttered.

'He definitely did not,' Sam confirmed. 'But we still have two and a bit weeks to figure it out,' she added. 'I'm sure we'll come up with something.'

*

Once again, the boys' team watched from the boundary as the women trained. The presence of the teachers had tempered their insults considerably, but they were not entirely deterred.

'I thought they would have tired by now,' said Meredith, frowning slightly.

'They're young and immature,' Diane responded. 'It's likely they resent us for playing when they don't have a team.'

'Well, they *have* a team, they're just not allowed to play. But that's no excuse for their behaviour,' said Nora. After a brief moment, she changed her tune. 'Or perhaps it is,' she conceded.

'Maybe we should have asked them what they thought about us playing,' Meredith suggested. 'It could be that they feel excluded.'

'You mean, ask their *permission*?' said Abby.

Meredith shook her head. 'No, not permission. But we could've let them know we were starting a team, perhaps asked if they wanted to be involved and help out at training.'

The younger players were not easily swayed.

'No one is stopping them from being a part of this,' said Kat. 'But clearly, that's not what they're interested in.'

'It's not like we stood on the boundary and yelled hateful things when we were told we couldn't play,' Eva commented.

'Yeah, same with me and my friends,' said Andy. 'We tried to start a team and when it didn't happen, when other people decided for us that it wouldn't be appropriate, we still came to every game and cheered for the boys.'

'Same with us,' Fi added.

'My husband keeps saying that it's disrespectful for us to play,' Diane said reluctantly.

There were murmurs of agreement from some of the group who'd been told the same.

'Oh, boo hoo,' said Charlie. 'They bitch and moan whenever

something doesn't go their way. So maybe just this one time, they need to grow up a bit and stop complaining. Maybe this one time, they need to consider what it's been like for *us* all these years to always be told that we can't play.'

The others started to nod enthusiastically.

'At least they know the reason *why* they're not allowed to play this season,' she went on, now on a roll. 'The only reason we're ever given is that we can't play because we're girls. That's not a reason. Yet time and time again, it's used as one. And I'm sick of it.'

Her thoughts tumbled out after years of suppression; it was clear why Charlie always did well in debates at school.

'I think, perhaps, they just don't understand,' said Nora. 'It's all very new to them, the concept of women playing.'

'I think they're worried we're trying to take something from them,' suggested Meredith.

'It's not like men *own* football,' Sam interjected with a note of defiance.

'Of course you're right,' Meredith said gently. 'But to most people, football's a man's game. Created *by* men *for* men. Even though women support footy –'

'And love footy,' Bess pointed out.

'Yes, exactly, even though women love footy and have been playing for decades, none of that registers with them. Without formal competitions, women's footy is just something that can be easily pushed aside.'

'What are they going to be like during the game?' Lou threw a sideways glance towards the boundary.

'I'd say they'll be the same as they are now,' said Bess.

'Well, that doesn't sound overly appealing,' Kat remarked.

'Nope, it does not,' added Sam.

'Definitely something to look forward to,' said Tully.

'But what's the alternative? We don't play because of what some people might say?' questioned Andy.

'But they're not just *some people*. They're our dads, and brothers, and guys who are meant to be our friends.' Abby looked at Sam. 'And boyfriends.'

'It's not just the men, it's other women too,' Jen chimed in. 'I've been told so many times by female family members that I'll get hurt if I play. That we all will.' She gestured to the group.

The team exchanged a look of understanding. They had all encountered at least one girl or woman who'd told them not to play, either because it was disrespectful, or because they would get hurt. Or perhaps the worst reason given: because it was a man's game.

'The boys get hurt every week!' said Kat.

'And we still get injured playing netball and basketball and soccer! So what's the bloody difference?' Tully cried.

'It's not like we're planning to be reckless and run into each other just for the sake of it,' said Abby. 'Well, most of us, anyway.' She stared pointedly at Charlie.

'Oh, seriously, Abs? I'm not planning on running into anyone,' Charlie shot back. 'At least, not intentionally,' she added with a sly grin.

'It's a valid concern,' said Gayle, 'but,' she held up her hand to stop the onslaught of objections, 'it's a worry we also have when the boys play. So as far as we're concerned, it's not a reason to *prevent* us from playing. We all know footy is a heavy contact sport, and we all know we're doing our best to prepare for that.'

'So how do we deal with people telling us we shouldn't play?' asked Kat. 'I mean, my dad's so happy that I'm on the team, but my mum isn't. And it sort of makes me feel as though we're doing something we shouldn't be.'

'I didn't know your mum felt that way.' Charlie turned to Kat in surprise.

'Well, it's sort of embarrassing that she's not being very supportive. I'm just . . . disappointed in her. So, I guess I didn't really wanna bring it up.'

'I get that,' said Abby. 'My mum's the same. She hasn't actually come out and directly said "I don't approve" but it's the way she gets when I leave for training and when I come home. She never wants to talk about the team or anything.'

'We're not doing something we shouldn't,' Rachel said suddenly. 'This, *us*,' she continued, locking eyes with all of them in turn, 'forming a footy team, training, getting ready for a game, there's nothing wrong with it. With any of it. But it *is* wrong that the people who love us are making us feel so guilty and causing us to have so much doubt.' Rachel rarely spoke for so long.

The group were nodding in agreement, but needed a final push of reassurance.

Jules gave a 'you're up' nod to Bess, who reluctantly tried to take the mantle. The problem was, she didn't know what to say. She still oscillated between wanting the game to go ahead and wanting to walk away from it. Today the pendulum had swung firmly to the latter, and there was nothing but a blank space where motivating phrases should have formed.

'You're right,' said Bess slowly. 'Um, but maybe . . . maybe right now we just try to ignore them and get on with training.'

Her words hung awkwardly and did little to improve morale.

'Come on, guys, let's get on with some drills,' she added curtly.

Bess deliberately avoided eye contact with any of the players. She could feel the disappointment seeping towards her and she was keen to avoid the splash.

The team reluctantly followed her lead and broke up into smaller groups, but they all seemed sapped of energy and lacked concentration.

*

A few minutes later, Kat handballed to Abby who attempted to handball, but found herself lifting her guiding hand way above her waist and half-throwing, half-handballing to a moving Ali.

'Christ almighty! You do that in a game and you'll be banned from the field! Just get back on the netball court where you belong!' Lucas called.

The now typical laughter from his lemmings followed, and Lucas revelled in the attention.

Bess turned towards the boundary and was surprised to see that Rick and Billy were also watching. She assumed they had arrived separately because they were standing apart. She had no idea why they were there, but was confident it was not to hurl insults at them. She also thought how awkward they seemed, standing alone, metres apart.

'Maybe you should spread the goalposts out! Otherwise you'll never score!' yelled Lucas. 'You know, *spread* them apart!'

'Oh gross,' said Abby. 'Does he mean what I think he means?'

'He's not that clever,' said Kat.

Before turning back to the team, Bess noticed that Rick and Billy glanced at each other, their expressions hardened. Still, they said nothing.

Bess tried not to look over at Lachie as he rested against the bonnet of his car on the east side of the field, his eyes shielded by familiar dark green sunnies. He was never one to buy new things. It wasn't that he was frugal – although he definitely was – but more that he hated to shop. Bess had to drag him to Denby before their high school graduation and practically force him into a pair of new trousers and a shirt. He complained so much, she'd literally had to undress him in the change rooms. Which, when she looked back, was probably exactly what he'd wanted.

*

Rick watched as the players worked in groups of six to move the football between them in a four v two scenario. Nora moved to try and tackle Kat, who had the option to handball or kick to Andy, Meredith or Charlie. But she held on to the ball and was wrapped up in the tackle.

'Okay,' said Andy, 'so that would be holding the ball.'

'Oh, is that what it means when the crowd yells "BALL" and the umpire sweeps his arms about,' Kat exclaimed, swishing both arms around her body like she was swatting a dozen flies away.

Andy looked amused rather than annoyed by Kat's limited footy acumen. She simply smiled and nodded encouragingly. 'Yep, that's exactly right.'

They tried again, but this time Kat dropped the ball and did not even attempt to handball or kick it.

'And that is also *not* what we're after,' said Andy.

'I still don't know why I'm not allowed to just drop it,' said Kat. 'I mean, it's my choice what I do with it, right? How can I be penalised for deciding I don't want the ball anymore?'

'Because, as we've gone over many, many times, it's an incorrect disposal. So, you need to make sure you stop dropping the ball every time one of us tries to tackle you, or we'll lose possession all game,' Nora explained, demonstrating the patience of a seasoned teacher.

'You're dropping that ball like it crawled up your skirt and bit you!' cried Lucas.

Nora turned in shock towards the boundary, while Kat went red in the face.

Rick glared at Lucas. 'You're a real dick, you know that?' he called from a few metres away. Then he jumped the fence and jogged over to the women. Lucas and his friends watched, stunned, mouths agape.

'Hey,' said Rick.

The players stopped and stared, unsure of what he planned to say or do.

'You guys need to learn where you are on the field and what your teammates are doing. Then when you actually play a game, you'll be able to find the gaps.'

He glanced around and tried to make sure he addressed all of them.

'When your team has possession,' he continued, 'it's your job to keep it that way, so you need to back each other up. You need to *talk* out here.' He paused for a moment. 'Footy is about trusting that someone will always be there.'

The women continued to stare at Rick; they'd never heard him make so much sense before.

'Here,' he said as he picked up a football, 'I'll show you. Bess, try and tackle me.'

Bess moved forward and Rick stepped back sharply and to the side. Nora was close by and had a go at tackling him, but he evaded her by faking to the right, then did a quick kick over the top to Meredith, who caught the ball.

He gestured to Kat. 'Now you try.'

Kat still seemed unsure about exactly what to do, but allowed Rick to guide her around the other players, showing her how to position her body for protection and how to move her feet.

'Let's keep going with this, and I'll come around to each group.' Rick stopped. 'I mean, only if you want. I don't wanna interfere. I just thought, maybe . . . I just thought maybe I could help?' he asked, suddenly timid for perhaps the first time in his life.

The players looked at each other and started laughing.

'Are you kidding?' said Eva.

'We'd love you to help, Rick,' Fiona added.

*

Billy remained on the boundary, but only momentarily. 'Ah, fuck it,' he muttered under his breath.

He too hopped the fence and joined the group. The younger boys, including Lucas, remained on the boundary.

Within minutes, the intensity on the field had lifted, with all players sprinting harder and calling louder.

Billy watched as Nora attempted to mark a kick from Meredith.

'Um, Mrs Phillips,' he said hesitantly as he approached Nora, 'I'm not sure if you're aware of this, but you close your eyes just when you're about to mark the ball. And I think that's maybe why you're not marking it.' He tripped over the words, clearly not used to telling an adult, especially a teacher, how to do something.

'You're absolutely right, Billy. I do close my eyes. I can't quite help it. I think I'm perhaps a tad scared of the pain the ball will cause if it hits me in the chest.'

'Oh, right,' said Billy, surprised she was aware of the issue. 'Okay. Um, well, I guess maybe try and tell yourself that it will hurt *more* if you don't open your eyes. You know, because the ball might smack into your face or something.' He almost wanted to laugh but also didn't want Mrs Phillips to think he was laughing at her.

'That's a very good point, Billy,' Nora agreed with a smile.

As Rachel ran past Lucas, who remained fixed in the same spot, she struggled to pick up a loose ball. A snide comment was enough to bring the upbeat atmosphere crashing down.

'Better lose some weight there, tubs,' Lucas commented loudly.

Rach stopped awkwardly. Still holding the ball, she turned to face Lucas, tears already forming in her eyes.

Nearby, Billy was beyond livid. As Lucas turned to his mates and laughed, Billy picked up a ball, ran full pelt towards the fence and smashed it directly into Lucas's face.

As his hands cupped his nose and mouth, Lucas howled, 'Fuck!'

Billy jumped the fence, clearly not finished. 'Apologise. Right now,' he demanded.

Lucas faltered, but seemed determined not to lose face in front of his friends. 'She's fat,' he stated, before aggressively spitting blood. 'I just call it how it is.'

'Do you have shit for brains?' asked Billy with complete sincerity.

'Why do you care?' said Lucas. 'What are you gonna do, join their team? So you can be some weirdo fairy like that dead kid?'

Billy's mouth opened slightly and his right fist clenched. With unexpected restraint, he spoke quietly. 'Did you even know him?'

'I knew he was a fucking poofter.'

The boys standing around Lucas shifted ever so slightly. It was as though the shield that had always protected Lucas had cracked and his true colours, ugly in tone and content, were exposed for all to see.

Billy thought back to games when words directed towards Danny were carried across the field like an intrusive song that you couldn't get out of your head. He'd stayed silent because he didn't believe that it was his battle to fight.

Billy's voice remained quiet. 'You know, I didn't stand up for Danny,' he said. 'Not once. I failed to help him when he needed it the most. But I should have. And you know why I should have?'

'No, why?' Lucas asked sarcastically.

'Because I could. I was in a position to say something and do something that might've made a difference. But I chose not to. And I made the wrong choice.' With a perfectly timed raised voice, he continued, 'Words fucking matter, you ignorant little shit. And you *know* that the player you just insulted is my big sister.'

Lucas remained in the same position, still holding his nose.

'In a few years' time, these guys aren't gonna be your mates,' Billy said, gesturing to the boys around him. 'They'll have figured out what a weak-arse shit-for-brains dickhead you are. If they ever bother to think of you at all, they'll only ever think bad things. So, go ahead, make your little comments. Enjoy how good you feel when you put other people down. Because it won't last. You will become irrelevant to everyone you have ever met.'

Lucas looked around nervously, as though seeking support, but his friends had increased their distance and continued to avoid eye contact, leaving Lucas to defend himself, alone.

Suddenly, Sam called from the field. 'Hey, Lucas!'

'What?' he yelled back.

'You're dropped!' Rather than wait for a response, she turned and headed off towards the centre circle.

Lucas stared after her, mouth open, nose dripping with blood. His friends sniggered.

'This is bullshit,' he muttered as he walked away, head back, pinching his nose.

Billy rejoined Rachel on the oval. She looked at him with a mixture of surprise and pride.

'I don't think I've ever heard you say so much before.'

He simply shrugged, and then gestured to the group in front of the north-end goal.

'Go on, get back into it,' he instructed her. He tried in vain to maintain his composure but was unable to stop the smile that formed as he watched his sister jog away.

THIRTEEN

Early Saturday afternoon, Rick approached a property with a red Ducati in the driveway and several bikes and an assortment of balls casually tossed across the lawn.

He rang the doorbell, and fourteen-year-old Will Lafferty opened the door.

'Hey, Will, is your brother home?'

'Hey, Rick. Yeah, he's here. I'll get him.'

'Thanks, mate.'

Rick leaned in slightly and could just make out a conversation between the brothers.

'I don't care, tell him I'm not home.'

'No, you tell him.'

'Will, fucking tell him I'm not here.'

After a brief wait, Will came back to the door. 'Um, sorry. He's out with Mum.'

'No worries. Can you get him to give me a call when he gets back?'

Will nodded, and closed the door.

*

Inside the house, Ben Lafferty was watching TV with a distracted expression and clasped, calloused hands. Will – a miniature version of Ben, right down to their chin-length blond hair – came back in.

'Why don't you talk to Rick anymore?'

'Mind your own business.'

'Fine.' Will used the remote from the edge of the couch to change the channel to the Essendon v Adelaide preliminary final.

'Change it back,' demanded Ben.

'Why? You weren't even paying attention,' said Will as he dropped onto the couch. 'And the game's about to start.'

Ben turned to face his brother. 'Change it back!' he repeated, anger rising.

'No,' said Will.

Ben jumped up and aggressively grabbed the remote from his brother's hand.

'Hey! Give it back!' Will stood and reached out in a failed attempt to wrestle it from his brother's strong grasp.

Ben shoved him down, hard, but showed a flicker of remorse as his little brother fell heavily on the couch, a stunned expression splashed across his young face.

'We're not watching footy. Not in this house. Got it?' said Ben, his face inches from his brother's. Will nodded vigorously as he watched Ben storm out of the room.

*

Late the next afternoon, Billy and Rick ran through the streets of Gerandaroo, matching each other stride for stride as they headed towards Ben's house. They came to a stop outside a partially open garage door, where they could hear a familiar pounding sound. Rick banged on the garage. 'Hey, Ben, ya decent?' he called.

The pounding stopped but there was no response.

'Come on, mate, can you open the door so we don't have to duck under? I mean, I'll do it, but I don't much feel like playing limbo.'

There was still no response from Ben, but the garage door started to open. The boys watched as Ben returned to punching the bag.

'How about taking a break from that and coming for a run with us?' Billy suggested.

Ben remained expressionless as he continued to work the punching bag. But after a few moments, he flicked his gaze towards them. 'Why?'

'Because you're looking a bit unfit,' said Rick.

'Yeah, you could use a good run,' added Billy.

As the corners of Ben's mouth edged towards a smile, he suppressed it. 'Nah, I'm good on my own,' he replied, followed by a one-two punch.

'You see, the thing is, mate,' said Rick, 'we've all tried to be on our own these last few months. And it pretty much sucked.'

'And what, you think running together is going to change anything?' Ben's tone was harsh, and his words hung briefly before crashing down on each of them.

Billy scoffed, and was about to take the bait, but Rick beat him to it.

'You think you're the only one suffering?'

Ben wiped sweat from his forehead with the edge of his grey t-shirt and went back to punching the bag.

'So, that's it then? You just plan to ignore us?' said Rick as a flood of energy surged through his body and landed in his fingertips. He opened and closed his fists to try to shake the tingling feeling that was starting to overwhelm him.

'No,' Billy said, his tone forcing them all to stop momentarily and focus on him. 'We know that running together isn't going to fix everything.' The boys followed Billy's gaze as he turned and stared at their grand final photo framed on the wall. After a brief but significant pause, he added, 'But it's a start.'

The honesty in Billy's voice forced Ben to drop his arms from their fighting position.

'Okay,' he said with a small nod. 'I just need to tell my dad that I'm going.'

*

Rick and Billy stood at the bottom of the Laffertys' driveway, waiting for Ben.

'I told you he'd come,' Rick said.

'He hasn't yet,' responded Billy.

'He will.'

Ben emerged from his front door

'Told you so,' said Rick.

The boys began to jog together, with Rick slightly in front.

'Wait, what? No, I don't want to go this way,' Ben said as Rick led them towards the gravel road.

'Just give us a chance to show you something,' said Billy.

Ben turned to run back home, but the boys blocked him.

'Ben, please, just wait,' said Rick, raising both hands. 'I promise it's a good thing. We just need you to trust us.'

Ben was breathing heavily, and Rick could tell he was fighting the overwhelming desire to flee. Or perhaps to fight. But he relented when he saw the pleading looks on his friends' faces. He reluctantly followed them to the footy oval.

'At first we thought it wasn't right,' said Rick as they watched the women warming up. 'You know, that they're playing after everything that happened.'

'But then we realised how much it always meant to us,' said Billy. 'And they've never been able to experience that.'

'And that didn't seem fair,' Rick added.

'Plus, they sort of suck, and could really use our help,' Billy said with a grin.

'Yeah, that too.' Rick laughed. 'You don't have to stay if you don't want too. But we'd rather do this with you.'

Ben looked between his friends on the boundary and the players on the oval.

'Okay,' he agreed quietly.

*

Near the centre circle, each player stood with her head tilted up towards the darkened sky.

'They said it was going to rain,' said Nora.

'But they never seem to get it right,' replied Tully.

'It feels like rain,' said Meredith.

The others nodded in agreement.

'And smells like it,' added Charlie. 'I love that rain smell.'

'You are so odd,' said Abby.

Then, as if on cue, heavy pelts of rain bucketed down.

The players were all momentarily frozen before they turned and sprinted to the boundary, with Tully calling, 'I guess they were right!'

*

Billy and the other boys were running towards the centre of the oval just as the women ran from it.

'Oh shit, our *teachers* are playing?' Ben whispered to Rick.

'Well, they don't teach us anymore,' said Rick. 'And it's been kinda fun, helping them get better. But I do feel a bit bad for all the crap we used to put them through,' he confessed.

'Where do you think you're going?' said Billy as the women dashed past.

Sam turned to face him. 'Ah, in case you haven't noticed, it's raining. Like a lot.' She took a few steps backwards, clearly keen to turn and continue sprinting from the field.

'And?' said Billy.

'And we're going home,' Abby called, still heading towards the carpark.

'Because you'll get wet? Seriously? What if it rains on match day?'

The women came to a reluctant stop.

Billy looked around the group, waiting for some sort of response, but was met with blank expressions. 'If you can develop your skills in the rain,' he said, 'you can really call yourselves footballers.'

'Is that actually a thing? Or did you just make it up?' asked Charlie.

'I just made it up,' he said, which drew a laugh.

'I'm in,' said Lou.

The rest of the team were shocked. Of all the players to speak up, the quietest seemed eager to stay and get soaked.

'So,' said Bess, looking around at everyone, 'we're still gonna train?'

There were mumblings and nods of agreement.

'Ah, we can do better than that!' Billy yelled. 'You gotta get pumped up!'

With his enthusiasm hard to ignore, the players turned and followed him back to the centre of the oval, sprinting hard.

*

Thirty minutes later and despite being drenched to the bone, the team were having an absolute ball. The glow of the floodlights cut through the dark sky as the intensity of the rain eased and the players could now see a few feet in front of them.

Billy had clearly decided to keep things simple. He said he wanted them to get used to where they were on the field and be able to judge distances. He had broken them up into groups, and each group had one of the male players for support.

And they really did provide support. It was as though they didn't need to actually *play*, but just be back around footy.

'Are you okay with this?' Jules whispered to Bess. 'I just realised that we never talked about whether we wanted the guys to help or not.'

'Are you kidding?' she said. 'I am beyond thrilled that they want to get involved. And that I don't have to plan all the training sessions now. I was getting to the end of my footy repertoire.'

'Could've fooled me.'

'Just look at them,' Bess exclaimed, gesturing to the boys. 'I've never seen them stay so focused on anything for this long. Even when they played, they could be real little shits at training. Used to drive Coach Macca crazy.'

All across the Gerandaroo oval, the boys could be heard shouting words of encouragement.

'Yes, yes, yes!' cried a jubilant Rick as Abby and Kat managed to handball a number of times, back and forth, without a fumble.

'That's it, Lou!' Billy called as Lou evaded a tackle from Charlie and handballed cleanly to Sam.

Andy booted a drop punt that landed directly in Ben's hands. 'Nice one, Andy!' he called.

As Bess walked over, Diane was speaking softly to the other teachers. 'Why couldn't they have been this attentive in class?'

'I think this is the first time I've heard Billy speak in complete sentences,' added Nora.

'I knew I should have taught with a footy in my hand,' joked Gayle, and the others laughed.

'It's nice, though. To see them smile again,' Meredith commented.

'Enough chitchat!' called Billy, half-joking, half-serious, and the group dutifully spread out to continue their kicking drill.

*

As the training came to a close, the rain had reduced to a spit.

Rick jogged up beside Bess. 'Have you heard from Tom?' he asked, his voice low, taking her by surprise.

'Um, not recently. We last spoke before I came back home.'

'So you don't know where he's living?'

Bess shook her head.

'Lachie said he hasn't heard anything either,' Rick said with a mixture of disappointment and resentment.

'I think Tom, he just . . . needs some time,' she offered.

'Time?' he scoffed. 'He should be here. Or at least let us know he's okay.'

'He's okay,' Bess defended.

'How do you know?'

'I just do.'

'He can't hide forever,' said Rick.

'He knows that. And he's not hiding. He's just, doing what he needs to do. To cope.'

Rick frowned.

'I think being here, it just became too hard for him,' she added.

'He's being selfish,' said Rick.

Bess didn't respond right away. Partly because she agreed, and partly because she didn't.

'Rick, if he knew *how* to be here, he would be here. He'll come back.'

'Well, if he's not back before game day, I'm going to find him and bring him back. I'll bring them *both* back. Whether they like it or not.'

They walked in step for a few more metres.

'I'll see you on Tuesday, Bess.' Rick jogged away, his voice sad yet determined.

Bess simply nodded. She knew how intense Rick could be, and how that intensity sometimes overwhelmed him. She knew that he was sometimes seen as aggressive and angry, but that he could also be surprisingly sweet. She also knew how restrained he had been lately, and how much he was holding inside.

And knowing all this meant knowing that he would go looking for his friends. And that he would bring them back. If they let him.

*

As the rain again increased in intensity and pounded the roof, Bess and Gayle came rushing through the front door. Exhausted, yet laughing, they dropped their bags.

Ian was sitting in his chair, a beer nestled in its Demons stubby holder held tightly in his right hand, the TV on mute.

'I'm literally soaked right through.' Bess shivered.

''Bout time you got home,' Ian grumbled.

Gayle looked at her husband, her smile immediately wiped from her face.

'Lachie came by,' he said.

Bess tried to sound uninterested. 'Oh?'

'He mentioned something about needing help on game day.'

'He asked you to help?' Bess's tone was optimistic. 'What did you say?'

Ian didn't answer, and instead took a sip of his beer.

'Mum,' Bess said, 'why don't you have a shower first and I'll start tea?'

'Thanks, love.'

Bess expected her dad to say something, anything, but he remained stubbornly silent. As a publican, listening and offering advice were well-honed skills. And for her entire life, Bess had never been in her dad's presence and experienced such lengthy periods of either no conversation or inconsequential talk. It was also the first time she didn't even have a hint of what he was thinking or what he planned to do. As the thoughts swirled around, she became increasingly frustrated.

'You know, Dad, this behaviour can't continue.'

Ian did not make eye contact with his daughter. Instead, he stood up and headed towards the front door.

'Dad, come on, please! Don't just leave. You always told us never to walk out on an argument.'

Ian turned. 'Is that what this is? An argument? Because it sounds like you're just telling me how I'm allowed to act in my own house.'

'It's my house too.'

'Is it now? Is it also Tom's house? Because you don't see him here. So as far as I can tell, I will do and say what I want. And if you don't like it, you can run off back to the city.'

Bess stood still, breathing deeply and trying furiously to blink back tears. Her dad had never spoken to her like that before. She struggled to make sense of his cruelty.

Ian's face softened, and Bess was certain he was going to apologise or at least say something, anything, to bring them back together.

But instead he turned and walked out the front door.

Bess jumped as it slammed shut. She stood in the same position for several minutes, wondering if the dad she knew, the dad who, despite his stubbornness, was unquestionably kind, had broken.

Bess was certain that he had.

She was also certain that she didn't have a clue how to help him.

*

Ian travelled several loops around town with no destination in mind. As he idled down Green Street, he had a sudden desire to buy crumpets and the expensive raspberry jam that came in a small jar – Bess's breakfast favourite.

With about ten minutes until the general store closed, Ian stood in the bakery aisle and reached to the top shelf to remove two packets of crumpets.

'Yeah, it's a bloody joke,' exclaimed a familiar voice from the next aisle over. Ian knew from the first syllable that it was Rob – a middle-aged Gerandaroo resident and owner of the Denby Hardware Store. He was that clichéd combination of racist, homophobe and misogynist – and an all-round prick.

'At least it'll be good for a laugh,' a deep male voice responded, one that Ian recognised but struggled to place.

'No way I'd let my wife or daughter play,' Rob added snidely.

'But your wife left you. And you've got no kids,' replied the other male with unintentional humour.

'That's not the bloody point! None of 'em should be playing. First we had fucking fairies prancing across our field and now we've got girls dancing on it!' Rob's voice faded, indicating he was walking away.

Ian was suddenly aware that he was not alone in the aisle. He glanced to the side and saw Rick.

'You know they're wrong,' Rick said quietly, but loud enough to be heard from where Ian remained standing metres away. 'The women, they really want this. And they deserve to play.'

Ian gave a small nod, small only because in that moment he realised how right Rick was, and he felt so deeply ashamed of how he'd acted towards Bess and his wife.

Rick turned and walked away, but looked back and smiled. Ian thought how grown up Rick seemed. From the hyper kid who'd liked to stretch the truth and demanded to be part of any and everything, he'd grown into a young man who recognised that playing footy had been a privilege, one afforded to him without issue simply because he was a boy.

Ian stared at the crumpets in his hand. Crumpets for his daughter who used to wear his guernsey and sit on his lap to watch VFL matches on the TV in black and white, and would clap for every goal scored, from *both* teams. The daughter who ran around with a small football and a Barbie doll, and would convince everyone that her Barbie was good enough to play for the Demons. The daughter who cried when Melbourne lost the prelim final in 1987.

But despite knowing all of these facts, he had never considered that Bess would actually want to play footy for *real*; he had devoted so much time and energy to supporting Tom to play, even when Tom resisted, that he'd failed to acknowledge that he had another child who was never even given the chance.

Back in the car, Ian found himself driving along nearly every street in town, before leaving Gerandaroo and heading towards Denby.

Driving was newly therapeutic; it helped his body keep pace with his mind, a reaction, perhaps, to his inability to make sense of recent events. For months now, whenever he left the house without giving any indication as to where he was going, he would drive. And then often walk. The combination had become an occasionally effective circuit breaker.

Acting on impulse, as soon as he arrived in Denby he circled the first roundabout and came straight back to Gerandaroo.

*

Returning just on midnight, rather than go to bed, Ian entered Tom's room and again sat at Tom's desk. He opened the bottom drawer and removed Tom's camera. As he held it in his hands, he was reminded of the last time he saw it.

It was the last week of February, early Sunday morning, when Ian knocked on Tom's door.

'Tom?' he called. 'I've made some pancakes.' He paused and waited for a response. 'Tom?' he called again, this time louder and more insistent. When there was still no answer, Ian opened the door and found an empty room. The bed looked like it had been slept in, but it always looked that way.

Ian noticed that Tom's camera was on his desk, but something was missing. The first photo Tom had taken with his camera was a portrait of Jinx. Lachie had made a wooden photo frame especially for it, and it usually took pride of place on Tom's desk.

Ian called to his wife. 'Gayle!'

She came running into Tom's room. 'What? What's happened?' She looked around. 'Where's Tom?' she asked, her voice rising with concern.

'He's gone,' said Ian.

'What do you mean? Of course he's not gone.'

She instinctively went to the wardrobe, only to find many empty hangers. She rushed to the dresser and pulled open the top drawer, which had been emptied.

She turned to look at Ian, who stood with Tom's camera in hand. They shared a look of panic.

'He's gone looking for him,' said Ian as he found himself sitting on the edge of Tom's bed, suddenly unable to stand.

Gayle could only nod. They both knew that Tom would not come home until he'd found him.

Bess, still awake despite the late hour, listened as her dad entered the house and tried to quietly lock the front door. She thought to herself how the quieter a person tried to be, the louder they usually were.

She could tell that her dad had not gone to his bedroom, so she ventured into the hallway and saw a light coming from under Tom's door. She entered the room and saw her dad sitting at the desk.

She hesitated. 'Dad?'

Ian did not turn around but held up a book entitled *The Backpacker's Guide to Australia*.

'I bought this for him,' he said.

'I remember.'

Bess could hear from his voice that her dad was crying. She moved forward to hug him, and as she gently wrapped her arms around his neck from behind, Ian reached and grasped her arm.

He made no attempt to stop crying. 'I don't know what to do, Bess,' he said between quiet sobs. 'You kids are everything.'

Bess gripped him tighter, aware that she had also started to cry. 'How about I make us a cuppa tea?' she offered.

Ian nodded and wiped his face with the sleeve of his jumper. As he rose, he turned and embraced Bess. It was the first proper hug they'd had all year. Her dad was the very best hugger and she had missed him terribly.

After making the tea, Ian and Bess sat on the couch and Bess put on *Back to the Future* on VHS. Growing up, they'd always had movie nights, not just with the family, but all their friends. Ian and Gayle loved having a full house. There was rarely a weekend in Bess's childhood without at least one visitor stopping by.

Neither of them spoke as the film started. There was a quiet understanding that they were both sorry. And were both forgiven.

*

Just after two in the morning, Ian returned to bed. He slowly moved closer to Gayle and gently cupped her shoulder so as not to frighten her. She turned, and with their heads rested on their pillows, they looked at each other in the dark. They remained silent as Ian reached out to stroke her face. Gayle clasped his hand and held it tight. She moved to rest her head on Ian's chest and he wrapped his arms around her, before kissing her softly on the top of the head.

They had shared a life filled with conversation, so in that moment, no words were needed.

FOURTEEN

13 days to Game Day

Inside the general store, Tully stood in front of the ice-cream freezers, thinking intently about her selection.

'Glad I'm not the only one to eat ice-cream when it's freezing out,' came a voice from behind her.

She turned to see Ben, his trolley half full, smiling. 'Hey, Ben. Yeah, my family think I'm nuts for always wanting something cold on a day like this.'

Ben moved to stand beside her. 'So, have you narrowed it down?'

'I can't decide between citrus or chocolate,' Tully mused.

'That is a tough one,' said Ben. 'I'm a big fan of the Twister Cups and the Mud Bucket. And the Boomy or a Pine Lime Splice. Oh, and Paddle Pops, but only the rainbow flavour. Or a Barney Banana. And Sunny Boys, but they're best on a super-hot day.'

'I always end up eating the cardboard,' said Tully.

'Same! Or maybe you could get a Choc-Wedge? Or a Ripper Dipper?' he suggested.

'Are you going to name everything in there?'

Ben laughed. 'Sorry, I just get excited by ice-cream. But, let's be honest, you can't go past a Golden Gaytime.'

'Definitely,' Tully agreed.

'Oh, look at this, are you both planning to have a *gay time* together?' Lucas broke the happy moment with his sing-song voice. 'But that wouldn't work, now, would it?' he added sarcastically.

Ben turned and stood tall. He had a confidence that Tully thought most people probably overlooked.

'You know, a black eye would go great with that crooked nose of yours,' he suggested.

'It's not crooked!' Lucas's hands immediately flew to his face. 'My mum said it's fine!'

Ben just grinned. 'And why would *she* lie?'

Tully knew Ben had no intention of punching Lucas.

'See you at training, Tully,' Ben said, before he pushed his trolley down the closest aisle.

Tully didn't feel abandoned by Ben, quite the opposite. He knew she could handle herself with Lucas. And so did Lucas.

He stared at Tully, giving the impression that he wanted to say something, but not sure what. Tully maintained eye contact; it had now become a staring contest. Lucas was the first to look away. He retreated and his lemmings followed.

Tully selected a Golden Gaytime and headed to the checkout where Mr Clark served her.

'I saw you running with your cousin the other day. You were bouncing a footy,' Mr Clark said.

Tully nodded. *Where is this headed?* she wondered. Mr Clark wasn't mean, but he wasn't exactly nice either.

'So, you're playing for that new team?'

She nodded again. She had no clue which side Mr Clark was on. *Is he about to launch into a tirade about how girls shouldn't play football? Don't get angry, Tully, just get your change and leave.*

'It's not an easy game,' he pointed out.

'No, it's not.' *Here we go . . .*

Mr Clark met her eyes as he handed over her change. 'That Lucas Cutler kid is a right little turd.'

Tully couldn't help but laugh out loud. She expected Mr Clark to at least be smiling, but he maintained his deadpan expression, so she composed herself and nodded. Again.

As she exited the store, she looked back, and Mr Clark gave her the slightest of nods.

He's on our side.

*

Bess slowed her pace close to home and decided to walk down her street rather than run. She wasn't sure why, but she wanted to take her time. Even though she wasn't working at the moment, her responsibilities with the team had placed her in a constant state of haste, as though she was always rushing to catch up. In fairness, she knew that her worries about the team had lessened considerably now that the boys had come on board and were running drills at training. But still, there was a nagging feeling that it was all about to come crashing down.

She realised that in the city, she never walked for enjoyment but only to *get* somewhere. She would run for exercise and this helped relieve stress from work and relationships and life in general. But as she ambled down her street, she wondered if perhaps she ought to try and walk, to maybe help her connect with her thoughts in a constructive way.

As much as she liked to think that things would change, she knew the sense of urgency that accompanied city walking was unlikely to abate, and that without the country air to soften the edges, she probably wouldn't follow through with this plan.

As Bess checked the letterbox, Tom popped into her mind. Tom loved receiving mail. Even when Bess lived at home, she'd always sent his birthday card via post. This meant not just putting it in their mailbox, but actually posting it with a stamp. That was the part Tom loved the most – something about how the letter had to travel to get to him.

She always added a short story that included people from around town. She would place them in far-off lands, sometimes real, sometimes fantasy. She never thought the stories were very good, but Tom always seemed to love them, and he kept them all in a shoebox under his bed. In Grade 3, he took one of the stories to school for show-and-tell. He read it out loud, complete with different voices. Bess was mildly horrified when she found out, mainly because she'd included Tom's teacher as a character in a less than flattering light. She became slightly less concerned when

Tom explained that the other kids had loved the story and laughed at all the right bits. He'd even seen his teacher smile.

As Bess opened the front door, she could hear her mum talking on the phone. She entered the kitchen, leaned over the countertop and caught the end of the conversation.

'Yes, I understand. Thank you for letting me know,' Gayle said, her tone more school principal than mum. There was a brief pause, then, 'You too. Bye now.'

'Who was that?' Bess asked as she poured herself a glass of water and Gayle slowly placed the phone back on the cradle.

Gayle didn't respond.

'Mum?' She took a gulp of water, her back against the kitchen cabinet.

'Yes, love?'

'Who was on the phone?' she repeated impatiently.

'The detective,' Gayle responded, but she didn't elaborate. It was as though she was running through a million and one thoughts and couldn't process the intrusion of Bess's questions.

'Detective Riley?' Bess prompted, and Gayle nodded.

'And?' Bess was becoming increasingly frustrated at having to prise the information out of her mum.

'He said all the Denby boys plan to change their plea to guilty.'

Bess gasped. 'You're kidding? *All* of them? Including Simon?'

'Apparently.'

'So, they won't go to trial?' asked Bess.

'No. It doesn't look like it. They'll attend court for the plea hearing and for sentencing. But no trial.'

'What else did he say?'

'He wanted to check that none of us had had any contact with Mitch.'

'So, they still have no idea where he is?'

'They're actively looking.'

'Obviously not hard enough,' said Bess with more than a hint of bitterness.

'Perhaps he'll come back on his own.'

'Mum, come on,' she scoffed, 'you seriously think that after all this time, Mitch Jacobs is going to do the right thing?'

'No. I don't,' said Gayle with sad resignation. 'But I can still hope for a better outcome.'

Mother and daughter stood in silence, each acutely aware that their lives, and the lives of the people they loved the most in this world, had long been impacted by the actions of Mitch Jacobs.

And they knew it was far from over.

Bess could suddenly hear it. Her heart beating. Fast, adrenaline pumping, but steady. And rather than persuade her to flee, it was guiding her to stay.

*

Bess was placing groceries into her car boot when Rick appeared behind her.

'Geez, Rick, creepy much?' she exclaimed.

'Your mum said you'd be here.' He glanced around to check that there was no one within earshot. 'I got Tom's address,' he added in a low voice. 'Or at least it might be his.'

'How?' Bess was surprised yet sceptical.

'My sister's ex-boyfriend Ronnie –'

'That guy who had the dreads?'

'Yeah, that's him. He lives in the same apartment block as Tom. Or, at least, he thinks Tom lives there.'

Bess frowned, unconvinced, so Rick continued.

'After he dumped my sister –'

'I thought she dumped him?'

'Bess! Can you please focus!' Rick insisted, his voice raised, much to Bess's amusement, even though she knew it was no laughing matter. It was one of those serious moments that almost seemed overwhelming, so Bess responded inappropriately by making light of the situation.

'Sure, sure, continue,' she told him, forcing a controlled tone.

'Well, we stayed in touch. He's a really cool guy. And I asked him to keep a look-out for Tom.'

'How does he –'

'He watched a few of our games,' Rick said, clearly anticipating the question, 'so he sort of remembers what Tom looks like. And he called this morning and said that he saw someone coming in from a run late last night that could be Tom.'

'So, it might not be him?'

'Maybe not. But it could be. And that's something, isn't it?' His expression was hopeful.

Although Bess didn't want to be too pessimistic, she also didn't want Rick to expect too much, or even anything.

'Rick, even if Tom does live there, he's not just going to come back with you,' she warned.

'I know,' he said, with an awareness Bess was not expecting.

For the first time, she saw Rick not just as her little brother's friend, but as an adult.

'I guess just be prepared,' she suggested gently. 'If it is Tom, he may not be too pleased to see you.'

Rick simply nodded, and gave a short wave as he walked to his car.

*

On the drive home, Rick reminded himself that it was a long shot. But he also held on to the persistent thought that someone had to do something before time created a distance between Tom and Gerandaroo that would become insurmountable. He decided that he was done giving the people he loved time and space.

*

Unsurprisingly, the news that the Denby boys planned to plead guilty spread rapidly. As the players trickled onto the oval and began warming up for their evening session, the mood was mixed. The chatter focused on whether the boys would serve any jail time; it was an outcome they had all considered but none had really vocalised until now. It was challenging to even think about because they all knew these boys in some capacity. Some of the women were former classmates of the boys' siblings, some knew their parents, others used to teach them. They weren't just random, faceless names. They were all part of the same extended country community, which was why their actions, the choice they all made, was so unfathomable. And heartbreaking.

Bess was reluctant to be drawn into a discussion, debate or argument about what might happen next. With the towns already so divided, it was challenging enough to focus on preparing for the game. To avoid giving her opinion, she stayed off to the side of the group and fixated on the sky beyond the west-side boundary, just before the bush took over. The clouds were moving faster than felt comfortable, as though they had somewhere else to be. Or perhaps they just didn't want to be here.

Bess became aware that the conversation had moved on, and the players were discussing if anyone would try to prevent the game from going ahead.

'You don't think they'll stop us playing, do you?' Kat asked no one in particular as she raised her left leg behind her and grasped it to stretch her quad muscle.

'What, you mean like physically restrain us?' joked Charlie, who was sitting on the oval stretching her hamstrings. 'Besides, there's no one who can actually stop us.' She looked around at the group. 'Is there?'

'Well, yes,' said Diane, 'there is. For starters, the league could renege on the agreement that Deb set up to let the game go ahead in Denby.'

'What reason could they possible give to back out now?' Charlie asked.

'There are plenty,' said Meredith. 'For one, there's been a lot more talk about how we'll get hurt. But I know we've already discussed it, so we just need to make it clear to everyone that we're aware of the risks.'

'There's also the potential for a major fight between spectators,' said Diane.

'And there are some people who think that the players will fight during the game,' added Nora.

'What? *Us?* Fight with the Denby players?' said Charlie.

'That, and the boys' teams fighting each other,' Nora continued. 'They don't want a repeat of all the retaliation fights that happened throughout January. None of us do. Remember, that's the reason they banned the Gerandaroo and Denby teams for the season in the first place.'

'But we're *friends* with the Denby girls. We all go to school together and we hang out with them. We're not like the boys who are ridiculous and stay in separate groups based on where they live.' Charlie was on a bit of a rant, clearly offended at being accused of potentially doing something she would never do. 'I mean, even after everything that happened, we didn't just stop being friends with them. They had *nothing* to do with it. Surely that's a better message to get across than stopping the game because of something that some people think will happen but never will,' she added, before finally taking a breath.

'We know that, Charlie,' said Meredith. 'We *all* know that,' she added, gesturing to the other teachers. 'That's exactly what we said at a staff meeting today.'

Nora threw a sideways glance at Meredith.

'Look, girls, we were going to keep this from you, but you do have a right to know what's happening,' continued Meredith.

Nora relented and gave a small nod of agreement. 'We were just worried that you would be upset about what's being said.'

'Of *course* we're upset, but that's not a reason not to tell us,' said Lou, surprising everyone. 'I know you just want to protect us, but we have a right to be able to defend ourselves. To be able to explain *why* we should play. Why we *need* to play. And it's not just about us. This town, *our* town, and Denby, I think we all really need something to look forward to.'

'Go, Lou,' said Andy with a playful punch in the arm.

'I know that there are people who don't want us to play, but they're not actively attempting to *stop* us, are they?' asked Bess.

The teachers all looked at each other apprehensively.

'There's a group of adults,' Diane started tentatively, 'including parents, some teachers, the Denby mayor and business owners, who have started a petition to prevent the game from happening. They plan to submit it to the District Football League board by the end of the week.'

'Apparently, they're meeting on Friday afternoon to discuss the game,' said Meredith.

'How did we not know about this?' questioned Tully.

Ali suddenly looked uneasy, and Tully noticed.

'Did you know?' she asked her cousin.

'Yes,' she admitted reluctantly. 'One of the other nurses warned me about it. I did some digging and it honestly didn't seem to be that big a deal. I think maybe things have escalated since the boys decided to plead guilty.'

'That's what we think happened,' said Gayle, nodding.

'We also think,' added Diane, 'that they tried to keep it quiet so they could get signatures unopposed. So rather than making a big song and dance about it, they only asked people they knew would definitely sign.'

'What a bunch of arseholes,' said Charlie.

'We also agree with that sentiment.' Diane gave a wry smile.

'But can they actually stop us?' asked Andy. 'I mean, do they have any power over what we do?'

'If we want to use umpires employed by the league, and play on the Denby oval, then yes, they can absolutely stop us playing,' Gayle explained.

'And I'm guessing the same goes for a game on our oval?' asked Jen.

Gayle nodded sadly.

'So, before the board meets, we just need to get more people to agree that the game should go ahead?' Kat suggested.

'In three days?' said Charlie. 'How exactly do we do that?'

'Easy.' Fi looked around at all the players. 'We do it together.'

The entire team turned to Bess, who was attempting to focus on her breathing.

Just breathe, Bess. Just breathe.

It didn't work. Each comment seemed to solidify her fear that the game would not go ahead, the team would be devastated, and it would be her fault because she was responsible for the team.

A car horn tooted three times in quick succession and momentarily deflected the shared expectation that Bess come up with a plan.

Sam had finally arrived. She pulled up in a new-model silver Land Rover driven by her dad.

'Why does she work in the general store if her family have money?' Bess whispered to Jules. 'Or do they just have a fancy car?'

'Her family's *loaded*,' Charlie whispered from behind Bess.

Sam jumped out of the car and removed a large cardboard box from the boot. As her dad drove off, Sam called to her teammates and waved them over.

'Hey, guys! I've got something to show you!'

With collective curiosity, the players made their way to the boundary.

When everyone was present, Sam made an announcement, clearly enjoying the spotlight.

'So,' she started, 'we all know that we don't have uniforms, and I really don't wanna look like some dropkick for the game. And my dad doesn't want that either. So . . .'

With a flourish she threw open the box and removed a clear plastic package. She checked the label and tossed it to Fiona, who looked down at it with surprise.

'You bought us uniforms?' she said.

'Well, yes and no. It was my idea, but my dad paid.'

'Sam, that was incredibly generous of him,' said Nora.

'I'll say,' said Ali. 'How on earth did you get this done so fast?'

'Dad was in the city last week, and he just . . . knows how to make things happen.'

'But, if he can afford to do this,' said Bess, 'why . . .'

'Why do I work as a checkout chick?'

Bess nodded.

'Yeah, so, my dad is, well, he's well-off, is the best way to put it, I guess. But he insists that I learn the value of money or some shit like that. You know, so I don't turn out to be a complete brat.'

'So, it's a work in progress?' suggested Diane.

Sam laughed. 'More or less.'

The team crowded around the box and removed the packages, eagerly searching for their own.

'I wanted it to be a surprise, so I had to guess sizes,' said Sam, 'but I'm pretty sure I got them right.'

Bess held up her guernsey – a number 1 was printed on the back.

Sam noticed Bess examining her number. 'I thought a lot about the numbers,' she explained. 'I decided not to give any of us the same number as a son or father, or cousin, or brother or boyfriend. I'd rather we start our own tradition, so everyone has a number that is just for them.' She shifted in place and glanced around at her teammates.

'I think it's a great idea,' Bess reassured her. 'Thank you, Sam.' She had to fight hard to keep from crying. These days Bess felt she was consistently on the verge of tears, which could be triggered by something as innocuous as a Qantas commercial. So, this current display of generosity was more than sufficient to push her over the edge.

Bess's genuine sentiment was echoed by all the players, who each held their uniforms with a sense of pride.

The poignant moment was broken by Charlie. 'I'm number 69,' she said dryly. 'Really, Sam? Really? Do the numbers even go that high in footy?'

Most of the team burst out laughing.

'Why is that funny?' Diane whispered to Gayle.

'I'll fill you in later.'

'I guess we have to make sure there's a game now,' said Eva.

'What? Why wouldn't there be a game?' Sam swung around, confused. When no one answered immediately, she started to spiral. 'Guys! Why wouldn't we play? What are you talking about? Somebody tell me what's going on!'

'All right, calm down,' said Fiona. 'We just need to fill you in on a few things. No need to hit the panic button. Not yet, anyway.' She looked to Bess. 'So, what's the plan?'

Bess looked around at the group, and for the first time in a long time, she listened to her insistent small voice.

'Well, I don't think we can do it alone,' she said.

FIFTEEN

Bess put the phone down and turned to face her mum who was making her famous lamb cutlets, something she hadn't done for months.

'What did Deb say?' asked Gayle as she added oil to a frypan.

'She thinks that a petition from both towns is our best chance of demonstrating support.'

'You don't sound convinced?'

'It's not that. It's just more work. And it could lead us nowhere.'

Gayle frowned slightly. 'Do you remember when you and Deb came to school in shorts in Year 9? You refused to wear the school dress for one more day.'

'Yeah, but that was different.'

'How is it different? You wanted something to change. And you and Deb, you've always fed off each other. Even though you were so competitive, you still came together for a common cause.'

'This feels a bit bigger than school uniforms. And that only worked because Mr O'Shea supported us.'

'It worked because you and Deb presented a united front. And you rallied everyone else to follow. You're both leaders, even if you don't want to be.'

'You're my mum – you have to say nice things like that.'

'No. My motherly duties extend to loving you and supporting you. They don't extend to lying to you.'

Bess remained unconvinced. That small supportive voice needed to build in strength before she could be optimistic.

*

All through primary school, Bess had loved day trips to Denby. They usually meant new clothes and a visit to the Light and Bright Cafe that served hearty scones with raspberry jam and clotted cream. Bess always had a cup of English breakfast tea, because that's what her mum ordered, but she would typically add more milk than hot water. Even after Tom was born, it was still something that just she and her mum did together.

Once she started high school, she travelled to and from Denby every weekday, and as much as she loved Gerandaroo, she spent most of Year 7 begging her parents to move to Denby. Before the end of Term 1, she'd grown tired of the commute and wanted to walk past more than one strip of shops. She was also desperate to hang out after school in Denby with her friends. Because her mum worked at the high school, Bess had to travel with her. This meant waiting at the school until her mum was ready to leave. Once Bess turned thirteen, her mum finally agreed to let her catch the bus home three times a week. Even though she pretty much had the run of Gerandaroo, she revelled in this new-found freedom. She and her friends would wander around town and usually end up on the banks of the Denby River. There was a retired tram from Melbourne that had been placed there in 1980 for use as a playground. They would clamber on board and chat and gossip and laugh; there was the occasional bickering, but it never lasted long. Everything felt so easy.

By virtue of tradition, the older high school kids owned the edge of the river that had a slope steep enough to be hidden from prying adult eyes; no one below Year 11 was allowed anywhere near it. They always seemed so cool, perched among pockets of smoke in their denim jackets as they chatted about music and R-rated films, which they hadn't seen but spoke of as if they had. Eva would often imitate them. She would flick her hair and hold a cigarette with a blasé expression, pretending to be one of the Year 12 girls and acting as though nothing fazed her and she could say and do anything she wanted, and no one would tell her off. Eva was the first of Bess's friends to actually take a puff from a cigarette, but it was only after a Gerandaroo dare from Rachel. She'd coughed and spluttered, which was enough of a deterrent for the rest of them.

Despite being a staunch non-smoker, Bess had been caught with a packet of cigarettes that Fiona had insisted they keep on the off-chance that one of the older kids asked for one. Unbeknownst to Bess, Fiona had slipped the packet between textbooks in Bess's backpack one afternoon, certain that her own mum would find them if she kept them. She was like a bloodhound when it came to things Fiona was not meant to have. This was reinforced years later when she found condoms in Fiona's room; confiscating them probably worked against her mum on that occasion.

On the drive to school one morning, as Bess had removed her science book, the packet tumbled into her lap. Gayle had pulled the car over and just stared at Bess, a tried and true tactic that immediately instilled guilt and extracted a confession. Bess covered for Fiona because that's what friends do. In her defence, she told her mum that she didn't even carry a lighter. This didn't seem to make a difference. Fiona promised Bess that she would make it up to her, and although Bess had never officially cashed in on this promise, she knew that Fi had long stopped owing her anything.

*

As she travelled the only road to Denby, passing sheep that seemed to always cluster in the same spots, never to venture beyond what felt familiar, Bess longed to be back in primary school or even high school, with her mum behind the wheel, letting her pick the music and listening to whatever she had to say. Instead, she was driving to Denby on a potentially pointless trip, with Andy beside her and Jen in the back seat. It was not the car trip she had in mind, but they'd both offered to come with her, and she wasn't quick enough to think of an excuse for why she wanted to drive alone. She wasn't up to chatting, but needn't have worried. Neither Jen nor Andy spoke.

Despite there being only a few years between them, and although they had both worked on Green Street since finishing high school, Andy and Jen were not exactly close. Neither even really classified the other as a friend, at least not until they started playing footy together. Andy saw Jen as someone who was a bit standoffish, bordering on aloof, while Jen considered Andy too outspoken to ever have anything in common with her. Becoming part of a team had altered their impressions, and it was definitely for the better. Jen realised how supportive Andy could be, and Andy was starting to recognise that Jen had a fire within her that was just waiting to be unleashed.

Bess glanced at Jen in the rear-view mirror and sensed that she was happy to simply be going *anywhere*. As a hairdresser, Andy was personable and always interested in what her customers were up to. But today, she also seemed content to sit quietly rather than converse.

Bess was starting to find the lack of conversation irritating. She shifted in her seat and sighed deeply in an unsuccessful attempt to quieten her thoughts. She knew what the problem was. When she didn't have to concentrate on what someone else was saying, her own self-monologue sprinted away, fuelled by her cycle of worry and doubt – and fear. She worried about Tom and her parents, her job, the game, Lachie . . . pretty much everything and everyone she cared about seemed to be struggling in some way. And she couldn't predict what was going to happen next, including if the worst was yet to come.

To cut through her inner ramblings, she turned up the radio. As R.E.M.'s 'It's the End of the World as We Know It (And I Feel Fine)' filled the space, Bess couldn't help but smile. The song had been released just before the end of Year 12 and by January, she and her friends knew it by heart – or close to; it wasn't exactly an easy song to memorise. She hadn't heard it for a while and hadn't sung it out loud for years, but as the chorus continued, Bess was surprised at the impact of the lyrics she once knew so well.

'I'm fine' had become somewhat of a habitual response from her.

The second chorus played out, and Bess realised that all three of them were singing low. As if on cue, their voices became louder, even though they all tripped over the same parts, until they were belting out the lyrics, each of them unashamedly tuneless. When the song came to a close, the women all shared a smile, but no one spoke. It was one of those moments that would have been ruined by talking, and they all knew it.

*

Deb was waiting outside the council offices as they pulled up, holding a manila folder. Bess realised this was the first time she'd seen Deb wearing work attire, rather than the shorts or tracksuit pants that had dominated her wardrobe during high school. Deb spent her primary school years in Gerandaroo, before her parents divorced and her dad moved interstate to start a new life, which included a new family. Deb and her three siblings had moved to Denby so her mum had a better chance of finding work to support them. Deb had held a job since she was fourteen and had an enviable work ethic. But she also knew how to really let loose. She had planned what had become known as the most legendary end-of-year blowout at the Denby River. Each year the graduating class tried to match it but never came close. There was an unspoken promise among the class of 1987 to never divulge to an outsider all that had happened that night, and to Bess's knowledge, that promise had been upheld.

'Hey, Bess,' Deb called as Bess opened her car door. 'Still driving the mustard Magna?'

'Yeah, I'll have her for a while yet,' Bess said as she, Jen and Andy got out of the car.

'I thought we'd head over to the gardens for a walk,' said Deb. 'Better than sitting in a stuffy office.'

Andy must have sensed that it would be better if just Bess and Deb talked, so she suggested that they meet back at the car in half an hour.

'How's Tom?' asked Deb as they waited for the streetlights to change.

Bess nearly answered instinctively that Tom was fine, but she didn't know that, not even remotely.

'He's . . .' she began, before a long pause. 'I dunno.' Looking down, she scuffed her shoe at an invisible mark on the pavement. 'We're not really talking much at the moment,' Bess explained.

'Seriously, Bess? You two were always irritatingly close.'

Bess pursed her lips and gave a shrug. 'Well, things change.'

Deb seemed on the verge of pushing, like she usually did, but stopped when she saw how sad Bess looked. 'You know, I never thought they were capable of doing something like that,' she said slowly. 'I've known Simon and the other boys for years, practically their whole lives. I cheered for them at every home game. Simon even helped out with the tree-planting drive last year and we talked about how he wants to be an engineer.'

Bess thought that people, most people, perhaps all people, were capable of doing almost anything – good and bad. She had spent an inordinate amount of time over the last few months trying to understand what had happened. All she could conclude was that everyone had thresholds, for any and every possible behaviour.

That night, too many people had reached theirs. And when that happens, the consequences can be devastating.

'Their parents are distraught,' Deb continued, 'and none of them have been able to start uni.'

Bess closed her eyes; she didn't care that it was hard for them and their parents, or that they'd had to put their lives on hold.

'I hope they get everything they deserve,' said Deb, 'and I really, *really* hope they find Mitch soon,' she added, her voice low but filled with anger.

Bess opened her eyes, not the least bit surprised by Deb's comments.

'So, how do we make sure we get to play?' said Deb, changing tack as they crossed the road.

Bess shrugged. 'I'm not sure there's anything we can do.'

'That's not quite the response I was expecting.'

'I don't have that much fight in me these days,' Bess explained with a hint of irritation, directed more at herself than at Deb. She was frustrated that the game couldn't just happen easily. Why did everything have to be such a battle?

'Well, you'll need to get some if we're gonna make this work,' Deb said. 'And besides, have you ever known me to back down from a fight?'

Bess threw her a side smile and shook her head. 'Do you think getting signatures is really going to make a difference?'

'I certainly hope so.' They sat at a picnic table close to the playground and Deb pulled out a piece of paper from her folder. 'This is what I've drawn up for us to get people to sign.'

She handed the page to Bess, who chuckled at the title phrased as a question:

WOULD YOU ONLY WANT TO ENJOY FOOTY
FROM THE BOUNDARY? NEITHER DO
WE! SUPPORT A WOMEN'S FOOTY GAME
BETWEEN GERANDAROO AND DENBY.

'I guess the plan is just to get as many signatures as possible,' Deb explained, handing the folder to Bess. 'And then just go from there. I've already got over a hundred signatures.'

'Christ, Deb, do you ever sleep?'

Deb just laughed.

'Can I ask you something?' said Bess.

'Sure.'

'Um, do you ever regret starting a team? I mean, it's just so much work.'

'I definitely don't regret it,' Deb responded firmly with a shake of her head. 'I was so sick and tired of only being able to watch footy. And I figured the only way to change that was to start my own team. It took a bloody long time, though. We've only been able to train consistently over the last two months or so. And I agree that it's a lot of work, but the best things usually are.'

'Yeah, I know,' agreed Bess, her voice still tired. 'And I know I should be grateful there were enough women in Gerandaroo willing to give it a go.'

'We only have eighteen,' Deb admitted.

'Us too!'

'We did have more, but some of the women couldn't really handle the abuse. Which I totally understand. There's been *a lot* of pushback.'

'How do you deal with it?'

'The way I see it, we have two options. We quit, and that's the end of it. No more football. Or we keep going. And I definitely don't always ignore the comments. Because, well, that's not my style.'

Bess couldn't help but laugh.

'But I think it means something. It feels like it does. Don't you think?' Deb mused.

'Yeah, I'm starting to think that. It is pretty exciting, you know? Like we *finally* get to really try and play, after all these years.' Bess paused and replayed what she'd just said; it made her feel calm, and alive. 'Thanks for doing this, Deb,' she added softly.

Deb just nodded, never one for overt displays of affection. 'I'd better get back,' she said, looking at her watch as she stood up. 'I've still got a lot more people to talk to, so I'll call you on Friday to let you know how many signatures I have.'

Bess nodded her goodbye.

'You'd better be match fit,' Deb called as she walked away. 'Beating you won't mean as much unless you're at your best.'

Bess scoffed. 'I didn't think it was possible for you to be any more arrogant,' she called back.

'I'm not arrogant,' Deb replied with mock indignation. 'I'm just confident.'

*

Bess didn't immediately head back to the car. She watched as a young woman let go of the hand of a small boy, aged about three, so that he could run towards a pile of leaves on the freshly mown grass. She assumed the woman, who looked about Bess's age, was his mother. The boy was wearing yellow gumboots and a knitted yellow jumper. He squealed with delight as his mum threw the leaves into the air and they fluttered high and landed on his head. As he shook his head free of the remaining leaves, he reached out to be picked up, and his mum happily obliged. Bess could hear her pointing out objects and colours to the boy. 'That's the blue sky,' she told him, pointing up, 'and the brown leaves,' as she held up a leaf, 'and the green grass,' pointing down. The boy settled his head on his mother's chest, his little hand wrapped warmly around her neck.

There had been a time, a brief one, when Bess's priorities had nearly changed entirely. In the fortnight before she left for uni, she'd thought she might be pregnant. A pregnancy test days later confirmed that she wasn't, but for those few days, she oscillated rapidly between her options. Her mum knew, as did Jules. They'd both offered the type of support and reassurance that would make most people envious. However, Bess had never shared the possibility of a pregnancy with Lachie. She knew he wouldn't tell her what to do, nor would he force her to do anything she didn't want to. But Bess also knew that Lachie longed to be a father, to start a family without trauma. And she knew how much he wanted that family to include her.

Bess didn't often feel regret. But in that moment, privy to the bond between mother and child, she did. Not a great deal, just a bit.

But the feeling was quickly followed by relief.

*

Gayle, Fiona and Eva sat at the kitchen table just after midday on Friday, cradling a second cup of tea as they waited for Bess to finish her call.

'Yep, you too,' she said, her expression increasingly optimistic.

'Well,' Bess said, taking a deep breath as she hung up the phone, 'Deb got a lot of signatures. And I mean *a lot*.'

'How many?' asked Eva.

'Two hundred and fifty-seven.'

'You're kidding?! Man, she gets stuff done,' Fiona said with admiration.

'She does indeed,' agreed Bess, not the least bit begrudgingly.

'So, we now have, what, around three hundred and thirty, right?' asked Eva.

'Yep, three hundred and thirty-four, to be exact.'

'Surely that's enough?'

'You'd think so. But we have no idea how many those arseholes got,' said Fiona.

'Fi's right,' said Bess. 'We really don't know if we have enough, or even if it matters. We just have to hope that it does.'

'So, what now?' asked Eva.

'Well, Meredith's husband said he'd stop by and pick up our list and take it to Denby for the meeting.'

'I guess all we can do now is wait,' said Gayle. The apprehension on her daughter's face and those of her childhood friends prompted Gayle to shift into mum mode, a role she had not played for some time. 'I'll make us a nice snack,' she suggested, rising from her seat.

Despite initial protests from Fi and Eva that it was unnecessary, and they must be getting home to prepare dinner before training, the women shared a look with Bess, who was simply smiling – their protests were futile.

Growing up, most afternoons had been spent at Bess's house. It wasn't just because Bess had the best stereo, and their backyard had secluded nooks where they could sit cross-legged and chat about any and everything in private, it was also because Gayle was the queen of the after-school snack. She spent Sunday afternoons baking slices and cakes for the week, always with the mindset that she was feeding a small army rather than just her own two kids.

As they all ate and chatted, it felt like how life should be. With old friends.

*

That night, the whole team was on edge. And just as Bess was about to start making them run some drills, Meredith's car pulled up beside Lachie's. The team jogged towards her and stood clustered around the boundary line. Lachie emerged from his car to hear the verdict, and he and Bess shared a small nod.

Charlie, too impatient to wait, yelled, 'How many signatures did they get?'

'Forty-seven,' Meredith replied as she closed her car door.

The response from the majority of the team was one of shock and joy.

There were cries of 'What?' and 'Seriously?' and 'That's it?'

'So, we're fine then, aren't we? We can play!' said Tully.

Judging from the look on Meredith's face, the older players weren't so sure.

'What is it, Meredith?' asked Bess. 'What did they say?'

'Well,' she said, clearly reluctant to share the news, 'even though both teams demonstrated overwhelming support for the game to go ahead, the board thinks it would be in everyone's best interests to postpone.'

'For how long?' asked Ali.

'Indefinitely.'

The unanimous outcry was loaded with genuine shock and confusion.

'What!?'

'Are you serious?'

'You've got to be kidding?'

'So that means cancelled, doesn't it?'

'What reason did they give?' asked Eva, her voice rising above the group.

'Well, first they said it was because they'd already banned Denby and Gerandaroo from competition this season and made a mistake telling Deb that we could play, but then they went on and on about safety,' Meredith explained. 'Apparently we can't play a formal game on our ovals because we're not covered by the league's insurance.'

'But what if we agree to waive that requirement?' Nora suggested.

'It won't matter. They can legally prevent us from playing on either the Denby or the Gerandaroo ovals. And they made it clear that they won't pay for the umpires. They kept saying that they've got enough bad press after . . .' She paused, head down. 'They just don't want any more,' she added as she took in the dejected faces of her teammates.

'But *not* letting us play *is* bad press. Isn't it?' asked Abby.

'I don't think it's that cut and dried,' said Meredith. 'I mean, yes, I think we'd definitely get support, but there will also be a lot of people out there who agree with the board. I'm not sure any of us are fully prepared to fight that battle.'

'Maybe you won't have to,' said Lachie.

They all turned to face him.

'For now, just keep training as though the game's still on, okay? And, Bess, can you tell Deb the same?'

'Um, yeah, sure. But, Lachie, what are you up to?'

'I just have an idea,' he said, his voice the most upbeat she'd heard it in years. 'Or at least, the start of an idea. I'm not sure if it'll work out. But just trust me.' He turned and jogged away. 'If you still can,' he called back after a beat, with a wide grin.

'Okay,' Bess replied, confused, but also keenly aware that trusting Lachie had never been an issue.

*

Lachie sat at his kitchen table, the first he ever made, scribbling on a notepad. He frowned slightly as he read a long list, concentrating hard, with 'Blue Sky Mine' by Midnight Oil his only company. He crossed out several lines of writing and added several more, nodding to himself. It would be a great deal of work, no doubt about it, and he would need help, lots of it. But to Lachie, the only thought that mattered was: *This could work.*

SIXTEEN

The game, and particularly the players, had become the talk of the town. Everyone seemed to have an opinion about whether the women should be allowed to play. It was an unwelcome experience for the team. Even when people expressed support, it boiled down to one thing: it seemed grossly unfair that there was even a question about the game going ahead. And that for some reason, they needed 'permission' to do what the boys and men of the town had been doing for nearly a century.

As the rumour mill churned, a growing group of townsfolk had been showing up at training to watch from the boundary. Initially, the players were worried they'd be subjected to an onslaught of abuse. But to their surprise, instead of having a dozen Lucases, most people seemed genuinely interested in how they were getting on. Some even called out words of encouragement as the women ran solo or in packs around the streets.

No matter the time of year, footy had always been a conversation starter. So, the prospect of Gerandaroo playing in a match, even if it was *only the women*, as many put it, and despite the fact that it wasn't part of any competition and therefore didn't seem to count for anything, was still enough to ignite those conversations. As a result, in a very subtle way, the darkness that had blanketed the town since New Year's Day began to lift.

There were still a number of detractors, though, too many to ignore, and they did impact the team's morale at times. The irritating thing was that none of the comments were particularly clever. They were all clichéd references to the women's gender or attire. Sometimes, a player would respond if she could think of a particularly snappy comeback.

This was reflected during a session when Rob – the same Rob who Ian had overheard bad-mouthing the team in the general store – called, 'I hope you'll all be wearing dresses for the game!'

'I'd borrow one from your wife, but she left town!' Andy shot back.

As the players and people within earshot laughed, Rob remained on the boundary for several moments, seething, before he left, muttering as he went.

On the whole, however, the team collectively decided it was best to just let the footy do the talking – even if their skills could only really muster a whisper rather than a roar.

*

The players focused on little else but preparing for the game. They found themselves engaging in additional training without ever discussing it; it just felt like the right thing to do. And, more importantly, they *wanted* to.

During a one-off session early one morning with a handful of the team, Ben tossed the ball into the air for Ali, Eva and Meredith, some of the tallest players, to practise rucking. They started at opposite ends of the centre circle and would run in, jump, and try to hit the ball out to the direction of another player. They had made decent progress over the last few weeks, and at least one of them would make meaningful contact with the ball more often than not.

That same morning, Billy convinced Nora to go for a jog with him, certain that a few more miles under her legs would help build her confidence. They made their way along a dry grass track towards the McNamara farm, owned by fierce Melbourne supporters and descendants of one of the town's founders, and the location of a legendary hill. Legendary to the town, that is.

It was on top of this hill in 1846 that three men had surveyed the surrounding land and determined where the town of Gerandaroo would be located. There was even a photograph that captured the moment on display at the Gerandaroo Primary School, considered one of the oldest surviving photographs in Australia. Just as the daguerreotype portrait of the three men was taken, the photographer – ironically a young gentlemen by the name of Edward Hill – had stumbled backward and ricocheted off every bump and divot for approximately thirty metres; over time, the distance was extended to a mythical one hundred and fifty metres. To everyone's surprise, he was completely uninjured, with barely a scratch or a bruise on him. Long considered a good omen, this act, affectionately known as 'doing an Eddie Hill', was replicated repeatedly over the decades, most notably by teenagers on discovering the impulsive and numbing effects of alcohol. Billy, and Nora for that matter, had been no exception to this Gerandaroo rite of passage.

Now adult Nora stood at the base of the hill, exhausted and slightly hunched over as she awkwardly sucked in air. She looked up, tried to slow her breathing with a long, deep breath, and after a nod of encouragement from Billy, she started up the hill with Billy beside her every step of the way. He knew what she needed. It wasn't trite slogans like 'You can do it!' but rather just someone to be there in silent support.

Neighbours Diane and Fi gathered with their husbands and kids to watch the Carlton v Essendon Grand Final at Diane's house. At half-time, they all flocked to the street to kick the footy around. Diane's husband had repeatedly questioned whether his wife had the ability to compete in an actual game, and he was more than open about his concerns for her safety and also the high potential for embarrassment. But his scepticism evaporated on seeing Diane mark consistently, and more importantly, when he saw the joy she exhibited. They never made it back inside to watch the second half, both husbands too intent on imparting as much wisdom as they could about how to kick 'accurately' and handball with 'purpose'. Diane's husband became highly animated when discussing the important height advantage she had over many of the other players.

'You're just so tall, Di,' he exclaimed, waving the football about as he gestured to her height. 'It's such a great thing for footy. And you're *so* coordinated,' he added, as though suddenly realising his wife was athletic.

'That's possibly the sweetest thing you've said to me all year,' she responded with a sly smile.

*

Bess and Gayle spent the day helping Jules on the farm. Her parents were interstate, visiting family, and it was easy for the work to pile up. In between providing feed and water for the sheep and checking the pens, the three women practised kicking long and discussed who should play what position and why. Bess thought back to a year ago, when she was consumed with anxiety over whether her students would be ready for their end-of-year exams. Never would she have believed that a year later, she would be on Jules' sheep farm of all places, talking about an upcoming footy match that she would actually be playing in. Although the catalyst for her return had often made her heart feel as though it would never beat easy again, she allowed herself to smile inside, just a little.

As the day came to a close, Gayle headed home while Bess stayed to have dinner with Jules. The two women took their bowls of spaghetti and glasses of red wine to the back verandah. With Molly asleep on the top step, they admired the pink sky that seemed so close you could touch it with one big jump on a trampoline. The air was mild with a welcome breeze.

'Do you remember when we first drank red wine?' asked Jules.

'Eva's parents' Christmas party in Year 11?'

'Yeah. And we all said how horrible it tasted so we switched back to soft drink.'

'A friend at uni told me that if you don't like wine the first time, you have to persist to develop your palate. I think we should be commended for our commitment,' Bess joked.

'Agreed,' said Jules, as they clinked their glasses.

'I still think you should apply to do your master's,' Bess said after a few mouthfuls of spaghetti.

'I know you do.'

'But I also understand why it's hard to leave this place.'

'If I leave,' said Jules, 'I know it won't be temporary. And Mum and Dad will definitely sell the farm. And they should,' she conceded after a beat.

'You really think so?'

Jules nodded. 'I think I've been holding on to a reality that won't ever happen again.'

'One where your brother is safe and well?'

'Yeah.'

'Jake has always been one of my favourite people,' Bess revealed. 'You remember how he'd say hi to us on the playground when we started Year 7? He was *so* popular and the other kids were *so* jealous. I can understand why you want that version of Jake to come back.'

'I think that's the problem. I keep seeing Jake as he was, not as he is. So maybe I'm expecting too much. But I think there's a balance between wanting him to feel better about who he is and the contributions he can make, but also not expecting so much that he pulls away even further and doesn't want me to be a part of his life.'

'Jake would never want that.'

'I hope not. But he can be impulsive. So, it's scary . . . to think about him alone, with no support, thinking that I don't love this version of him.'

'Have you ever told him this?'

'I tried. Once. But it wasn't the right time.'

'Maybe you just have to keep trying. And I know you are,' Bess added quickly. 'I know you think about him every day and that you try so hard to track him down. And that's more than a lot of families would do.'

'It's different with Tom,' Jules reassured her. 'He doesn't need you to go and bring him home.'

'That's exactly what Rick plans to do.'

'Maybe that's for the best – that a friend goes and not his big sister. Maybe it's something they need to work through together.'

Bess sighed, but nodded. 'Well, J, I can still push *you* in the direction I think you should go,' she said, half-joking, half-sincere. 'And there's no harm in applying. It's okay to give yourself permission to try and have the reality you want.'

'Maybe.'

'I'll tell you what,' said Bess, 'if I kick a goal in the game, you have to apply.'

'Is that a dare?' Jules was smiling.

'Nope. It's just a promise between two friends.'

'Deal,' Jules agreed, as Molly rose, stretched, and ambled over for a pat.

*

At the mechanics the next morning, Jen was sitting behind the reception counter, handballing to herself as the day, like most of her workdays, was impressively slow. She tried to lightly tap the ball on the same spot on the ceiling, but the phone rang. Startled, she knocked over her mug of tea as she tried to catch the ball and reach for the phone at the same time. She let out a snort of laughter and was still smiling when she answered, 'Gerandaroo Mechanics, Jen speaking.'

A few shops down, Andy paced the length of her empty salon bouncing a football, with 'Hells Bells' by AC/DC blasting through her radio. She enjoyed the satisfaction she experienced every time the ball hit the ground at the perfect angle and bounced expertly back into her palm, her confidence building.

Even after the sun had set for the night, and with only weak streetlights to guide them, Rach and Billy continued to kick a football in front of their house. They didn't talk. Not because they didn't want to, but because they didn't need to. They simply kicked back and forth, back and forth, creating a rhythm that had been absent from their lives, until the night closed in and they could no longer track the ball.

*

The following day, Sam, Charlie, Kat, Abby, Lou and Tully, dressed in their phys ed uniforms, stood in a relaxed circle on the Denby High oval during their lunch break and practised handballing to each other. Even without the football, the appearance of these girls together would have drawn a crowd, or at least gossip. It was therefore no surprise that students started to gather on the fence to watch. Andrew Finch was among them, although he stood off to the side, mindful that his mother would be enraged with even his mere peripheral presence around women's footy, and certain that she would find out.

A fumble between Lou and Abby brought immediate laughter and Lou's face flashed red.

'Hahaha,' cried Mike, a Year 12 student with untidy brown hair and a half-tucked-in school shirt.

'What are you laughing at, Mike?' Abby shot back. 'You never even made the footy team. You can't kick a ball to save your life.'

Andrew tried suppressing a laugh but ended up half-snorting.

Mike threw an aggressive glare at him before turning back to the field. 'I kick better than you!' he yelled at Abby.

'Prove it!' she fired back as she stormed towards him. 'I set a Gerandaroo dare for you to kick a goal from thirty metres out, directly in front. And that any one of us,' she gestured to her team-mates, 'will do the same. You can pick who to kick against.'

'Wait, what?' said Kat, who looked at the others in surprise, and more than a little fear. 'I can't kick –'

Charlie silenced her with a harsh, '*Shhhh.*'

'Any one of you?' Mike mocked. 'You can't even handball from one foot away, what makes you think you can kick?'

Instead of responding, Abby headed towards the goal square. 'Hurry up, Mike, we don't have all day,' she called over her shoulder as the team followed.

A pestering chorus from the surrounding students – 'Come on, Mike, it's easy!' and 'You can at least kick better than a girl!' – gave Mike no choice but to agree.

As the students hopped the fence and made their way to the goal square, Mike reluctantly followed, slightly ashen-faced.

'So, Mike, who do you pick?' asked Sam as she handballed high to herself and then to Abby.

Mike surveyed the team as Kat maintained a solid stare, her attempt at intimidation. It must have worked because she wasn't selected.

'Lou,' said Mike with a snide smile.

Off to the side of the oval, Mrs Phillips, Mrs Harron and Mrs Carson stood watching the interaction unfold.

'Should we let this go ahead?' said Diane.

'I think so,' said Nora. 'It's their turn to prove they can play.'

'And if Lou misses?' asked Meredith.

'Then she misses.' Nora shrugged. 'But she won't.'

Lou, who had been avoiding eye contact, looked up to face Mike and swallowed hard.

'Good pick,' Sam said briskly after seeing sheer panic flash across Lou's face. 'Lou's one of our best players.'

'You've got this, Lou,' said Tully.

Abby handed Lou the ball and her teammates continued to shout words of encouragement.

Lou's feet seemed to be glued in place and her eyes were terrified. Abby guided her over to about forty metres out from goal and whispered to her. 'I was hoping he'd pick you.'

Lou turned to Abby, confused. She couldn't possibly have meant that, could she? Or did she mean it as a joke on her? But when she looked at Abby's face, she realised she was being genuine.

Abby moved forward and scuffed a line in the grass approximately thirty metres out.

'Come on, Lou!' she called, clapping hard, with the team joining in. Abby noticed that Andrew was clapping along with them. She briefly smiled, long enough for Andrew to know that it was meant for him.

Lou suddenly felt her shoulders relax. She took a deep breath and rotated the ball once in her hands, kept her head down and started a short run in, right foot forward first, just as Billy had taught her. After one, two, three, four slow steps, she then quickened her pace; five, six, seven, eight steps, and on the ninth, she guided the ball so it landed perfectly over the shoelaces of her right runner. She kept her body forward and drove her right leg up and watched as the ball spun high between the goalposts for a textbook goal.

There was a sweeping cheer from her teammates and onlookers, with the obvious exception of Mike, who looked like a stunned mullet.

'Shit, Mike,' said Hayden, his supposed best friend, who couldn't stop laughing. 'No chance you'll do that.'

Lou locked eyes with Mike; he swallowed sharply, his eyes darting to the merciless horde of peers that seemed to be growing. The prospect of humiliation was something Lou grappled with often, and the rush of sympathy she felt towards Mike was only slightly tempered by his belief that she could not kick a goal. She had never liked Mike. He was the kid who continually interrupted classes with crass jokes and comments, and who had pushed all the girls off the monkey bars in primary school – except Charlie, who always pushed back. He really was quite a jerk.

The bell sounded for the end of lunch.

'Oh well, maybe next time,' Mike said, actively avoiding Lou's gaze as he hurried towards the lockers.

'We'll hold you to that, Mike!' Kat called after him.

SEVENTEEN

5 days to Game Day

On his early-evening run, surrounded by high-rise apartments, office buildings and an ever-growing array of cafes and restaurants, Thomas slipped past people and shopfronts without anyone recognising him. His anonymity persisted even when his colleagues passed him at the closest supermarket, unaware he was a night shelf-packer.

He preferred the night. In the daylight there were too many people. People led to questions. Questions provoked uncertainty. And he didn't have the answers. He'd experienced this during his first month in the city when working at a video store. The other employees, similar in age to Tom, were friendly but far too nosey for him to feel comfortable enough to stay, even though they weren't asking anything unusual. They wanted to know where he went to high school, what sports he played, where his family lived, if he was going to uni. He'd considered telling the truth, but he couldn't form the words; his heart would race, his mouth would go dry, and his mind would either fill with a thousand thoughts or go completely blank. He then tried to make up the answers, but he'd never been much of a liar. So, he sought a job that allowed him to blend in and which suited his current night-owl status.

As Tom reached the substantial parkland, boxed in by main roads, he joined the throng of Tuesday athletes. He liked to create backstories for the people he passed. It was a game that he and Bess used to play on family road trips growing up, and he was always jealous of how easily Bess could come up with funny yet believable anecdotes for complete strangers.

Tom could usually spot the individuals who seemed determined to make up for a weekend of inactivity and had perhaps made a silent promise to do more – a promise he suspected was seldom kept. Today a stocky bloke in his forties fit that description. As Tom ran past, the man maintained a weary yet dogged expression, as though he desperately wanted to stop but knew he would regret doing so. Tom thought that he probably had a wife and four, possibly five, rowdy kids at home, and that his dog, a black labrador named Harvey, was the only one in his life who didn't demand anything of him.

He caught up to a trio of women who were jogging and all talking at the same time, with barely a breath taken between them. He easily pictured them working together, clamouring for the same promotion. It would not end well.

An extremely tall woman in her early twenties headed towards Tom. She appeared athletic, focused, running in pursuit of a particular goal. Tom saw her as an assistant to a news anchor who longed to be in front of the camera, but had been told she'd have to shrink a few inches before that would ever happen.

A guy nearby was straddling a shiny new bike. He seemed completely out of place, wobbling from side to side as he tried to slip his runners into the toe clips. Tom imagined that he had entered into a bike race to impress his girlfriend, and that she would dump him as soon as she saw what he looked like in Lycra.

Tom wondered if any of these people were struggling in some way and using exercise as a form of escape. It was no secret to him that he ran to cope. And it had worked – for a while at least. But his thoughts were becoming more insistent and harder to ignore, and he worried they would soon overwhelm him. So he ran, the distance and intensity growing by the day.

The constant hum of city life was only partly muffled among the greenery. The intermittent ding of trams, not-so-distant sirens, honked horns and slammed brakes could all still be heard. They mixed with the clicking of bicycle chains, the push of strollers and the pounding of the pavement. And unlike conversations in Gerandaroo, the general chatter never included that season's crop, with discussions about the weather typically focused on social rather than economic plans. Tom had started to think that you either got used to the busyness or you didn't. He wasn't sure what side he was on.

He circled back along a curved track and into the surrounding streets, where he passed a group of young footballers warming up on a nearby school oval. As a ball sailed over the boundary fence on the outer east wing and into his path, he found himself caught between the gentle pull of the footy field and the mixture of emotions it triggered. He hesitated, and despite the pleas to 'Kick it here!' he ran around the ball and sprinted away.

Moments created and collected from years of playing footy seeped into his consciousness. There were snippets of training sessions, long bus rides to other towns, Coach Macca's excited tone as he explained his game plan that no one else understood, and conversations with his dad about next week's opponent. He heard his own voice calling out to Danny for the ball, and repeatedly telling Billy how glad he was to never have to play against him. He saw himself high-fiving Ben after he scored his first goal and handballing to Rick who always seemed to find space. He saw his mum waving to him from the boundary and heard Bess cheering louder than everyone.

Before each run, he would promise himself that the physical distance he covered would help push unwanted memories aside. He tried to believe that if he ran for long enough, perhaps he would forget.

Today was particularly challenging, and as hard as he tried to distract himself by making up stories about the people around him, he was consumed by two conversations with Danny; each fought to be the dominant one.

Danny and Tom stood a few metres apart on the oval, beer cans in hand.

'I don't know what to do. I mean, I just . . . I thought it would go away,' said Danny. 'When Tristan . . . when we stopped seeing each other or even being able to talk, I missed him. But I thought

that maybe it was just him and not . . . not me. And that I was just confused. But I wasn't. I'm not. But I still don't know what to do.'

With anger spilling over, he hurled his beer can high into the air and watched as it landed disappointingly without a sound on the grass.

Tom moved to comfort his best friend, concern etched across his face, but Danny pulled away.

'Dad . . . when he saw us that time, just talking in my room. The look on his face. He knew what it meant. What we are to each other. He'll never . . .' He swung around to face Tom. 'Do you remember that teacher we had? For Year 7 Maths? Mr Greenville? He was the best teacher.' The words tumbled out rapidly. 'Then Dad . . . he took me out of his class because he thought Mr Greenville was gay. He went on and on about how he shouldn't be allowed to teach. And then Mr Greenville . . . he just – he left. All because of me.'

'Danny,' Tom started, but Daniel interrupted him.

'And Tristan. As soon as his family moved to Denby, Dad just . . . he hated them. For no reason. And we never did anything wrong. We just, Dad knew . . . and he . . . the things he said. I've never been so ashamed. And then he threatened Tristan. And his parents. Even though Sophie and Luke . . . they're such good people. Just like your mum and dad. So I made him stop calling. I was so awful to him.'

Tom spoke gently, determined to try and help his friend. 'But Tristan came back. He knew you were only trying to protect him.'

'But he shouldn't've!' exclaimed Danny, eyes wild. 'I can barely protect myself from my dad. How can I possibly protect him too?' He paused. 'How is it that your parents and Tristan's parents understand and are just happy if we're happy, yet it makes my dad so hateful? How is that fair?' His voice had risen, but the anger quickly dissipated.

'I know you heard them again during the game the other week. And I heard what you said to Simon.'

'Well, yeah, I mean, of course I'm gonna say something,' Tom replied.

'They're only words, though, right?' said Danny, almost talking to himself in an attempt to shrug it off.

'Well, Simon's a real aggro dick. He'll say anything to get a rise. And the others, they just do what he says. But I'm not the one they talk about, so I'm not gonna say they're only words.'

'You know that Tristan quit?'

'I didn't,' said Tom, shaking his head. 'But I can get why. There are some real arseholes on that Denby team.' Tom looked directly at his best friend and spoke with a steady voice. 'Danny, don't give anyone the satisfaction of letting them make you feel like you're only one thing. Being gay, it's just a part of what makes you, you. And you're a pretty fucking great guy. I mean, you're not my type. Being male and all,' he added with a playful punch on Danny's arm. 'But seriously, Dan, it doesn't have to define you.'

'It does, though. It already has.' Danny's voice was laden with defeat. 'But just to clarify, you're not really my type either,' he said with a small smile.

Tom moved forward to hug his friend, to hold him and tell him everything was going to be okay. Even if he didn't know that it would be.

Tears slipping down his young face, Danny embraced his friend, his brother. As the night closed in, they tried to hold on to a feeling of comfort, and to ignore the world that was not yet ready to accept people for who they are.

Tom continued running, moving his head from side to side to try to shake the memory from his consciousness. As he did, another conversation pushed through.

'You can't just leave,' Tom insisted as Danny threw open his wardrobe door.

'You're not my keeper, Tom, so stop telling me what to do,' Danny responded with unexpected bluntness.

Tom stood back and watched as Danny ripped clothes from hangers and tossed them into the aged brown suitcase open on his bed.

'What about Lachie? Are you even going to tell him?'

'I've written him a letter.'

'A letter? Are you for real? After everything he's done for you? After everything he's sacrificed, you're just going to up and leave without even talking to him about it?' As Tom peppered Danny with truths, both boys became increasingly angry.

'He'll understand,' said Danny. 'Why can't you?'

'You're right. I don't understand. Not even a little bit.' Tom reached out to grab Danny's arm and forced him to face him.

'Dan, can you just stop and talk to me? Just explain why you have to go like this.'

Danny threw off Tom's grasp. 'Tom, I hate it here. I hate everything about this place. Everything. Everyone I have ever loved has died here.'

Tom watched as Danny finished packing, tears and fury mixing.

As Danny pushed past him to the front door, Tom called after him. 'You're wrong. People you love are still here. And you'll regret this – running away.'

'I'm not running away, Tom.' Dan turned to face his childhood friend. 'I'm just leaving.'

With that, Danny walked out and did not look back.

Tom had broken into a sprint as he headed down a no-through road towards a set of rundown apartment blocks. After about four hundred metres, he slowed and then stopped completely when he saw an unexpected and unwanted visitor sitting on the top step of his building.

Rick's face lit up, but when Tom didn't reciprocate, his smile faltered.

Tom and Rick looked at each other for several moments, neither speaking.

'How did you find me?' asked Tom with a hint of annoyance. He was breathing heavily and used his t-shirt to wipe sweat from his face.

'I wasn't sure I had. I mean, until now.' Without any response from Tom, Rick hesitated. He swallowed deep and shifted on the uncomfortable concrete before continuing. 'Um, Shell's ex-boyfriend, you remember Ronnie?' His eyes met Tom's and he gave a small nod. 'Well, he lives here.' Rick pointed to the apartments. 'He saw us play those few times and he recognised you.'

'Did you tell my parents?'

'No.'

'But you told Bess?'

'How did you know?'

Tom didn't respond, but was exhausted from his run, so he moved to sit beside Rick. 'I don't think I'm ready,' he said after a minute.

'I know.'

Tom could feel Rick watching him and he knew that he sounded different, tired and a bit sombre, and that his expression matched his tone. 'I can't make Danny come home,' he said.

'That's not why I'm here.'

Tom looked at Rick, unconvinced.

'Okay, it is. But not in the way you think. You might never *want* to come back,' Rick said, 'and I understand that. Or at least I'm starting to. But we have to start somewhere. And it's time for you *and* Danny to come home. Lachie won't tell me where Danny is, but I'm pretty sure he knows. So that just leaves you.'

With no validation either way from Tom, Rick continued. 'You do know where he is, don't you? I thought maybe, before you left, he would have written to you to tell you?'

'Even if I do know, what makes you think I can make him come home? *I* don't even want to go back.'

'You know,' said Rick, 'I hated you for leaving the way you did. It was hard enough when Danny left, but then you just . . . you up and left in the middle of the night without saying anything. To *anyone*.'

Tom shifted restlessly, as though on the verge of standing and walking away. But he remained sitting.

'I would have come with you,' Rick said quietly.

'No. You would have tried to stop me.'

'Yeah. Probably,' said Rick, smiling. 'You went looking for Mitch, didn't you?'

Tom didn't respond.

'Do you think the police will find him?'

'I dunno,' said Tom. 'Mitch was a cop. Even though he was shit at his job, he still knows how to disappear. Remember how often he went camping, but we never knew where? He used to leave Danny and Lachie home alone, sometimes for weeks on end, even when Lachie had only just started high school. And then my mum would find out and they'd come and stay with us until he came back. So, yeah, I'd say he's pretty good at staying off the radar.'

'He'll get what's coming to him. He has to,' said Rick.

'I don't think that's how things work.'

'Well, I *really* need to find Danny.'

'Why?' Tom frowned.

Rick waited a moment before answering. 'I need to apologise.'

'For what?'

'For not stopping Simon and those other guys.'

Tom didn't respond, but stared straight ahead.

'When you were helping your dad at the bar,' Rick continued, 'the rest of us – me, Ben and Billy – we were out the front.'

'Yeah, I know,' said Tom.

'Yeah, but we never told you that we saw them leave after Danny and Tristan. And we did nothing.'

'Did Simon ask you where Tristan was?'

'Yes.'

'And you told him that he left with Danny?'

'Yes.' Rick's voice was small as he looked away.

'Did you know Danny and Tristan were going to the footy oval?'

'No.'

'So, you didn't actually tell Simon where they were?'

'No, but we said that they'd just left together. *I* said they'd just left together.'

'Did you know Simon and his lackeys were going to try and track them down?'

'Not exactly. But I mean, why else were they asking after them? I knew they wanted to find them. I just . . . I don't think I even thought about it. I just wanted them to leave.'

'Did you know they were going to find them on the oval and punch and kick Danny repeatedly?'

'No.'

'Did you know they were going to hold down Tristan while they beat Danny?'

'No.'

'Did you know they were going to leave them in a bloody mess and not call for help?'

Rick stopped answering.

'Did you know that Mitch would be on the track when Danny and Tristan arrived at the oval, and that he'd remain in the shadows, watching them? And that he would stay hidden while Simon and the others beat his son to a pulp?'

Rick's head was down, his breathing rapid.

'Hey, look at me!' Tom pulled Rick's arm, forcing him to face him, determined that Rick's heart heard his words.

'Did you know that Mitch was going to wait until the Denby boys left, walk up to Tristan, and punch him with so much anger that he'd fall and smash his head on the ground, stop breathing and die?'

Rick's eyes flooded with tears as he shook his head.

'Did you know that Mitch was going to walk off the oval and leave his battered and bleeding son to run for help for his already dead boyfriend?'

Rick continued to shake his head, his face wet.

'Then how could you have stopped them?'

'When they said things to Danny at school and during the Grand Final. And then that night, at the bar. I just . . . I just ignored it. I always . . . *always* pretended like I didn't hear.'

'Everyone did,' said Tom.

'*You* didn't.'

Tom answered slowly. 'You can't change what happened. None of us can.'

'Then why won't you come home?'

'Because you're right. I went looking for Mitch.'

When he failed to elaborate, Rick prompted him. 'And?' he asked.

'And then I just . . . stopped looking,' said Tom with a defeated shrug.

'Were you worried that if you stayed, there would be more fights?' asked Rick.

Tom focused on a passing group of high schoolers who were talking too loudly, and taking up the entire footpath.

'Tom?'

'After what happened,' he said, 'I didn't *plan* to retaliate. But when I saw Simon and the other guys, they were just . . . they were acting like *nothing* had happened. And some of the things they said . . . it was like they were baiting me, they *wanted* to fight me. To fight us. And I couldn't handle it. And I know I shouldn't have reacted the way I did, but I couldn't stop.'

'I never thought I'd ever see you actually punch someone,' said Rick. 'I mean, I was more than happy to get in there and defend you, and I'd do it again. But it was a bit scary to see you like that.'

'I know.' Tom's voice was low. 'I think that maybe I decided to stay here because on some level I couldn't trust myself to be anywhere near them. I don't ever want my default response to be violence. That's the last thing Danny or Tristan would want. So Gerandaroo . . . it just . . . doesn't feel like home anymore.'

'And this wonderfully shitty apartment block does?' Rick gestured behind him.

'No,' said Tom with a reluctant smile.

'Tommo, here's the thing.' Rick faced his childhood friend. 'I know that I'll stay in Gerandaroo and probably work at your dad's pub or get a job on a farm. I know that the furthest I'll ever move, *if* I move, will be to Denby. Billy's the same. And I always knew you'd leave Gerandaroo. And that Danny would, and Ben too,' he added after a pause. 'And you know, I'm fine with that because I always hoped that you'd come back to visit. I *know* my place in this world. And it's fine if you don't know yours, but you'll never figure it out if you cut yourself off from the *one* place that knows you the best. From the people who will call you out on your bullshit. And who will be there to help you celebrate when something finally goes right. And who'll find you and bring you home, even when you don't wanna come.' Rick looked expectantly at Tom with a mixture of pleading and compassion.

'Did you practise that?' asked Tom.

'A little, yeah.'

'Well, do you really think that piece of shit car is going to make it up the coast and back?' he asked, with a nod towards Rick's car parked opposite the apartments.

'I'm almost certain that it won't,' said Rick as the two friends shared a smile.

EIGHTEEN

Late that night, two and a half thousand kilometres away, darkness had recently settled in. Despite the ceiling fan spinning on high, the day's warmth lingered, with not even a faint breeze from the open window to offer relief. Against the wall beneath the window, Danny lay awake, the aged single bedframe and sagging mattress shrinking beneath his strong build.

The streetlights provided a constant glow that formed a halo on his ceiling, but the road was quiet, with only the occasional cicada to remind him that he was not alone. As he drifted into a restless sleep, his defences weakened and the memories that he tried so hard to suppress morphed into his most frequent nightmare.

Surrounded by darkness that held a high bright moon, he felt the cool air the moment Tristan relaxed his grip and took his last breath.

He smelled blood as it seeped from the split skin under Tristan's left eye.

He felt the blood that easily escaped as he cradled Tristan's head.

He tasted metallic blood in his own mouth.

He heard his heavy heart beat both slow and fast.

He felt his ribs crack with each breath.

He watched the man he loved lie motionless, eyes and mouth slightly open.

He heard his voice break when he cried for help.

And he realised he was alone.

A brief thought formed: Please don't let this be how I always see him.

This was followed by a series of horrific moments, as if time were in reverse, that seemed to stretch for hours but which Danny knew, even in his nightmare, had lasted only minutes.

It began the moment he struggled to break free from Simon and Jason, who'd pinned his arms behind his back. Lewis and Keith held Tristan down, his face forced to the right so he had to watch. Alan's punches rained down on Danny's face and stomach, one after another after another, until he could no longer stand and his legs collapsed beneath him, blood streaming down his face.

The air carried Tristan's cries as he pleaded with them to stop, and Simon suddenly released his grip and let Danny fall sideways, before kicking him in the face.

Then came the moment that Simon picked up a stick, lunged at Tristan, and ripped down his pants.

The other boys jumped back in surprise, but did nothing to help.

And then, fuelled by adrenaline but driven by love, Danny surged towards Simon and tackled him. He wrapped both hands around Simon's neck and the other boys tried to tear him away. Simon struggled to breathe, hands grasping wildly.

As Simon started to lose consciousness, Tristan pleaded with Danny to stop.

Danny woke up, his breathing erratic, his body drenched with sweat.

He could still taste blood in his mouth.

He could still hear Tristan's desperate cries.

And he could still feel his hands around Simon's neck.

NINETEEN

Danny watched as the sun stirred and took over from the moon. He used to do the same in Gerandaroo, always with his mother and Lachie. She would wake them before dawn, and they would climb through Lachie's window and onto the roof. Mitch never joined them, and likely never even knew it was something they did. Their house was one of only three on the street and it sat upon an unusually high slope, which gave them a clear view of neighbouring streets and surrounding farms. His mum always brought blankets and they would huddle together and watch as the sun gently filled their small town.

Danny could remember feeling envious of the constant exchange between the sun and the moon. They had a place. They knew their role. Meanwhile he harboured thoughts that he did not fit neatly into the world. At least, not the way other boys seemed to.

It would be ideal to think that life was simpler back then, but it wasn't. It did, however, hold more love, or at least a different kind of love. His mother's death just after he turned seven had left not just a void, but an ever-expanding chasm. Lachie had tried to fill it, but he was only twelve. Their father continued to drink like a fish, only he would now claim that it was to cope with grief.

It wasn't.

Mitch was beyond selfish, bordering on sociopathic, with his violent outbursts and manipulative nature well known across town. He drank before his wife became unwell and throughout her illness, even to the point that he was consistently unable to drive her to the city for treatment. That burden fell to the O'Neill family, although they never saw it that way.

Gayle and Ian tried to make up for Ruth's death, and Danny knew that without them he never would have made it through primary school, let alone high school. But he found himself feeling more jealous than he could ever admit out loud. And sometimes that jealousy turned to resentment, which made him feel small.

He had come to the conclusion that leaving Gerandaroo was the only way to start a life without everyone around him knowing his sob story. Without the pity and the stares. Without the judgement and the whispers. Without the rumours and the changing truth.

The day he left town, Danny had spent a night in the city, but had known he couldn't stay. There was so much going on around him that he found it suffocating. So, he boarded an early-morning train for the first leg of a long journey to Queensland. It didn't take him long to get a job at the Grand Pub, located about a hundred and forty kilometres inland from Townsville; it was a fairly respectable establishment that also had rooms for let.

Danny was a hard worker and didn't care for gossip. He also spoke little of where he was from, which only served to make him more mysterious to the other employees, particularly the younger women. He knew that telling them, or anyone within a fifty k radius, that he was gay would be like a rag to a bull. Telling them he was from Gerandaroo also might have raised unwelcome questions, so he kept largely to himself.

One tradition that he maintained was an early-morning run. He used to run alone, or with Tom or Lachie. Every few weeks he would meet up with some of the guys from the team, usually Rick, and sometimes Ben and Billy. Along with Tom, they would go for a longer run beyond the town's border. It was never something they planned, they just seemed to find each other when out running and there was this rhythm they fell into when they were together. This was probably one of the things he truly missed about home. Not that he'd admit it, and when this thought arose, he was quick to suppress it.

As he trekked along the dusty main road, he could feel heat radiating through his soles to the balls of his feet, and he reluctantly admitted to himself that he would have to buy a new pair of runners.

Lachie always used to take him shoe shopping. Even though their dad tried to get Danny to wear his brother's old shoes, Lachie would take the money meant for him and buy Danny a new pair. He then endured a beating from their dad, but Lachie would keep this from Danny until he was too old, and too stubborn, to do what Lachie asked and stay in his room. He remembered being nine years old and hearing raised voices. Lachie had long told him that whenever he heard his dad and Lachie argue, he was to go into his room and put his radio on. But for the first time, Danny had decided to investigate.

Fourteen-year-old Lachie, his recent growth spurt a blessing, had his back flat against the front door, and Danny realised that he was trying to prevent their dad from leaving.

'Not like this, Dad. Just stay here tonight,' pleaded Lachie, his grip on the car keys turning his knuckles white.

Mitch started screaming, 'Get the fuck away from the door!'

For the next few minutes, Danny felt completely paralysed as he watched his brother and dad participate in what would become an all too familiar and increasingly volatile exchange.

Mitch eventually relented, but Danny soon realised that was a rare outcome. In the years that followed, Danny became an expert at recognising when Mitch was not just angry-drunk, but violent-drunk, and when he was drunk but not too drunk to drive, even though he knew that wasn't actually a thing.

By the time Danny was in high school, he and Lachie had become skilled at navigating their father's moods and doing everything possible to keep him on an even keel, or at least close to one.

As a young teenager, Danny once argued with Lachie that they should just let their dad drive drunk if he wanted to, and if he killed himself, it would be his own fault. Lachie explained to Danny that it wasn't so much their dad that he was looking out for, but anyone else on the road. He reminded Danny that they had a responsibility to keep everyone around them safe from their dad.

It was such a hard concept for Danny to accept.

He would repeat the line, 'I have to keep everyone safe *from* my dad.'

The man who was a police officer, which did not just imply but demand that he be the one doing the protecting. The man who had never offered Danny any manner of protection, certainly not in the form of love or support the way a parent was instinctively meant to.

So, Danny grew up faster and more unevenly than a child should.

But he still believed that his dad was capable of change. And he still sought his praise, his approval.

From his tenth birthday, Danny wished in terms of 'more'. He wished that his dad was kind, that he cared, and that he listened.

From his fifteenth birthday, he wished in terms of 'less'. He wished that his dad would drink less, be less violent and not as cruel.

On his seventeenth birthday, he wished that his dad would leave, disappear, or die.

And sometimes wishes come true, just not in the way you think.

*

Danny had just started the Friday lunch shift, his back to the customers as he unloaded gin bottles, when he heard a familiar voice.

'I can definitely see why someone would decide to stay here.' A voice that belonged to the boy whose name was one of the first words he spoke.

'Oh absolutely,' said another familiar voice. A voice that belonged to the boy who'd taught him how to kick a torp and clean a fish. 'It's the kwa-noa of the place,' Rick added, pretending to be serious.

'I think you mean keen-wah,' said Tom. 'Remember it's that rice stuff that Ben's mum always tries to get us to eat? But I think you actually mean feng shui.'

'Yeah, right, that's the thing Mr Donaldson was always going on about?'

Danny turned around, and without a hint of recognition he took out two beer glasses and filled them with Carlton Draught. He placed the beers in front of his best mates without making eye contact. 'I'll need to see some ID,' he said.

Rick and Tom both placed their driver's licences on the countertop.

'We're a long way from home,' said Tom – a loaded statement.

Danny finally locked eyes with him and gave a nondescript nod.

'Right, okay, I can't stand this,' said Rick. 'Danny, you *know* why we're here.'

'To drink beer?' Danny offered, and Tom smiled.

'Yep, we drove over two thousand k's in a car that's not meant to travel more than a hundred k at a time, just so we could sit at a bar in Woop Woop and drink beer that has too much froth.'

'Thought so,' Danny replied.

'Been for any good runs?' asked Tom.

'Some. There's a creek about five k's east. It's best at dusk,' he said, and Tom nodded. 'You?'

'Not really. Too many people in the city. Makes it hard to find a rhythm.'

Danny began wiping down the counter. 'Read any good books lately?'

Tom shook his head. 'You?'

'Seriously,' said Rick, 'this is what we're going to talk about? Runs and books? What the fuck, guys?' He looked from Danny to Tom, increasingly incredulous.

They shared a smile.

'We don't have time for this. We have a game to get to.'

'What?' asked Danny, suddenly serious as he put down his cloth.

'Not us,' Tom said. 'The girls.'

'The girls?' repeated Danny. 'What girls?'

'*Our* girls,' said Rick. 'Or women. It's both. Both our girls and our women. Oh, actually that sounds a bit off, doesn't it?'

'Denby and Gerandaroo have both put together a team of women to play each other this Sunday,' Tom explained.

'Seriously?'

'Yeah, it came together pretty fast. Bess helped to start things.'

'*Bess?*' said Danny. 'What's she doing in Gerandaroo?'

'That's a great question,' said Rick. 'One that we can happily discuss once we're in the car – on our way home. All of us. To Gerandaroo.'

Danny was summoned by a patron at the end of the counter and he reluctantly left his friends to serve her.

*

As Danny moved out of earshot, Tom leaned towards Rick. 'Cool it, okay?' he whispered. 'You can't just dump all this on him and expect that he'll come back right away.'

'Yes. I can,' Rick said, choosing not to whisper. 'That's exactly what I can do and what I expect to happen.'

'Just back off a bit, you'll –'

'What? I'll run him out of town? Out of the state? To a far-off land covered in red dirt? Literally everything here is covered in dirt. See?' He ran his finger under the countertop and held up an orange fingertip. 'It sticks to everything. Danny doesn't want to stay in Queensland.'

Tom just looked at Rick and sighed deeply.

'And before you go thinking that you should have done this without me, remember you wouldn't even be here if I hadn't tracked you down.' Rick slid off his stool and stood, stretching slightly. 'And if you recall, it took all of five minutes to convince you to come and get Danny,' his voice now raised as he walked backwards to the bathroom, 'so, I'm pretty sure it'll only take another few minutes to convince Danny to come home.'

*

When Danny returned to Tom, an awkward tension pulled between them.

'I tried to find him,' Tom said after a few moments.

Danny kept his head down.

'I couldn't, though. Find him, I mean.'

'At least you tried.'

'Dan,' Tom began tentatively, 'I don't know if Detective Riley has been in contact, but Simon and the other boys, they've apparently told their lawyers that they'll plead guilty. To all charges.'

Danny froze. He slowly formed a fist, his other hand gripping the edge of the counter in a frantic attempt to remain upright.

His breathing became erratic; swallowing was an unpleasant challenge. He was only vaguely aware that Tom was still talking.

'The cops said you could leave the state, but you'll still need to come back and . . .'

The words slipped past Dan as the ceiling and the floor and all the walls hurried towards him. He reacted in the only way his mind would permit.

He fled.

He didn't remember walking out from behind the bar, nor did he hear Tom calling for him to stop. He didn't see his boss Max, a man short in stature but big in heart, coming towards him. He couldn't feel the patrons he pushed through to get out the front door.

He had no memory of walking faster and faster until he was running. His first conscious moment was Tom standing in front of him in the warm air, one hand on each shoulder, calmly but firmly, in a voice laden with concern and desperation, and love, reminding him how to breathe.

'In and out, Dan, just in,' Tom took a deep breath and Dan followed suit, 'and out,' Tom said as he exhaled slowly. This went on for several minutes until Dan could feel his body again and could form slightly coherent thoughts.

'Does that happen often?' asked Tom.

'Only when you're around.' Dan gave a small smile.

The friends stood quietly as Tom watched Danny to make sure he kept breathing, and continued to hold his shoulders to stop him from fleeing. Danny watched him and mirrored his breathing, and feeling the firm touch of his friend's hands on his shoulders helped keep him in the present, helped keep him grounded.

'Dan, I need you to really listen to every word I'm about to say,' insisted Tom. 'When anything or everything is out of sync, when you can't make sense of what you're thinking or feeling or doing, know that this,' he gestured between the two of them with his head, 'us, our friendship, and Lachie, and Bess, my parents, and your friends, including Rick,' he added with a smile, 'we're the ones who will be the rhythm and the compass you need to keep going. Even if that means you need to stay still for a while. Because that's what you do for us. Without you, everything has been hard. And sad. And . . .' His voice started to trail off as he blinked back tears. 'And just – we're lost, Danny. We're all lost without you.'

As Danny held back tears and reached up to hold the arms of the boy who had always helped keep him steady, the two friends, now young men, fell into a familiar embrace.

*

Rick was leaning against the bonnet of his car as Danny and Tom approached. ''Bout bloody time,' he said. 'Oh, I just resigned for you and packed up your stuff,' he added, looking at Dan. 'You know you really should learn how to fold your clothes better.'

'You what?'

'Your suitcase is in the back. Now let's get going. You'll need to take first shift because we pretty much drove flat out to get here. And we both had a beer, or a few sips of beer froth. But still.'

'Wait, just wait. I have a job. I can't just up and leave right this second.'

'Yeah, so Max, really cool bloke, he said he knew you'd need to head home to Gerandaroo. And that it would likely be with short notice.'

'What are you on about?'

'Turns out Max grew up in Melcot. His great uncle is Arthur Brinks, you know that old codger who lives out at the farm next to the Trayfords' with the rocket ship for a letterbox?'

'What?'

'You know the one, it's got the tip of the rocket above the –'

'Not the letterbox, Rick!'

'Oh, you mean about Max?'

Danny nodded, and drew a long breath.

'Well, he knew who you were when you rocked up,' Rick explained. 'He figured that maybe you needed some space. So that's what he gave you. And now he wants to give you even more space, by letting you come home, without notice.'

Seeing the look of surprise turn to anger on Danny's face, Rick quickly went on, 'Oh, but don't worry. He's not pissed off or anything, like I said, he's a cool guy. He gets it. And he knows what happ—' He suddenly stopped himself. 'Well, he knows that you're dealing with some pretty heavy stuff and is happy for you to come home.'

'Rick,' started Danny, exasperated, 'do you ever just stop to think before acting?'

Rick lowered his gaze.

'Just wait here, okay?' Danny gestured for him to stay put before he turned and hurried inside.

*

Rick hadn't meant to make light of the situation. He just wanted them to all be on the same page again. But after seeing the conflicted expression on Danny's face, a mixture of sadness and shock, he didn't know what else to say or do to convince his childhood friend to come home.

'You really are something else,' said Tom with a sideways glare at Rick.

'My mum always said I was a special boy,' he said, throwing both hands up in the air.

The duo waited in silence and hoped that Danny would return.

TWENTY

2 days to Game Day

'You're seriously not going to tell me where we're going?' asked Bess, irritated and intrigued in equal measure.

'Nope,' said Lachie, enjoying the suspense. 'But if you're as smart as you think you are, you'll figure it out pretty soon. And Deb already knows about it.'

'This is so frustrating,' muttered Bess. 'And I still can't believe you haven't got your air-conditioning fixed,' she continued as she rolled down her window. 'And why does it smell like wet dog in here?'

'Ya done?' Lachie smiled. 'It's probably Jinx. I took him to the lake last week when you were in Denby.'

'Really? I didn't know you still did that.'

'Is that a problem?' he asked.

'Of course not. He loves his trips with you. I just didn't realise it was something you still did.'

'Not everything has changed.'

Bess remained tight-lipped. This was typically the moment she would throw in a sarcastic comment, or even one with a bit of malice. But she decided not to indulge that version of herself.

Lachie graciously changed the subject. 'So, do you miss teaching?'

'Um, yes and no. It's a lot of work, which I thought I was prepared for because of Mum, but it can be a bit overwhelming. Some parents think the sun shines out of every orifice their kid has, and those kids are usually lacking in the intelligence department.'

Lachie laughed. 'Are you meant to refer to students like that?'

'Not really,' Bess said with a grin. 'But there are some real mouth-breathers in my Year 10 class. I mean, we thought we had some thick ones in our day, but these kids are next level.'

Lachie kept laughing. 'Isn't it your job?'

'To what? Teach them to be less thick?'

'Something like that.'

'Probably. I don't know. Sometimes I just can't be bothered.'

'I'm sure our teachers felt like that all the time.'

'I'm certain they did.' Bess paused. 'I was about to quit,' she admitted.

'Seriously?'

She nodded and focused on the passing scenery. 'Everything started to feel . . . wrong. I don't know how to explain it. It was like I was going through the motions each day but not actually engaging with . . . well, with anything really. Have you ever wanted your thoughts to just slow down enough for you to make sense of them?'

'I think everyone has. Did you tell your boss that you wanted to quit?'

'Yeah.'

'Bet that felt weird.'

'Why do you say that?'

'You, being honest about your feelings.'

Lachie was right, and Bess didn't know how to respond.

'What are the good parts of the job?' he asked.

'What makes you think there are any?'

'Because when I asked you if you missed it, you said yes and no. So, there must be some parts you enjoy.'

Bess had forgotten how good a listener Lachie was.

'I guess I miss the actual teaching part. So, in class, when the kids have read a novel and they're starting to put everything together and we end up having a lively discussion, it can be pretty satisfying.'

'Well, I guess you won't have to wait long to have that again.'

When Bess didn't say anything, Lachie pressed her. 'I figured once the game was over, you'd be heading back to the city?'

'It's not like I came home to play footy,' Bess said pointedly. 'Remember, there wasn't even a team when I came back.'

'So, you still consider Gerandaroo your home? Even though you haven't lived here for nearly six years?'

'It's just a figure of speech. Home is usually where your parents are, until you get married or have kids of your own.'

'So, where's mine?'

'Your what?'

'My home. Mum's dead, Dad's AWOL, I'm not married and I don't have kids.'

Bess felt both sadness and a bit of anger towards Lachie. He knew she didn't mean to imply that he didn't have a home, but she also knew she'd been insensitive. She decided to let the question hang unanswered.

'Why did you really come back?' he asked, with just a hint of animosity.

Bess took a moment to consider his question. 'Why did you stay?' she shot back.

Lachie shook his head slightly, but said nothing.

'I've dated people,' she blurted, surprised at her own admission.

'That's nice,' said Lachie, which only fuelled her desire to hurt him.

'Have *you*?' she asked, even though she knew she didn't have any right to.

'Not really.'

'What does that mean?' Bess turned to face him, trying to get a read.

'It means I haven't really dated.'

'It's a yes or no question.'

'Is it? I think there's scope for a variety of responses.'

'Fine.'

'See, it comes down to how you define *dated*,' Lachie insisted. 'Does it mean taking someone out, seeing them more than once, referring to them as your boyfriend or girlfriend?'

'Okay. So, how many women have you *not really* dated?'

'Does it matter?'

'Depends on the answer,' said Bess.

'Well, how many men have you dated or not really dated?' asked Lachie.

'A few.'
'Same.'

*

After about ten minutes, during which neither of them said a word, they passed the defunct *Welcome to Melcot* sign.

'The oval in Melcot?' exclaimed Bess. 'That's it, isn't it? We can play there?'

'Took you long enough,' Lachie said, before he pulled to a stop a few moments later. But there was no malice in his response.

'I haven't been here since, what was it, Year 8? I can remember how upset Mum and Dad were. The town tried so hard to stay afloat,' Bess murmured.

'I remember,' said Lachie. 'But the fire damage was just *so* extreme. And as soon as they decided not to fix up the hotel and most of the shops, there was really no hope.'

Bess gazed through the windscreen at the oval. 'How on earth did you do all of this in just a week?'

'Well, it was in surprisingly good nick,' he explained, climbing out of the car. 'We were pretty lucky.'

'We?' asked Bess as she closed her car door.

Lachie became fidgety. 'Yeah, um, your dad helped. I first asked if he would score on game day, but he shut me down pretty hard. Then when everything was falling apart, he really came through. Actually, without him, this wouldn't have been possible. He got all the stuff we needed and got together blokes from home and from Denby who he knew were on our side. We've been out here day and night to get it ready. And he also organised umpires,' he added, the words rushing out.

'You're kidding?' Bess tried to process what Lachie had shared. 'Dad hasn't said anything about *any* of this,' she said as she surveyed the oval.

It was definitely a hard surface, but it always had been. The grass, recently marked with precision white lines, was fairly evenly spread. She stepped across the boundary line and her eyes traced over the fifty-metre arcs, the centre square, the centre circle and the goal squares. It was one of the smaller ovals in the region, which made it ideal for their first game.

'I think maybe he wanted it to be a surprise,' Lachie said quietly. 'Or maybe he just didn't want to get your hopes up in case it didn't work out.'

That was more like it, thought Bess. Her dad always wanted to protect her, even when he knew he couldn't.

'Where did the footy posts come from?' she asked.

'Ben's uncle works for the supplier, and he got the company to agree to donate them if we put up a sign saying just that. And Ryan drove down from Wylie Creek a few mornings in a row to do all the ground markings,' he added, gesturing to the boundary line.

'That was good of him.'

'I think he did it hoping Jules would see it as some sort of romantic gesture.'

'She probably will, you know,' said Bess. 'Who are the umpires?'

'You remember Jed and Brendan?'

'The brothers who took over the feedstock store?'

'Yeah, that's them. They played for the VFL reserves for a few seasons, and they also did a bit of umpiring. Your dad reached out to them and they were really keen to be involved. And they were able to convince a few more guys to umpire with them. I think your mum was like their favourite teacher in high school.'

Bess nodded slowly, suddenly feeling overwhelmed that the game might actually go ahead.

'Deep breaths, Bess. Deep breaths,' said Lachie with a knowing glance.

Those words, said by him, triggered a response Bess could not have prepared for.

'Why didn't it work out,' she asked, 'with the women you didn't really date?' Her voice had lost its sharpness, and she sounded mature but young, all at the same time.

She watched Lachie's Adam's apple bob up and down, as though he knew the answer right away but thought it best to take a beat.

'They weren't you,' he replied with a shrug, equally young, equally mature.

*

Throughout their final training session on Friday night, not a single thing went right. Communication, accuracy, confidence, everything was off. And if Bess heard one more player use the 'bad dress rehearsal, great opening night' analogy, she was literally going to scream as loud as her lungs would allow. Her frustration was obvious, so the rest of the team tried to remain upbeat to avoid inflaming the situation – with the exception of Sam, who pushed the boundaries by providing a running negative commentary.

After a kick that went clean off the side of Kat's boot and out on the full, Sam was quick to respond. 'Well,' she said, hands in the air, 'I think that confirms that we should well and truly call it quits. Don't you?' she added, to no one in particular.

As Charlie missed a handball from Tully, Sam called, 'Yeah, that's pretty pathetic. Sums up our whole team, don't you think?'

And as Ali went to tackle Nora and slipped before making contact, Sam yelled, 'I don't know why we're even bothering with this charade!'

It would have been funny if it didn't irritate the hell out of Bess.

'Sam! Do you think for once in your life you could just keep your comments to yourself?' she yelled.

'No!' Sam yelled back. 'I'm pretty happy to keep commenting!'

TWENTY-ONE

Game Day

After two restless nights, Bess and Gayle sat at the kitchen table on Sunday morning dressed in their footy gear, Bess's left foot tapping. Both stared at the pieces of toast in front of them, smeared with butter and Vegemite, but neither could eat.

'I'm really nervous,' said Bess.

Gayle looked as though she wanted to say something encouraging but couldn't find the words, so she just nodded.

'Do you want to go early with us?' Gayle asked Ian, who had just walked in. 'Or will you come later?'

'Ah, I don't think I'll make the game,' he replied.

Gayle and Bess shared a glance.

'What do you mean? You're not coming?' asked Gayle.

'I've just got, I've got things to do,' he said as he opened the refrigerator.

'Like what?'

Ian didn't turn around to face them. 'I just can't,' he said quietly.

Gayle stood up and wrapped her arms around Ian's middle. She turned her head so that it rested on his back.

'It's okay,' she said softly.

'Dad, it's fine. It really is,' added Bess. 'You've already done more than enough to make sure the game can go ahead.'

As they prepared to leave, Ian still couldn't bring himself to look either of them in the eye.

'Good luck,' he said, his voice quiet and genuine as his wife and daughter walked out the front door.

*

Ian thought about how he hadn't watched or listened to a footy match all season and how it was the first year since he turned seven that he hadn't been to the 'G. Even though he'd been able to help Lachie get the Melcot oval ready, he just couldn't bring himself to be so close to an actual game. He desperately wanted to support the women in his life, but he didn't feel he could be a part of this next stage without Tom. Because every time he thought about footy, he could hear Tom telling him that he only played for him. And he could see Tom crying over his friend. And he could see Danny covered in blood, and Tristan covered in blood. And the Gerandaroo footy oval at the centre of it all.

Ian remained standing in front of the closed refrigerator and stared at the collection of photographs on the door, all held in place with fruit-shaped magnets. His favourite was front and centre – it was of Bess and Lachie age eleven, and Tom and Danny age six, camping at the lake; a white and reddish blur at the side representing two-year-old Jinx, who had refused to sit still. Only the kids' heads were visible, poking out from a tent opening. Every time Ian looked at it, he could hear them laughing and he could feel their joy. It was taken about a year before Lachie and Danny's mum died, before all the kids lost a layer of innocence that would never be recovered. Ian focused on the pineapple magnet that held the photo in place and wondered if he had the capacity to help the kids, now adults, to find their place in the world. And he realised that perhaps that was not his role; his role was to make sure they always had a place to come home to.

But despite this, he still couldn't bring himself to go and watch the game.

*

When matches were played during the seventies and eighties, more than a few fists, elbows and knees landed heavy blows behind the play, but it was the cross-town rivalry between Gerandaroo and Denby supporters that was sometimes more deeply felt. The spectators regularly engaged in verbal stoushes that led to the occasional tussle, however, more shirtfronting than fist-throwing occurred. These instances were typically amusing rather than alarming, and petered out when the instigators became more concerned with drinking beer than following through with threats.

The teams competed yearly for the Den-Roo cup, an unfortunate nickname that started when the two towns couldn't decide on an appropriate cup name. The match was always played in Round 8, and the Demons held a commanding lead of cup wins over the Cats. After Gerandaroo could no longer field a men's side, the cup became a tradition between the Under 18s. The recent season, however, was only the second time since the cup's inception in 1948 that it wasn't awarded.

The absence of either a Gerandaroo or Denby boys team was a hotly debated topic, and during every match supporters from other clubs would inevitably start discussing the likelihood of either team competing next season. And everyone seemed to have an opinion. The one constant that people from all the surrounding towns agreed on was how distant Gerandaroo had become. Folks from Denby in particular noticed a difference. This was not solely due to football. A metaphysical distance between the towns had steadily grown over the last decade, spurred by the development in Denby and the apparent stalemate that Gerandaroo found itself in. Even without a footy team, Denby was on the up and up, but for Gerandaroo, the growth in the larger town had seemed to be a catalyst for them to fall further behind, as though someone had hit pause, and they were just waiting for permission to get moving. Matches were associated not only with revenue on game day, but also a spirit that attracted newcomers and convinced families to stay. Now with the women's match upon them, even if footy only returned for the day, the townsfolk seemed to have regained some of their passion. And the residents embraced their new-found energy.

*

Unlike the Denby oval, which had recently installed a seven-row grandstand, the Melcot oval had only a single aged structure with a forest-green tin roof. It provided some protection during light rain; heavy rain, however, blew in from all sides, forcing everyone to huddle closer than was comfortable. But there was a gradual hill across the entire south side that extended partially to the west, making it ideal for foldout chairs and rugs. There was also a continuous wooden bench that wrapped itself around about a quarter of the oval. Unless you enjoyed removing splinters from your thighs, sitting on it with bare legs was not advised. There were no change rooms and never had been, bar an ancient two-toilet block with the dreaded long-drop toilets. It would be easy to dismiss the surroundings as inferior, but the women from both teams knew of no other female players who had ever trained on the oval, let alone played a game on it. And that made them feel connected to it in a way they couldn't quite describe.

Deb approached Bess as she removed footballs from her gym bag.

'Ready for this?' asked Deb.

'I'm bloody nervous,' said Bess.

'Same. Do you think maybe it would be a good idea to get both teams together? Just to say a few words?'

'Um, yeah. Sure.'

'Hey, guys!' Deb called to her team, who were wearing borrowed guernseys. 'Let's everyone come over here for a minute.'

As the Denby players gathered near the Gerandaroo team, all the women exchanged nods and hellos in a friendly manner; they pretty much all knew each other in some capacity. Despite the long-held rivalry between the two towns, which the women were happy to maintain, there was a general unspoken feeling that there was no need for any pre-game intimidatory tactics.

'So, before we start warming up and get things going,' said Deb, 'I thought maybe it would be nice to just acknowledge how great it is that we made it this far. I am so, *so* proud of everyone for sticking with training and getting to a point where we can play a game.' She turned to Bess expectantly.

Bess bit her lower lip; blood rushed to her face. And just as rapidly, she felt it drain away, because in that moment all she could think about was Tom. Had Rick found him? Should she have gone with Rick? Would Tom ever come home? She felt light-headed and had a sudden urge to sit down and close her eyes.

She was aware that all the players were waiting for her to say something inspiring, so she tried to bring herself back to the present. But while she had thought quite intensely about the speech she would deliver, she suddenly had an overwhelming thought: *Playing a game of footy won't solve anything.* 'Ah, yeah so, well, um . . .' Bess paused, her heart pounding. 'I think Deb said it all.'

'Yeah, great,' Deb said, surveying Bess with a concerned rather than judgemental gaze.

As Deb and her team jogged back to the other half of the oval, Bess felt the heat radiate once again from her face and neck. Her teammates were still watching her. Trying to be subtle, she turned away from them and pretended to focus on the spectators. As the crowd grew, she swallowed hard, her mouth increasingly dry. Her motivating voice remained silent, or perhaps she just couldn't hear it. Instead, her mind raced to the last game she saw

Tom and Danny play in. And all she could think was, *What am I doing here?*

*

Anyone passing by would likely assume this was a regular match to be played between men. Spectators wore navy and white scarfs and beanies for the Denby Cats, and royal blue and red ones for the Gerandaroo Demons. A handful of supporters also carried flags. And the air was filled with that footy feeling, created in anticipation of the first bounce. The indisputable fact about footy supporters is that they don't just show up, they go all in. Supporters could spend their time doing any number of things, but they repeatedly and without hesitation chose to stand on the boundary or sit on uncomfortable seats, in all temperatures, to clap and cheer and boo, and perhaps mutter or scream the occasional obscenity. And in doing so, they got to celebrate every victory and commiserate in defeat, however peripheral the experience.

But despite knowing all of this, and despite being grateful that people had actually taken the time to come and see them play, Bess felt the rise of unwanted nervous energy, and she struggled to process her cycle of thoughts:

Am I just nervous that I might not play well?

Am I scared that people will laugh?

Or do I honestly believe that this was a bad idea?

As Bess looked towards the carpark, she realised that all throughout primary school and high school, her dad had watched her compete in every athletics event, every cross-country and swimming race, and in every netball game, basketball game and soccer match. It didn't matter the time of day, he would always make a point of showing up, even if that meant closing the pub. So now, it felt unnatural to be playing for Gerandaroo without him.

*

Facing the crowd that had grown to over a hundred, Ali and Tully shared an anxious look.

Charlie noticed their apprehension. 'You guys right?'

'Yeah.' Ali nodded, but it was unconvincing. 'It's just . . . you never really know what's gonna happen, what people might say.'

Charlie looked to the crowd then back to Ali and Tully. 'Fuck 'em if they've got a problem,' she said. 'They'll have us to deal with.'

She put her arm around Tully and squeezed her shoulder. Ali smiled, but the worry inside did not abate.

Abby glanced around at the spectators and caught Andrew Finch's eye. As usual, he was off to the side, standing on his own. She was surprised to see him, but also not. There was a brief moment between them, where Abby knew that despite his mother's over-bearing influence, Andrew was there to offer support.

As the players gathered for the obligatory pre-game pep talk, there was an excitement and nervousness in the air. No one was entirely sure what to expect. In the Demons' huddle, Bess looked around at the players and knew she still had no idea what to say. If she was honest, she would have said that she was terrified and regretted the decision to ever form a team. Instead, she fumbled through a few sentences with an energy more suited to consoling a stranger before surgery rather than motivating a team of friends before their first ever match. Throughout the entire non-pep pep talk, Tom and Danny crowded her thoughts, and no matter how hard she tried, she couldn't shake the feeling that without them there, nothing felt right.

*

As Lachie watched from the boundary, he could tell from the way Bess tensed her shoulders, avoided eye contact, and kept crossing and uncrossing her arms, that she was flailing. He was certain her words matched her movements, and that whatever she was saying was not going to be enough to fire the women up. Not even close. He wanted to run to her and tell her to get out of her head. To enjoy the game. To remember that this was never about winning. But he resisted the urge and remained still, arms folded. Lachie reminded himself that it was not his place to interfere. Bess needed to get there on her own.

*

With about a minute to game time, the players, as well as the umpires Jed and Brendan and the friends they'd recruited, took their respective positions around the oval. Diane started off in the ruck with Fiona as centre, Andy as rover and Ali as ruck rover. Diane jumped on the spot several times as she shook her hands, and could hear her husband cheering above the crowd.

'Carn the Dees!' he called, followed by a near perfect two-fingered double whistle.

Sam and Jules were placed at half-forward, Lou and Gayle in the forward pocket and Tully at centre half-forward. Sam stood after retying her bootlaces. She stared at the crowd for several moments, and then bent down to tie them again.

With Eva and Kat positioned on the wings, the backline consisted of Nora and Jen at half-back, Charlie and Abby in the back pocket and Meredith at centre half-back. Nora repeatedly tugged at her footy shorts. She couldn't remember the last time she'd showed this much flesh in public.

Bess took her position as full-forward and stared down the barrel of the oval to Rach at full-back. The oval suddenly seemed a whole lot bigger than she remembered.

*

Neither team had an off-field coach. Deb acted as captain–coach for Denby, with two Year 11 Denby High boys working as runners to relay messages between Deb and the other players. In Rick's absence, Ben and Billy took up the runner mantle for Gerandaroo, and Bess assured them she was happy for them to guide the team however they felt appropriate.

The clapping and cheering grew in intensity, and as the start siren sounded, a resounding roar broke out. The first bounce was met with a failed attempt by both rucks to hit the football towards a teammate. Players threw themselves at the loose ball, resulting in a ball up only seconds later. There was an awkwardness to the players' movements, a mixture of nerves and uncertainty. This was not helped by the laughter emanating from some spectators, who seemed content to deride rather than support the women.

The ball was knocked out of a pack of about seven players, and landed at the feet of a nearby Cats player who managed to chip it short towards the wing. It bounced off the chest of the intended target, which triggered laughter from the crowd. Meredith and Charlie were close by but made a bungled attempt to clear the ball out. It made its way into the hands of an imposing Cats player with a tank-like body, who ran towards goal and kicked with reasonably good form, but only managed to score a point.

Rach took the kick in but remained in the goal square for an extended period as there were no leads. She opted for a long kick but the ball only made it to a Cats player about twenty metres away. Players toppled over each other to get to the ball, creating a domino effect of falling bodies that accompanied continued laughter from the boundary.

Ben and Billy glared at the spectators, which had zero impact.

Bess stood at the top of the goal square and looked on with frustration as Sam and Kat argued near the centre of the field.

Fifteen minutes now seemed like an unbearably long time. While most of the players were reasonably fit, there was a difference when it came to match fitness. The adrenaline and excitement had worn off after about five minutes, and now it all just seemed like a hot mess.

As the quarter came to a merciful close, the score 0 to 1, with Gerandaroo only able to get the ball into their forward fifty twice, the players collapsed on the ground. Ben and Billy were at a complete loss as to what they should say, and the players felt the same. It was likely the first time a team was silent at the break.

*

Midway through the second quarter, Denby maintained the lead. Which wasn't saying much considering the score remained 0 to 1. Number 4 for the Cats had possession just within their fifty-metre arc. The player sprinted past Jen and was nearly brought down by Abby, but managed a wobbly yet remarkably accurate kick to Deb, who marked directly in front of goal. Deb lined up with confidence and easily slotted it through. Her team mobbed her; the joyous celebration infectious. While the Gerandaroo players found themselves clapping, they were also slightly resentful that they were not the first to achieve this milestone.

Following a clean tap-out by Eva, play made its way to the east side of the oval. Rob, beer can in hand, leaned over the fence as Ali jogged by, her opponent close behind.

'Would you look at that, fellas,' he proclaimed loudly as he raised his beer as if to toast Ali, 'a girl ape pretending to be a boy ape.'

The comment drew sniggers from several spectators standing with Rob.

Ali stopped, the words cutting through her like a shard of ice, her breath momentarily lost. She exhaled slowly, opting not to turn around. Her opponent Mel stopped beside her.

'Ya right?' asked Mel.

Ali nodded, unsure of what to say.

'Pretty impressive to be so fucking insulting with so few words,' Mel said.

'At least he's consistent.' Ali gave a slight shrug of the shoulders. Rob had long thrown racist insults towards her brothers and cousins over the years and her family always made a point of sitting far away from him at matches.

Mel glared at Rob. 'Yeah. Consistent at being an ignorant dick.'

The two players shared a brief laugh before sprinting off towards the play.

With no leads, Nora, doing her best as a half-back flanker, turned and attempted to chip the ball back to Charlie, but kicked too long. Charlie sprinted and almost marked near the outer wing, but couldn't get there in time. As the bounce went against her, the ball rolled slowly out of bounds and there was yet another ball up.

Meredith tapped it towards Kat who managed to handball off to Sam. Sam was brought under pressure and tackled to the ground. The cry of 'Ball!' from the crowd was accompanied by the umpire's whistle, and the Demons lost possession.

A Cats player kicked towards a lone teammate who marked near the goal square. The player turned with speed and decided to play on, but Jen managed to reach her in time and lay a decent tackle.

'Nice one, Jen!' called her brother Tim, who'd made a surprise trip from Sydney to support his sister.

As possession was turned back to the Demons, the players tried to spread out and create leads. There was no cohesion, largely because there was no leadership. The runners were doing their best to guide the players, but with each passing minute, they seemed to shy away from even *trying* to play the game. Exhaustion, being made to feel like fools by many in the crowd, questioning why they were even doing this, all worked against them.

In the final minute, the Demons managed to get the ball close enough to try to score. Lou, hanging back from a pack of six players, watched as the ball trickled out and landed at her feet.

'Straight to goal, Lou!' cried her granddad, who typically remained quiet on the boundary.

Lou awkwardly gathered the ball, nearly lost it, and despite being in a position to run to the goal square, she just dropped ball to boot and watched as it bounced once, twice, towards the outer point post. It landed just over the white line and came to a somewhat pathetic stop. They had their first score. A solitary point. But Gerandaroo did not celebrate, because unless a single point wins the game, nobody claps and nobody cheers, except the opposition.

The siren sounded for half-time and all the players looked relieved. The score was 1 to 7.

*

The Demons gathered under a red pop-up gazebo set up at the base of the southern boundary incline. Most found their way to the ground, content if they never had to move again. With a blanket expression of defeat, they had little left to give.

Bess briefly opened her mouth as though on the verge of speaking. The women focused on her, apprehensive with a tinge of eagerness. It was up to her to rally them, but she closed her mouth and said nothing. And all the players remained silent.

As they handed out water bottles, Ben and Billy tried to improve the team's morale by pointing out things they had done well, but the list was short.

When the time came to head back onto the field, the team filed out dejectedly.

Jules caught up to Bess as she walked through the fence opening.

'B, what was that? Why didn't you say anything?'

'Why does it always have to be me?' Bess shot back. 'You could have said something. Anyone could have.'

'You still don't get it, do you?'

Jules did not wait for a response, and instead headed to her position near the outer west fifty-metre arc. Pissed off, but also confused, Bess watched her go.

TWENTY-TWO

Tom stared out the window as they passed the familiar sights along the highway. He knew how sparse and repetitive it must look to an outsider. While he'd never considered farming as a career, he knew the promise the land held, and he appreciated the solace of the countryside. Even if he never shared this with his dad.

There was a simmering darkness though, kept at bay by the tireless efforts of the individuals who worked the land. They battled endlessly to stay one step ahead, to not let the demands of daily living and the unpredictability of the seasons overwhelm them.

Tom hoped that perhaps one day he could use photography to show others this world he'd grown up in. The world where he learned to kick a football and drive a car, where he was taught to always check on a neighbour if they hadn't put their bins out, where he had his first kiss by the lake, eavesdropped on his sister and her friends, snuck his first beer, and where he'd watched close family friends sell their possessions to pay down debt accumulated from a failed farm. And it was the world where he'd learned to love a friend like a brother, and where he watched that brother break into pieces, some buried, others scattered far and wide, with the rest trying fiercely to hold him together.

His grandfather Percy used to tell him that in the not-so-distant future, new highways would be built that bypassed towns like Gerandaroo. This would be seen as progress, shunting small towns aside as though they were an impediment, with speed the priority. And he had been right.

As they approached the *Welcome to Gerandaroo* sign, Tom felt increasingly agitated, like he could crawl out of his own skin, afraid of where his thoughts were headed. He closed his eyes so he would not be tempted to demand that Rick turn the car around.

But all he could see was that night and the same ending that he knew would never change.

Jinx ran to the front door, seemingly alerted to something outside. His sense of urgency led Tom to follow. When he opened the door, Tom jumped back slightly as Danny fell from a sitting position, his head landing beside Tom's feet, his shirt, hands and face covered in blood.

'Bess!' Tom cried out as he kneeled to cradle his best friend and check for wounds.

He could see blood spilling from Danny's nose and from a deep cut below his swollen right eye, with bruises forming rapidly.

'Bess, call an ambulance!' His voice was louder and more scared than it had ever been. 'Danny, Daniel! What happened, what's . . . where's the blood coming from?' Tom frantically lifted his friend's shirt, concerned he'd been stabbed.

Jinx, now whimpering, started to paw at Dan's chest.

'It's not all mine,' Danny whispered as his eyes fluttered open. 'The oval.'

'What? What about the oval?'

'He's on the oval.'

'Who? Danny, who's on the oval?'

'Tristan. I couldn't stop . . .' His voice drifted.

'Stop what?'

'I couldn't . . .' he repeated, his voice barely audible, before he lost consciousness.

'Stay with him,' demanded Tom.

'Tom, no! You're not going out there alone!' Bess insisted, as she kneeled beside Daniel, her face ashen. 'We don't know what's happened!'

Tom ignored his sister's pleas, took her car keys, and drove full pelt towards the oval.

He arrived in complete darkness.

He turned on the high-beam headlights, which tracked an almost sinister path across the grass that merged close to the centre square. He couldn't make out any shapes, aside from the goalposts, but that was only because he knew exactly where they were.

He climbed over the fence, and cool air whipped around him like an angry spirit. He swallowed deep, fear starting to mix with adrenaline. He didn't know what he was looking for. Or what he might find.

As his eyes struggled to adjust to the black, he could just make out a shape near the centre circle. He headed towards it, and as he closed in, he knew it was a body.

'Tristan!? Tristan, it's Tom.'

The trees, despite being a hundred yards away, offered an eerie response, with a rustling that grew more intense.

He dropped to his knees beside Tristan and stared at his unblinking eyes. He placed a hand on his chest and felt for a pulse at his left wrist. He could see the blood that had recently flowed from a wound at the back of Tristan's head and settled around his neck, and the blood from a cut under his left eye had trickled slowly towards his ear.

Tom reached out to touch Tristan's face but hesitated. He looked around, even though he knew he was alone.

And that Tristan had died.

And that he was too late.

He heard a car pull up, just as fast as he had, and turned to see his dad and Lachie sprinting towards him. He remained kneeling as they approached and processed the scene. Their movements slowed when they realised that Tristan was dead.

'What happened?' asked his dad as he kneeled beside his son.

'I don't know. Danny was at the front door. Covered in blood.'

'I just arrived home and was in the driveway when Lachie came looking for Dan,' his dad explained. 'We found him with Bess, waiting for the ambulance. He was conscious.'

'What happened?' asked Tom, with the voice of a child.

His dad shook his head and took a deep breath. 'I . . . I don't know,' he replied, his voice crippled by uncertainty and concern. And fear.

Lachlan was silent. Although his eyes were focused on Tristan, Tom knew that his thoughts belonged to Danny.

*

Back at the oval, the third quarter was underway with a ball up at the east of the centre of the oval. The Cats had tried to come out strong, kicking two points in quick succession.

A strong tap by number 17 for the Cats landed the ball directly in the hands of a shortish Cats forward pocket player, but her kick was cut off by Abby. She tried to swing it across the field but kicked to an uneven contest and Diane, suddenly on the ground, surrounded by several Denby players and unsure what to do, inadvertently pulled the ball underneath her body and the Cats took possession. A few short handballs and play was back in the Cats' forward fifty. The ball was soccered off the ground and tumbled through for another point.

Jen took the kick in and drove it towards Abby and Charlie who were jostling among three tall Cats. Although the ball ricocheted off Charlie's chest, she was able to gather it back. But she was caught in a tackle and couldn't complete her kick to Meredith.

A Cats player won the ground contest over Andy and sent it deep past the centre circle. Ali managed to lay a tackle with force, but wasn't rewarded and there was a ball up. The Cats had the numbers in their forward fifty and managed to handball several times before number 11 chipped a short one to number 8, who took an easy mark against Nora. She lined up to take a shot at goal, but pipped the post for a behind.

Rach drove a high kick to the wing, but it fell short of Kat, who struggled to play the ground game. Number 14 for the Cats collected the football and opted to drive it down the line. The Cats number 18 jumped slightly to mark, and turned to play on, but her kick towards goal was mercifully touched off the boot by a jumping Abby. The score was now 1 to 12.

Rach gestured to Meredith to have a go at the kick in and Meredith, somewhat reluctantly, sent it low to the east, towards Jen and Charlie. Jen marked and handballed fast to Diane, who copped one high, earning her a free kick. She sent a mangled kick less than ten metres to the right and players from both sides descended on the ball, resulting in a ball up.

Andy tapped it to Ali, who took a few steps and a bounce before launching it high. But the Demons gained little ground, as the ball went up and came straight back down. Fiona got hands to it but couldn't bring it under control and had to fight it out with two Cats defenders. Bess collected the ball and streamed into open territory, before a hard tackle stopped the play.

Minutes later and a boundary throw-in caused a congested group to flail about and struggle to clear the ball out. A scooping handball by Jules sent it towards Gayle, who tried for a clearing kick but couldn't get enough power behind it. Still, it landed near Tully who managed to keep it in, before sending it inside fifty towards Bess and Sam. Sam fumbled the mark, but recovered to collect the ball and kick towards goal, but only managed a point.

The Cats sent it towards the east-side boundary and a mark was taken by Eva, who decided to send it backwards with a handpass to Lou, who sidestepped one opponent only to be crushed in a sand-wich tackle by two more. A kick by Cats number 24 hit the target in number 35, but a handpass was intercepted by Diane, who sent it towards Fiona at centre half-forward. Fiona gained considerable territory with a few bounces before kicking towards goal, but again only managed a point.

The kick in by Cats number 16 sent it directly in front of goal, for a ground game between four players, including Bess and Tully. Tully decided to snap it high and as it nearly pulled back to sail through the goalposts, the Demons players held their breath, but it stayed left for a point.

Cats number 16 again sent it down the middle, but this time it was taken cleanly by number 27, who sprinted off the mark and towards the wing. She slipped through a tackle from Kat and sent a short kick to number 19. After holding the ball for too long, the umpire called 'Play on!' and Kat again tried for a tackle. Kat held contact and kept possession. She was nervous about kicking so handballed to a nearby Eva, who sent it forward to Jules. It fell just short of Jules and was picked off by Cats number 33, who struggled to decide what to do, before a hurried handpass landed between players and a scrum ensued.

A ball up allowed Meredith to tap successfully to Diane, who kicked across the field towards the west for some space. Nora was the closest to the ball, but couldn't quite gather it cleanly. Players crowded around and the ball was knocked out the back towards Jen, who managed to handpass to a moving Ali, but she was pinged for taking too many steps without bouncing. Frustrated, she threw the ball to a Cats player and stood on the mark, hands over head, breathing hard.

As the kick sailed into a contest, Ali turned and sprinted, determined to make up for her mistake. The Cats number 18 had the ball near the boundary wing and a loose target in the goal square, but she was brought to ground by Ali, much to the cheers of the crowd.

Ali took a few moments to compose herself, adrenaline pumping, before a booming kick directly to Abby, who almost cried out in pain as the ball slammed into her chest. She turned to see her options and decided to send it to the right, but misjudged and the ball sailed over the head of Charlie. She waved her hands in frustration and Abby called, 'Calm down! It's not like I did it on purpose!'

'Well, next time don't do it at all!' Charlie shot back.

'Charlie, just cool it, okay?' said Andy, who was within earshot.

'You know what? Playing it cool never got me anywhere. So I think it's about time I got a bit fired up and see how that works out. Is that okay with you?' she said angrily to Andy.

'Okay, okay, do what you want,' she replied, throwing up her hands.

Moments later, a kick out of bounds on the full by Eva set something off in Fi, who yelled, 'Keep an eye on the boundary!'

'Yeah, thanks for that, Fiona! Like I bloody planned to kick it there!'

As the ball made its way towards the Cats forward-half, Meredith and Diane found themselves clashing over it.

'Oh goodness, Meredith!' Diane cried. 'Watch where you're going!'

'I could say the same thing to you!' Meredith retorted.

A few clean handballs and a high kick saw the Cats line up for another goal. Abby was meant to be on the mark but opted not to.

'Abby! What the hell?! Get on the mark!' Kat yelled from the wing.

'You do it!' Abby shot back as she walked away from the play.

After the score by the Cats, the ball was brought back to the centre. The scoreboard displayed a lopsided 4 to 18.

'Hey, Eva!' Sam called. 'Do you think you could try and hit it just once our way?'

'Excuse me?' she replied. 'Are you being serious? How about you try and do something with the ball rather than handballing to air and hoping someone will catch it.'

'That's not what I'm doing!'

'That's *all* you've been doing!'

'Guys, let's just take it down a notch, okay?' said Jules.

'Oh, stay out of it, Juliet,' said Eva, which caused Jules to take a step back.

'Fine. Argue, for all I care. It only makes us look like fools.'

Eva looked immediately apologetic, but said nothing.

The football bounced high, and Eva ran in, jumped up, and made excellent contact, sending it directly towards Ali, who chipped it low to Sam. Unfortunately, Sam turned and handballed to space, with no Gerandaroo player nearby.

'I bloody told you so!' called Eva with immediate regret. 'Hey, no worries,' she said as she jogged over to Sam.

'Don't pretend you care how I feel,' said Sam. Her face flushed a deeper red before she ran away towards the play.

'So, you know how Rick is always telling them they need to talk more on the field?' Ben said to Billy as they watched the increasingly adverse interactions from the boundary.

'Yep,' replied Billy.

'I don't think he meant that they should argue.'

'Yeah, Rick probably could have been a bit clearer.'

'What do we do?'

'Nothing,' said Billy. 'I think we just have to let them play it out.'

'I didn't take you for the philosophical type.'

Billy laughed. 'Not even close,' he said. 'But do you remember that game against Wylie Creek in Year 11? When we were all fighting on the field because of some argument we'd had on the bus?'

Ben nodded.

'And Danny brought everyone back together by doing that running tackle from, like, forty metres out to stop a goal?' Billy continued. 'Well, Coach Macca told me on the bus ride home that when you're out there on the field, sometimes you have to learn how to communicate the hard way. And that sometimes starts with fighting.'

'So, we just let them figure it out?'

'I think so.'

'Well, they've got one quarter to go, so they'd better figure it out soon.'

*

Bess had also watched these heated exchanges but didn't intervene. Partly because she didn't have the energy, partly because she didn't want to, but mostly because she just didn't know what to say.

She felt light-headed again. She knew why but wished she didn't. Since the siren had sounded for the start of the game, she had been replaying the night that Tristan died. It was as though her mind was stuck on a loop and she inadvertently and repeatedly held her breath, hoping each time for a different ending. Even when the football was in her hands, she still felt like she was holding Danny in her arms as they waited for the ambulance. As play continued around her, she intermittently experienced the same motion-sickness feeling she'd had when she'd travelled with Danny to the hospital in Denby. And she felt the same fear and heaviness she'd experienced when the police arrived, and she instinctively reached out to hold Danny's hand the way you only do for someone you love with your whole self.

From the moment she had arrived at the Melcot oval, Bess had never wanted to be as far away from anything as she did from football.

*

Tom's breathing became fast and shallow as they approached Gundry Crescent. On arrival at his house, he felt a pull between comfort and nausea. As he got out of the car, Jinx came hurtling over from a mat on the verandah where he'd been sleeping, bounding around him like a puppy.

Tom dropped straight to the ground to greet Jinx, equally happy to see him again. He nestled his face deep into Jinx's neck as the dog showered him with small kisses.

Ian stepped out from behind the hood of his Landy and wiped his hands with a red rag.

Tom paused before he slowly stood. Father and son looked at each other, their eyes reflecting the same sadness and regret.

Ian took the first step, and Tom quickly followed. As Ian opened his arms, Tom fell instinctively into his dad's chest. His dad held him close, and Tom felt his heart and mind relax for the first time that year.

After they pulled apart, Ian clamped a hand on Tom's shoulders and gave a gentle but definite nod – a quiet resolution.

At that moment, Danny emerged from the back seat.

If Ian was surprised to see him, he didn't show it. Tom watched his dad walk towards Danny, who remained still. Ian reached out to shake his hand, clearly tentative, but Danny stepped forward and embraced Ian, who held him tight, taking his full weight. Ian pulled back and cupped Danny's face the way a loving father would, just as Jinx wedged himself between them to greet Danny.

Rick emerged to break the emotional tension. 'If we're done with the love fest, we've got a game to get to,' he said.

They all laughed, and Jinx settled on the verandah while Tom and Danny piled back into the car.

'If we're lucky, we'll be able to catch the end of the fourth quarter,' said Ian.

'What?' exclaimed Rick. 'Doesn't the game start at two?'

'Ah, no, it started at midday.'

'Oh shit. How did I get that wrong? Wait – why aren't you at the game?'

'You know, Rick, I've been wondering the exact same thing,' Ian replied with a shake of his head.

As Rick hurried into the driver's seat, Ian turned and headed towards the house. 'Just hold on a minute,' he called.

He emerged moments later with Tom's camera. Tom hesitated, but only briefly, before he accepted it.

TWENTY-THREE

As the match approached the end of the third quarter, the Demons still trailed the Cats 4 to 18. The spectators had started to take bets on whether Gerandaroo would even score a goal and the odds were stacked heavily against them.

Rob was particularly vocal and insisted this'd be the last time any of them would see a women's match, or as he referred to it, 'girly-girls pretending'. This drew the ire of some, but Rob was eager to defend his position, confident he was right and that anyone who disagreed was simply 'not living in reality'.

'Do you seriously think only men will ever play footy?' asked Sam's mum.

'Oh, I'm sure you girls will have another go, but it won't come to anything,' insisted a defiant Rob. 'Just look at 'em.' He gestured towards the players. 'No skill, no fitness, no aggression. They can't tackle, or kick straight, and they throw rather than handball. I don't even think all of 'em know the rules.'

'And did you come out of the womb knowing all those things?' asked Kat's oldest sister, who had travelled from the city to support the team.

'Come on now, don't get all hysterical. I'm just stating facts,' said Rob.

'You wanna know a real fact?' called Ben, who was standing close to the boundary. 'Fact is, you're a real dick. Who cares if they don't know everything yet? At least they're trying. They're not afraid to get out there in front of judgemental people like you and give it a go. And that's more than most. I'm pretty certain that's more than you've ever done.'

A hush fell over the spectators who were nearby. Ben was known as a larrikin, remembered for his pranks and oftentimes aggression on the field. He had the ability to intimidate. He wasn't a bully as such, but also wasn't known as someone who went out of their way to stand up for anyone.

'So why don't you just shut up and watch the game,' Ben continued. 'And if you can't do that, bugger off, because nobody cares what you think.'

Supporters from both sides clapped loudly and Rob sat down, sulking.

The Gerandaroo players seemed ready for the final siren to sound, almost as though they didn't want to play out the fourth quarter. Bess observed the women sprawled around her, all breathing heavily and taking gulps of water. They were the very picture of defeat, bordering on broken. Her first thought was, *This is all my fault.*

But then, finally, although she couldn't explain it, the small insistent voice broke through, and she had an epiphany. *No, it's not all your fault. It's all your doing.* Along with the voice, the images of her brother and Danny in a state of despair melted away, and she pictured them having an absolute ball, just playing as kids. In that moment, she knew they would want the women to finish the game.

She thought about how far her team had come in a matter of weeks. The fact was, she loved football. It had everything: speed, power, agility, and players needed to be able to both attack and defend. But beyond the skill level required, Bess knew that truly great teams only succeeded because they were filled with team players. And that success did not have to always include winning.

Before her was a group of women who, independently and without coercion, and in the absence of any assurances that it would all work out, had made the decision to play. In helping to build this team, along with Denby, she realised they'd started something that would endure long after the final siren. And she recognised how important it was that they continued to play, and that anyone who wanted to, was able to play without fear, without harm, without prejudice.

Bess stood up with a new-found energy and addressed her team-mates. 'I took . . .' she started, as the players all looked up at her. She swallowed hard. 'I took this town for granted,' she continued. 'When I lived here I was happy, but I still wanted to leave. Then when I left, I expected Gerandaroo to always just stay the same. That nothing would change.' She paused. 'Then everything changed.'

All the players watched Bess, listening intently now.

'For decades we've watched this game that we absolutely *love*, from the boundary. We've watched brothers, sons, boyfriends, husbands, fathers and friends play for our town. And now, we just wanna do the same. But nothing's the same and everything feels different. It's like we don't belong.'

She looked across the oval to the spectators, then back to her team. 'But . . . we *do* belong. And I think we all know that forming this team, it was never about winning some game. It might have started out like we wanted to prove to everyone else, and to ourselves, that we *deserve* to play.'

The players nodded in agreement, which gave Bess the courage to continue.

'But it's not about that. At least, not in the way we thought. I think . . . I think it's become a chance to show that we all belong, just as we are. Even if we didn't realise that's what we've been doing.'

She took a few deep breaths and steadied herself. 'Tristan and Danny, they both loved footy.'

It was the first time Bess had spoken about Tristan since he was killed.

'And they were made to feel like it was okay to love a game but not each other. And right now, there are people watching us who don't want us to keep playing. They think it's only acceptable for us to love this game so long as we don't ever set foot on the field. Now, I'm not saying that what we've experienced compares at all to what happened to Tristan and to Dan, but the only way we stop that hateful rhetoric and abuse, the only way we show people that something *isn't* wrong, is to keep playing. And we can play this game with more passion than anyone ever has.' Bess paused. 'Every heart beats true.'

One by one the players stood, and a chorus of 'For the red and the blue!' rang out.

The tension, the expectations, the pressure, all of it was released, and Bess could see in their faces that each Gerandaroo Demon knew she was exactly where she was meant to be.

Sam wiped tears from her eyes.

'Oh, Sammy.' Charlie chuckled as she reached out to put her arm around Sam.

'It's just sweat!' she insisted, but she fell into a side hug with Charlie and smiled, as all the women's eyes reflected tears – the type that only emerge from a mixture of joy and relief.

Gayle moved to embrace Bess and they held each other, not only as mother and daughter, but as teammates. As they pulled apart, Bess felt liberated; that small insistent voice was now loud and encouraging. And although she knew that not everything was okay, it was at least headed in a better direction.

Finally feeling like a team, a real team, the players ran to their respective positions, determined to finish what they'd started, together.

*

'Come on, Rick, put your foot down,' said Ian as they headed for Melcot.

'Um, so here's the thing, Mr O'Neill, Rhonda here is not really designed to travel to Queensland. And back. And she's also not built for speed. And I don't think you should be telling me to go any faster – I'm already doing ten k over the speed limit.'

'Son, I respect all of that, but if you don't pick up the pace, I'll climb up front, push you out while Rhonda's still moving, and take over. Understand?'

Rick accelerated, and the car travelled about two hundred metres before coming to a spluttering stop, smoke billowing from under the bonnet.

'I don't want to say I told you so, but I definitely told you so,' said Rick, with a furtive glance at Ian in the rear-view mirror.

'Oh, Christ almighty!' Ian exclaimed, already jumping out of the car.

Rick popped the hood and they all gathered to inspect the damage. It was obvious the car would not be going anywhere anytime soon.

'Right, let's hoof it then,' said Tom. 'We're less than two k out.'

They all turned and began running – not jogging, but running, including Ian who had long held records for cross country.

The four men fell into a rhythm with ease; they knew they had to get to the oval before the final siren. They had to see the women they grew up with, the women they loved, the women they admired (and sometimes feared), play some footy. They just had to.

Still sprinting as they made their way up the path to the oval, they could hear shouts and cheers.

They all looked up at the scoreboard:

Demons	Cats
0.4.04	2.6.18

Nora's husband approached them, stubby in hand.

''Bout two minutes to go,' Jeff told the breathless group. 'The Dees may not have scored, but they've kept the Cats scoreless this quarter. It's bloody brutal to watch. They just can't get a goal. Couple have come close, though. On the plus side, I never knew my wife could handle a ball so well.'

Tom caught his mum's eye as she ran past on the east side of the field. Gayle beamed and waved high as relief washed over her face. He smiled back. Only his mum would wave from a footy oval when the game was in play.

A Cats player looked sure to score a goal. She was on the run with an open goal square. Rach, who'd initially misjudged the incoming kick, caught up with the player and approached from behind to lay a perfect tackle.

'That's what I'm talking 'bout!' cried Billy.

Billy and his dad high-fived over the fence while her other brothers cheered.

Rachel hurried to get it downfield. She turned and swung the ball to Nora with a deep kick.

Nora positioned herself confidently and threw off her opponent to land a chest mark. For the first time, her eyes were wide open.

Jeff cheered wildly from the boundary. 'I told you, didn't I tell you!?' he exclaimed to no one in particular. 'She's bloody brilliant, is my wife!'

Nora weaved a handball between two Cats defenders to Diane, who had made her way from the wing to be in a position to help. Jen shepherded an oncoming player, as did Charlie, which allowed Diane to take a bounce before handballing cleanly to Abby, who had to pass it high over a player to reach Meredith.

Meredith faked right and delivered a short kick to Eva. It wasn't quite ten metres, so Eva was called to play on. She handballed to a fast-moving Andy, who bounced cleanly, once, twice, before kicking short to Tully, who handballed long to Kat on her right.

Kat was brought under pressure but managed a left-foot kick across her body that connected with Ali on the corner of the centre square.

Ali tried to slow the play down to give her team time to position themselves in the forward fifty. Without any open leads, she was forced to kick backwards to Abby, who had made her way downfield from the back pocket.

Abby unexpectedly ran off the mark, and a fast-moving shepherd from Fiona helped Abby kick across the centre circle to Tully. Lou created a quick lead, and Tully kicked short. Aided by a shepherd from Sam, Lou kicked high across the field to Jules, who leaped into the back of number 6 for the Cats. Jules took the mark while airborne and her eyes filled with surprise when she was still holding the ball after landing.

Jules looked to the boundary and watched as Ryan, who seemed caught between winter and summer wearing a Melbourne Demons beanie with a t-shirt and shorts, made the play on movement. Jules knew that time was running out.

Out of nowhere came Gayle, streaming past Jules, calling for the ball. Jules considered kicking forward to Bess but handballed – the right decision.

Gayle evaded one opponent and was nearly tackled by Deb, but Tully, her feet firmly on the ground, landed a hard bump and knocked Deb down, a clean hip and shoulder.

Gayle wasted no time chipping it high to a contest outside the goal square. Bess ascended above the pack of Cats to take the mark of the game in the right-hand forward pocket, on a fifteen-degree angle from goal, just before the boundary. A challenging shot even for the most seasoned player. The whistle blew; Bess composed herself and lined up to kick. A hush fell across the crowd.

'No way she'll make this,' said Lucas. 'Zero chance. Even her brother wouldn't be able to.' He fidgeted on the boundary. 'Come on, Bess,' he whispered under his breath.

Tom and Ian exchanged a smile.

Tom raised his camera and captured Bess spinning the ball between her hands. The click cut through the silence, broken by a smattering of claps that escalated into all-out cheers.

Bess, her back grazing the fence, took steady steps forward, head down, and as she crossed over the boundary line, she released the ball and it landed perfectly over her left boot. It sailed high and snuck through on the right side of the post for the Gerandaroo women's first ever goal. The siren sounded, and for perhaps the only time in history, the townspeople of Gerandaroo and Denby celebrated as one.

The final score:

Demons	Cats
1.4.10	2.6.18

Bess was mobbed by her teammates, and even the opposition cheered, as much for Bess as themselves.

Ian was the first to hop the fence, and he made his way straight to Gayle.

Rob could be heard from the boundary, 'What are they celebrating for? Don't they know they're the losers?'

A hand clamped down on Rob's shoulder and gave a firm squeeze. Ali's dad Nathan said nothing as Rob stared at him, slightly startled. After several moments, Nathan removed his grip and left to congratulate his daughter and niece. Rob stood still; even if he had a comeback, no one was listening.

Close to the boundary, Lachie turned and saw Danny. They locked eyes and both knew that one event had played continuously for the last nine months.

'Dad! You're not coming in here!' yelled Lachie. 'We've already called the cops!'

'You open the fuckin' door, you lying piece of shit!' Mitch screamed. 'The phone's been out for a month! You haven't called anyone!'

Danny stood in the hallway, just as he had as a child. This was the first time he'd heard his dad's voice since that night, seven days ago.

The night he told Dan, 'I know what you are.'

The night when Danny and Tristan had tried to walk away rather than respond, and his dad had murdered his boyfriend.

A warrant had been issued for Mitch's arrest, but he was good at hiding. He always had been. And he was right – the phone was out, and he also knew that the Camerons, the only neighbours within earshot, had been away for weeks and would not be back until next month.

Lachie turned to face Danny as he pushed against the door, desperate to keep it shut, 'Dan, go out the back and break into the Camerons' house and call the police!'

Danny didn't move. He couldn't hear Mitch anymore. The banging had stopped.

'Danny, go!' Lachie pleaded.

Suddenly, there was a series of bangs as bullets pierced the door. Lachie jumped backwards and Danny ducked as Mitch's fist smashed through the splintered wood around the doorhandle and he gained entry.

Wild with anger and hate, he headed straight for Danny. Lachie tackled him from the side and a fight broke out. With both men throwing very real punches, Danny cried out for them to stop. And when Lachie pinned their dad on his back, his hands forming tightly around Mitch's neck, Danny was frantic with fear.

'Lachie! Stop!' He pulled his brother's hands away from their father's neck and all three of them remained sprawled on the floor, breathing heavily.

Mitch was the first to stand. He stumbled to his bedroom and packed his things. As he stepped through the broken front door, he gave them a warning, 'Follow me, and I'll fuckin' kill you both.'

After Mitch had reversed his car down the driveway and sped off, the brothers waited several minutes before going to the Camerons to call the police. But they knew it was already too late.

That would be the last time they saw their father.

They spent the night at the O'Neills', but by morning, Danny was also gone. He headed back home in the early hours to pack his things. When Tom realised Danny wasn't asleep on the pull-out bed in the living room, he caught up with him and tried to stop him. But he couldn't.

Lachie told them that it was Danny's choice to leave or stay, and he wasn't going to go after him.

That was the last time they had all been together.

Danny remained in place and watched as his brother approached him. He could feel his body start to shake, not from fear, but because the internal barriers he had built up were finally starting to fall. And with each breath, he felt the weight of every moment, every decision, every regret, leave his mind and his heart and merge into Lachie, as though he could take it all.

And he did.

As Lachie watched the tears spill from his brother's eyes, he shook his head briefly and reached out to pull him into a bear hug. Danny wrapped his arms around Lachie and squeezed tight. Lachie held the back of his brother's head and spoke through his own tears.

'You little bugger,' he told Danny, his tone dominated by relief and love. 'Took you long enough.'

*

Deb sidled up to Bess as the players celebrated around them. A sense of relief and satisfaction crowded the atmosphere.

'So, that was pretty fun,' she said. 'Except for that knock at the end – that bloody hurt.'

Bess laughed. 'Yeah, you went down hard.'

Deb also laughed. 'Maybe next year we can try and play a few games, get some other towns involved?'

'Sounds good. See you at Redlegs later?' Ever since her dad had been the owner of Redlegs, he'd made sure it was always open after a Gerandaroo match. And Bess knew that by coming to the game, he would keep the tradition alive.

'Yep.' She gave Bess a quick pat on the back before she joined her team.

Tom continued to take photos but remained standing on the boundary, unable to bring himself to walk onto the oval.

Bess watched her brother as he let his camera settle comfortably around his neck. He looked up and they made eye contact. She picked up the nearby game ball and kicked it high over the crowd.

Tom took a step back and marked it, his hands stretched above his head. He looked at the ball and spun it in his right hand – a familiar feeling. He held it up in acknowledgement to Bess, along with a nod. She smiled wide in return.

She made her way to the boundary, and Jules fell into step beside her.

'How did you know this would work?' Bess asked.

'I didn't,' Jules replied.

Bess turned to her, eyebrows raised.

'Lachie saw you driving down Green Street the day you arrived home and he asked me to do it – to get you to agree to start a team,' Jules explained. 'He said if I dared you, you'd never back down.'

'Seriously?' said Bess.

'Yep.'

'What if I hadn't missed the pool shot? Then what?'

'Yeah, so, funny thing about that,' said Jules. 'Bess, you *made* the shot, but you forgot. Clearly. So, about an hour later when you spoke to me about training sessions and you practically forced me to draw up that flyer, I just went along with it. I'm quite clever like that.'

'So, we actually had a conversation that night about training and the flyer? I didn't realise I was that drunk.'

'Not the first time that's happened.'

They both laughed, a relaxed and genuine laugh that neither had heard in a long time.

Fiona's girls, Lily and Daisy, came bursting through the crowd towards Bess, arms outstretched, with their mum close behind.

'Mum said we had to ask you if we can join the team!' cried Lily as she hugged Bess's side tightly.

'Can we?!' cried Daisy, taking hold of the other side.

'Of course!' Bess exclaimed, bending down to give them both a proper hug. 'But I thought you both wanted to be basketball stars?'

'Who told you that?' asked Fi.

'Um, Mum did,' replied Bess.

'I told her that over a year ago,' said Fi.

'Yeah, I know. That's when she told me.'

'And you remembered?'

'Yeah, of course. Even though I don't live here anymore, I still care about the people who do. And I guess talking about you all makes me feel like I'm still a part of the town.'

Fiona gave a smile and shook her head. 'You really are something else, Bess.'

*

That evening, residents from both towns celebrated. Long-overdue sounds of relaxed chatter and laughter once again filled every corner of Redlegs, with Ian and Rick behind the bar, taking orders and making jokes with patrons.

As Tom and Danny entered the pub, Bess watched Billy put down his pool cue and head towards them, with Ben close by; Rick ducked out from behind the bar and joined them. There was an awkward silence as they stood in a tight circle. Danny seemed unable to look any of them in the eye.

Bess couldn't hear what was being said, but she knew that Rick was apologising, as best he could, with the others equally sorry. When Rick finished, they all stood in silence once more, not expecting forgiveness, but keen to let Danny say whatever he wanted or needed to say.

Danny raised his head, close to tears, but in control. He gave a small smile and a nod. They were forgiven, not because he believed they'd done anything wrong, but because he knew they were trying to make things right.

*

Lachie came over to Bess, who was standing with a few teammates. He caught her eye and indicated to the front entrance with a tilt of his head. Bess gave a nod and followed him out the front door.

They stood side by side and breathed in the brisk night air. 'Throw Your Arms Around Me' by Hunters & Collectors drifted out and created a warm space between them.

'Not a bad kick,' said Lachie.

Bess smiled but said nothing, not quite making eye contact.

'Will you be back for Christmas?' he asked.

'Ah yeah, I will be.'

'Good.'

'Will . . . you be here?' she asked.

'Yeah, should be.'

'Good.'

The two finally looked at each other, and shared a smile. The same smile Bess always gave before kissing him.

TWENTY-FOUR

February 1994

Gayle stood at her office door with a girl, about thirteen. As the girl walked out, she passed a young boy sitting on a lone orange plastic chair and threw him a dirty look. He watched her walk down the hall, the bright green paint still glistening across the back of her blue plaid school dress.

Gayle looked sternly at Bobby and gestured for him to follow her.

'Bobby,' she said as she sat across her desk from him, 'even if you don't like someone, it doesn't mean you can put green paint on their seat.'

'But I like Sally,' implored Bobby. 'It's just . . . it was a Gerandaroo dare. I *had* to do it.'

A grin twitched in the corners of Gayle's mouth that she struggled to suppress.

'Right. Well, I think we're going to have a chat about what sort of dares are appropriate during school time.'

He nodded in agreement, eyes downcast.

'But, Bobby, just so you know, you're not the first one to get in trouble for doing a dare involving green paint,' Gayle explained gently.

'Really?' he asked.

'Really.'

*

In Redlegs, with the afternoon sun bearing down, Ian held a clipboard and was making a series of ticks as Rick, perched on a ladder, counted out their inventory. An empty dog bed was visible beside them.

Two new framed photographs, both taken by Tom, had joined the collection of Gerandaroo moments that filled the walls and fed the soul of Redlegs. There was a group shot that included all the women from both the Denby and Gerandaroo teams; the players were mixed together, arms around shoulders, giving the camera a collective smile. Nearby was a black and white photo of Tristan and Danny at the lake, one of the few photographs that existed of the two teenagers together. It was candid – Tom had managed to capture them both laughing while looking directly at each other. Danny was happy for it to be shared; he hoped its presence meant Tristan would not be forgotten, and their relationship, however brief, would never be hidden again.

Just as Rick started to climb down the ladder, Jinx strolled past and settled on his bed, his eyes closing with contentment. Moments later Specky, Rick's border collie pup, nuzzled his way into Jinx's side and fell asleep.

*

On the Gerandaroo oval, an evening game of Marks Up was taking place. Billy, Andy, Rach, Kat, Ben, Tully and Jen were joined by several boys who had recently graduated and some Year 11 girls. Jen kicked the ball high and long and, as they all jostled for prime position, Kat reached out and tickled Ben just as he was about to mark.

'Hey, illegal!' he cried with mock indignation.

'Nope! Totally legal!' said Kat as she picked up the loose ball and kicked it directly back to Jen.

*

Early in the morning, Jules was in a packed campus bookstore, standing in a long line with several textbooks in hand. She turned slightly and smiled wide when she saw Sam a few students back, juggling five textbooks. Sam looked up and returned Jules' smile. They gave a nod in unison as the line progressed.

*

Tom kneeled as he finished writing a postcard, using his copy of *The Backpacker's Guide to Australia* as a rest. He placed the postcard and guide book in his backpack, and hurried towards a narrow sandy track that was surrounded by native shrubs. He followed the track for about thirty metres and emerged on a near deserted beach, the setting sun sinking into the blue-green waters. He kicked off his thongs and dropped his backpack, the soft sand warm under his feet. In the distance, he could see Danny standing on wet sand as a set of waves petered out close to his toes. Tom lifted his camera from around his neck and captured the moment.

*

In the city, Bess sat at her work desk with postcards from all over Australia pinned on a corkboard to her right.

'Do you need a lift home after training?' asked a colleague, poking her head around the edge of the door.

'No, all good, thanks,' said Bess. 'Lachie's checking out a few more workshop spaces and he'll swing by after.'

Bess made her way outside and up a set of concrete steps, a bag of footballs in hand. She arrived at the school's oval where around thirty girls were waiting, ready to play.

AUTHOR'S NOTE

Women have been playing Australian Rules Football for over a century. On 3 February 2017, the inaugural Australian Football League for Women (AFLW) began. Athletes across eight teams competed over a seven-week season. The first game, Carlton v Collingwood, was a lock-out, and will go down as a turning point in Australian sporting history. In the season one Grand Final, the Adelaide Crows defeated the Brisbane Lions. In season six, the Melbourne Demons played in their first Grand Final, but lost to the Crows. In season seven, 2022, eighteen teams competed across a ten-week season, and the Demons won their maiden premiership against the Lions.

To anyone who wants to be a part of footy, we belong.

ACKNOWLEDGEMENTS

My deepest thanks to Pan Macmillan Australia for accepting unsolicited manuscripts, with special mention to Cate Blake and Brianne Collins. Cate, I am so very grateful that you gave this story a chance. Brianne, thank you for your infectious enthusiasm and insightful feedback. I am also extremely appreciative of all the efforts by the copyeditors, and the design, marketing and sales teams, particularly Lily Cameron and Allie Schotte.

To my parents Carole and Stephen, your unwavering support and love is an endless gift. Thank you for teaching me that finding meaning in what I do is a worthy pursuit. My sister Hayley, thank you for all the times you came outside to play.

My heartfelt thanks to the friends who always ask, with genuine interest, *'How's the writing going?'* Charlotte, thank you for believing in this story from the very beginning, and for an enduring friendship that celebrates every joy and shares every heartache. Jacquie (aka Jay-Quel-inn), your exceptionally supportive and delightfully entertaining friendship made this book possible. Thank you for promising to read it, even though you've never watched an entire game of footy and don't follow 'sports'.

To the dogs I've been lucky enough to share stages of my life with, Cassie, Bella, Rosie and Homer, you helped ensure there will always be a 'good dog' in every story I create.

And to all the individuals who play sport, watch sport, and barrack from the boundary, there is no oval, no court, no body of water, no rink, no course, no field, no velodrome, no pitch, no track, no stadium, and no arena where we don't belong.